The Lost & Found

No Matter What
Book 2

Jennifer Carr

Edited by
Ashley Andrews

Chapter 1

Jess

I watched and listened from the doorway as the pair walked around the tree, oohing and ah-ing over the lights and the ornaments. This had become a daily ritual since we put the tree up after Thanksgiving. At five, Hayley was enamored with the sparkles and magic of Christmas. I loved watching my husband indulge Hayley's fascination, telling her where the different ornaments came from or pointing to and naming colors.

When he noticed me watching them, he whispered loudly, "And that," he pointed in my direction, "is the most beautiful mommy in the world."

Hayley squirmed to get down. She ran toward me with an arm outstretched.

"Mommy! Come see the Christmas tree!" Hayley squealed as she pulled me toward the tree.

"Good morning to you, too, my angel," I said as I ran a hand over her silky brown hair. "And good morning to you, Sheriff Collins," I said as I leaned over and kissed my husband.

"Good morning, Mrs. Collins. How are we this morning?" Mark put his hand on my growing belly.

I smiled and sighed contentedly as I moved his hand slightly to the left.

"One of us is very awake."

Mark's eyes grew wide.

"You aren't kidding. Well, awake or not, you really are the most beautiful mommy in the world." He said softly before he kissed me, again.

"Thank you," I smiled and touched his cheek.

"Now," I turned to Hayley, "Who is ready for breakfast? Because I am so hungry, I could eat all the pancakes!"

Hayley laughed, "UH-uh! I already ate them!"

I chuckled. "You did? Well, then I guess I will just have to have something else."

With Hayley content to continue inspecting the tree on her own, Mark and I moved to the kitchen.

"Any leads on the robbery at Mason's?" I asked as I sat down at the island.

Mark handed me a coffee and my usual English Muffin.

"No, and it's frustrating." He sighed. "There are no cameras anywhere, inside, or outside. Nobody saw anything, and because it's such a public place there are too many fingerprints to narrow it down to a single person."

I listened as I chewed.

When Mark made the decision to move to the farm in Kentucky to be with us, he left behind a thriving exciting career with the FBI. At first, he enjoyed the change of pace and thought he could embrace the lifestyle. It took about three months for him to confess that he loved the idea, but milking cows and mowing grass was not quite enough excitement for him. I laughed and told him I'd known before the first week had come to an end but had wanted him to find his own rhythm in his new environment.

When he made his admission, I encouraged him to talk to the local law enforcement and find out if they could use a former FBI agent on their team. Just a few months later, Mark ran unopposed in a special election and was elected county Sheriff. Tim Stephens, the interim sheriff who was also the coroner, was more than happy to hand off the badge.

A year into his service, the most challenging undertaking he'd faced was responding to noise complaints made by Vernon Wilkins about his neighbor's bluegrass band practicing after 9:00 P.M. The raucous caused his Yorkie to bark incessantly which led to his wife being extra ornery, so Vernon was always insistent the Sheriff address the situation when it would arise.

Mark never seemed to mind the simplicity of the job. By his own admission, he had fallen in love with the town and the people almost instantly. And the people loved Mark. The older ladies especially took a liking to him, always bringing him sweets and baked goods. The older men enjoyed trading war stories with him once they learned he was a Marine veteran. The teenage boys wanted to be him, and the teenage girls would blush and giggle when he walked by. It was obvious that Mark had found his calling.

"I'm going back to Mason's this morning to ask him a few more questions about what was missing and talk about some better security measures he could put in place. The initial list of missing items he gave was a little odd, but he was also a little flustered when we talked yesterday," Mark said as he picked up his tan Stetson from the counter and dusted invisible dust from it.

"How was the list odd?" I asked as I finished my coffee.

"It wasn't a list of things someone would steal for the usual reasons. It included a single pack of batteries, two cans of chili, and a blanket."

"How did Mason know a single pack of batteries was missing?" I asked, my brows drawing close together in confusion.

Mark laughed. "I asked the same thing. Apparently, he has a very specific set up in his store and he knows it by heart. Knowing Mason, I didn't doubt him. It's just going to make it difficult to pinpoint the person or people responsible. How am I supposed to track a single pack of batteries?"

I suppressed a smile.

"If anyone can do it, the hottest Sheriff in town can. I hear he's former FBI. And have you seen him in Wranglers? Oh, my." I fanned myself and let my eyes flutter closed.

Mark's cheeks turned pink right before a look of promise flashed in his eyes. The moment was interrupted by an abrupt question coming from the living room.

"Mommy, when are we going to Sadie's?" Hayley asked as she rearranged ornaments on the lower branches of the Christmas tree.

Mark checked his watch and I slid off the barstool and stretched my already tired back.

"Do you want me to drop her off on my way to town? That way you can move at your own pace and not that of a sugar-filled five-year-old?" Mark asked as he watched Hayley sing to the reindeer ornament in her hand. His look of endearment at her melted my heart.

"That would be amazing," I said as I rested my hands on my lower back.

Mark took a few steps and closed the space between us, placed his hat on my head, then put his arms around my waist.

"Consider it done. What else can I do?"

I closed my eyes and relaxed as best I could into him.

"Hmm."

My eyes popped open, and I exclaimed, "Oh!"

Mark stood at attention and moved his hands to my stomach.

"What?" his voice was strained and breathy.

"Marí invited us to dinner with her and Cal this evening."

Mark relaxed. "You can't make those noises for reasons like that," he laughed nervously. "You scared me. Dinner with Marí and Cal sounds good. I'll be home by 6:00."

I wrapped my arms around his neck and teased, "Sorry for scaring you. I'll try to keep all exclamations to a minimum unless absolutely necessary."

I gave him a quick kiss on the lips.

"Good," he smiled and pulled me close for a long minute. "OK, I've got to get going. Hayley-bug, are you ready?"

"Yes, sir," she said as she made her last arrangement of the tree.

With one last kiss, Mark took his hat from my head.

"I'll see you at dinner," I told him then turned to Hayley. "I'll see you at Marí and Cal's in a little while, OK?"

"OK, bye, mommy."

I leaned down and kissed her head.

"Race you to the truck!" Hayley yelled.

Mark and I both laughed as he took off after a giggling Hayley.

The smile on my face lingered as I rubbed my tummy and said, "Alright, now, let's see if we can't get ourselves ready and out the door without needing a nap, today. OK, sweet baby?"

Chapter 2

Jess

After my routine doctor's appointment, I thought I'd drive through town and surprise Mark at his office for lunch. However, before I made it to the courthouse where his office was located, I was distracted by the two Sheriff's vehicles parked outside of Judy B's 5 & 10. I parked across the street and made my way over to the sidewalk where Ms. Judy was talking animatedly to Deputy Mike Whitson. He held and patted Judy's hand, assuring her everything was going to be OK.

Once he walked inside, I stepped in next to Judy.

"Oh, Jess! Hello, sweetheart! What are you doing out here? Look at you!" Judy patted my stomach.

Until I was an adult, there were very few people I allowed into my personal space close enough to make physical contact with me. I was not always capable of preventing myself from having an intense internalized biophysical reaction. Depending on the person who was making the contact, it could be painful. It was part of a skillset I'd had since I was a child that allowed me to read people either through their microexpressions, body language, physical contact, or a combination of the three. It took years of research, study, and application to learn how to consciously engage and disengage the process.

While I was still wary around new people, I'd learned over the years to embrace figuratively and literally those I felt safe enough to allow to get close to me. Thus, Ms. Judy had the privilege of her physical greeting that I returned with a gentle hug.

"Hey, Ms. Judy. What is all this about?" I asked motioning toward the vehicles with flashing lights.

With a hand fluttering around her chest, Ms. Judy was clearly flustered.

"Oh, Jess, it's just awful. I came in this morning and found the store had been broken into. I called your husband as soon as I saw the mess. First Mason's and now here? What is going on? We haven't had this much trouble in twenty years since that motorcycle gang rode through town and vandalized the park after their concert was shut down earlier than they wanted."

I slowly rubbed circles on her back trying to calm her.

"I don't know. But I do know Mark is going to work nonstop to get to the bottom of it."

I paused and looked through the store windows. "Ms. Judy, what was taken?"

The woman was wringing her hands. "Well, that's the funny thing. It wasn't anything big, just a camping chair and a few boxes of soap. If the soap hadn't been part of a display, I probably wouldn't have noticed it. And the chair wasn't even new. It was the one Marv sits in by the door every day."

Eyes fixed on the store, I muttered, "That is an odd combination."

Judy's sister Estelle waved from across the street. When Judy excused herself, I made my way to the familiar white F-150 pickup truck with the Sheriff's insignia and waited for Mark.

"Ma'am, I'm going to have to ask you to step away from the truck," a voice said, catching my attention.

I had let my eyes and mind wander over the town as I waited.

The man's voice brought an immediate smile to my face. When I turned my head, my favorite blue eyes were sparkling at me.

"You got me. I'll go willingly this time, Sheriff," I said as I stood, throwing my head back dramatically and holding my hands out for cuffs.

"I think I can let you off with a warning this time," he said with a wink.

"What brings you here?" he asked.

"I thought I'd stop by after my visit with Dr. Reynolds and see if you were free for lunch. Looks like you might be a little busy," I nodded toward the storefront.

Hands on hips, Mark looked back at the store. "You would think, but I'm kind of at a loss. Let me tell Whitson I'm stepping out and then you can tell me about your doctor's appointment over lunch."

We managed to wedge ourselves into a booth at the Downtown Diner.

"Sheriff Collins, Mrs. Jess, what can I get for y'all today?"

Barbie was my favorite server at the diner. When she was working, I always ended up with extra fries whether I ordered fries or not. And this pregnancy had me craving salty food so badly, I welcomed the crunchy, salty, deep-fried goodness.

"Something warm," I said brightly. "Not chili. This baby does not like chili," I added, pointing to my stomach.

"Got it. Sheriff?"

He looked up at her, his eyes kind. "How's your mom, Barb? Is her recovery going, OK?"

Barb perked up. "Yes, sir. Dr. Reynolds says she'll be back to shuffleboard and horseshoes by New Year's."

"That's great! I'll have the cheeseburger."

Barb made a note on her ticket pad. "Alrighty, give me just a few minutes and I'll have some fries out for you."

She was really good at her job.

"You're the best, Barb!"

Mark put his hand out and I gladly took it.

"Seriously, you were made for this job, Mark."

He rubbed his thumb over my knuckles.

"I never thought I'd ever truly love my job, but I really do."

The baby decided it was a good time to squirm causing me to shift in my seat uncomfortably for a moment. Mark looked concerned.

"This baby has no more room and far too long to keep growing," I laughed. "Dr. Reynolds thinks he or she could come early but doesn't want me to get my hopes up for that."

Mark shook his head in disbelief. "You are amazing. And beautiful."

He knew exactly what I needed to hear and when I needed to hear it. What's more, he meant every word he said. I sighed dreamily and traced his fingers and the lines on his palm with my finger.

"Thank you. Now, tell me about today's excitement."

We ate and Mark recapped the two break-ins.

"It sounds more like someone that needs things trying to only take what they need," I said as I munched on a French fry.

"I agree. And I have a suspicion that there are kids involved. The windows used at both stores were far too small for an adult to fit through."

A heavy weight landed in my chest.

"That makes it even worse. Have a plan?"

"Yeah, this afternoon I'm going to Bob's to see if he has any window alarms. If he does, I'm going to visit the main street businesses and encourage them to put them on any of their business windows that open. If he doesn't, I'll still meet with the owners and encourage them to double check any locks and make repairs if necessary. I know it's not a guaranteed deterrent but it's more than what they have right now."

I nodded thoughtfully, "That is a great plan."

With a glance at my watch, I realized we both had places we needed to be.

"I guess I should go relieve Marí and Cal of Hayley. Maybe she'll want to go home and take a nap with me before dinner."

"That sounds like a good way to spend the afternoon. I wish I were free to join you," he ran a hand up my arm.

"You and me, both. But it sounds like your afternoon is spoken for. Maybe we can schedule a naptime when you aren't fighting crime and saving the day."

Mark left cash on the table then stood and helped me to my feet. He helped me get my jacket on and took my hand as we walked toward the exit. We both said several hellos and goodbyes as we left.

"I never imagined being married to such a celebrity," I teased as we walked outside.

"Funny, I was going to say the same thing."

Arms draped around each other, we walked across the street and down the sidewalk to where I had parked earlier.

"Have I told you lately how thankful I am for you?" Mark asked.

"Hmm," I pretended to consider the question.

"If you have to think that hard about it, then it's well overdue."

We stopped at my car.

"I don't think words are enough to tell you how thankful I am for you, but it's important to me that you know that I love you, and I am grateful for you. Because of you, I have a relationship with God, I have a family, I have friends, and a career that means the world to me. You are the reason I wake up every morning and work to be a better man. So, thank you for being you."

Blinking back tears, I put my hands on either side of his face and pulled it to mine. He wrapped his arms around me and rested his forehead on mine.

"You really don't understand the volatility of a pregnant woman's emotions. We'll have a private conversation about it, later."

He chuckled, "I look forward to it. For now, though, I have to get back to work and you have a nap to take."

My entire body tensed before I let out a slow focused breath at his chest.

"Jess?"

I inhaled sharply trying to control my breathing.

"Jess, what's wrong?"

As the tension left my body, my breath whooshed out with relief. I paused before answering to catch my breath.

"That was unexpected."

Mark pulled away searching my face and my body for indicators of what had happened. He tried to mask the panic I could clearly see on his face.

"Are you, OK?" He asked, brushing my hair from my face.

My heart hurt for him as I watched every emotion flicker across his face, the strongest one being fear.

"I'm good," I smiled at him trying to assure him I was fine. "I think between the doctor's visit, two plates of fries, and the walking, I triggered some Braxton-Hicks contractions. They tend to sneak up on me and take my breath away."

"You scared me. Again."

Mark rested his hands on my belly. I held his hands in place and tiptoed to kiss him.

"I'm fine, I promise. I'm going to go pick up Hayley and go straight home for a nap. Sure you can't join me?"

The tension in his shoulders relaxed.

"If I could, we wouldn't be standing here. Maybe call Marí and see if Hayley can stay with them until we get there for dinner. That way you're guaranteed some rest."

I kissed him once more before getting in the car.

"You are full of good ideas, today."

Chapter 3

Jess

As I suspected, Marí was more than happy to have Hayley stay with her for the afternoon. Sadie, Marí's granddaughter, was at school and Cal was working in the barn with Carlos, so Hayley became Marí's baking buddy for the day. Kicking my shoes off and crawling into bed on top of the covers, I was thankful to have a few hours of quiet to myself. Wrangling an active and inquisitive five-year-old while being eight months pregnant was exhausting. It didn't help that I was five, almost six years older since having Hayley, and felt every bit of it.

As I considered how much time had passed, one hand had automatically gone to the pendant around my neck and the other to my round stomach. The pendant had been made from the engagement ring given to me by Hayley's father, Bryan. The mornings I woke thinking about my first pregnancy, I felt compelled to put the necklace on trying to keep a connection to the past. Granted, it was a past that had been fraught with so many emotions and memories.

And it was hard not to think about this pregnancy and compare it with my first. I'd had morning sickness and headaches constantly during my first pregnancy. This time, it had been smooth sailing from the beginning, and I was thankful. The trouble was, the more I thought about my pregnancy with Hayley, the more I thought about Bryan.

My first husband, Bryan, had gotten caught up in an investigation of a series of cyber-attacks on the U.S. Army databases that consumed him and ultimately led to his murder. His obsession had driven a wedge between us that grew wider over the period of a year before I took matters into my own hands. We had only been working to close that gap for about six months before he died. At first, I wore the necklace compulsively as a token reminder of him but on occasion I would forget to put it on and eventually, I stopped wearing it altogether. When I got pregnant, memories and thoughts of the life I left behind in D.C. revived the habit.

Honestly, I knew that I was fighting an underlying guilt of having moved forward with my life. It was a familiar feeling that I'd wrestled with for a long time even before I fell in love with Mark. While I have never been one to carry much weight when it came to the opinions of others, I cared greatly what my closest friends thought. It took a tear-filled evening of baring my heart and soul to Deborah, one of my dearest friends, who'd also happened to be a surrogate mother figure to Bryan long before he and I ever met, and asking for her permission to live my life after Bryan. It had been a low, desperate moment for me, and I was amazed how readily she hugged me, cried with me, then chided me for even feeling like I had to ask. There were still days after that conversation that I had to replay it in my mind to remember to give myself time and grace as I navigated a path I had never expected to be on, especially at my age.

I also knew I would never forget Bryan. I saw him every time I looked at my daughter, whose green eyes were identical to Bryan's. But my life had indeed moved forward. I was married to someone else, a man whom I adored and loved more than my own life. And I was bringing this man's child into the world, soon. My eyes began to close as I wondered if maybe it was time to put the necklace in my jewelry box permanently.

"Are you kidding me?" I muttered through gritted teeth as I juggled a crying Hayley in one arm, an overflowing laundry basket in another, and was trying to step over the puddle of water I just created by knocking my tumbler off the table. "Bryan!" I called out trying not to startle Hayley and send her even deeper into hysterics.

Bryan had been in the office most of the day even though it was Saturday. We were slated to have dinner with John and Deborah in just a few hours, but I desperately needed to catch up on the laundry that should have already been done. But time seemed to have a mind of its own and it kept getting away from me. Between work, caring for a newborn, and having a very distracted husband, there were days I considered merely surviving the day a huge success.

Dropping the basket of clothes onto the couch, I readjusted Hayley so I could hold her with both arms and bounced her several times, shushing her as I held her close. It had been her usual afternoon nap time and she had fallen asleep quickly, but something caused her to wake up twenty minutes later and she had been wailing ever since. We nursed, tried gas drops, her pacifier had apparently turned into a torture device, and the wearable baby carrier was still hanging to dry because it had become one of the latest victims of an exploding diaper.

My patience with everything was wearing thinner each day but particularly with Bryan. I knew things at work had been stressful even though he never really talked about it. He'd spend hours locked away in the office even after coming home late from work. For all intents and purposes, I was a single parent even though my husband was fifteen steps away from where I stood.

Hayley had calmed to more of a whimper. I slowly bounced her while walking toward the office. The door was only pushed closed, so I toed it open and discovered Bryan looking wild eyed and muttering to himself. His hair looked like he had run his hands through it constantly as it was standing out all over his head. He had his hands balled into fists pressing them into the desk on either side of his computer.

He hadn't noticed the door creep open, so I cleared my throat trying not to startle him or disturb a finally calm Hayley. Nothing. Two steps closer to the desk and another slightly louder clearing of my throat and still no response or flicker of acknowledgement.

There was a twisting in my gut and a sensation running up and down my spine that made me stop where I was standing. My throat tightened, my breathing went shallow, and I felt dizzy. The temperature in the room dropped as I stared at the profile of the man I'd married but hardly recognized. I tried to say his name and no sound would come out.

Bryan's entire body went rigid and stilled. My heart raced and I wanted to leave but my feet felt bolted to the floor. Hands flattened into palms, Bryan turned his torso slowly to face me. Staring back at me was a ghostly white expressionless face that looked familiar but was more like a shadow. In the center of his chest was a bullet hole and his shirt was covered in blood.

Gasping, I pushed myself up onto my elbows then slowly sat up the rest of the way. I had to blink several times before I could process where I was and what was real. My face was wet with tears and as I attempted to swipe them away, my sleeve caught on the pendant around my neck. Once I had it detached from my shirt, I reached around and unclasped the hook. The chain draped over the side of my hand with the pendant resting in my palm. I rubbed my thumb over the sparkling jewels before wrapping my fingers around it and walking it to the dresser where my jewelry box sat.

Grief can be a funny thing, as I've learned. There are days it makes you grateful for the time you had. Then there are moments like this that dredge up parts of the past that hurt and bring up reminders of days best forgotten. And that's something else I've learned – Time may heal old wounds, but the scars left behind are never erased, unable to be forgotten. Bryan was my first love. That place in my heart will always be his. But, he's no longer here for me to love; and if he was, these memories and dreams would be fiction.

Without another look, I opened the organizer and positioned the necklace behind several other pieces of jewelry. There would never be another day when I wore it, but I would hold onto it for Hayley. Maybe one day it would be a way for her to connect with the father she never really knew. Until then, it would be safely tucked away and left in the past.

Chapter 4

Mark

As planned, I made visits to all the downtown businesses, walking through each storefront and making recommendations for better security measures that could be taken. Several office windows were found to be unlocked while others had locks that were broken. Bob Avery of Bob's Electronics had arranged to order the window alarms for any of the owners who wanted them. The smalltown charm of such open trust in humanity was vastly different from the bars-on-windows and multiple locks on doors mentality of D.C. It was clear how easy it was for the townspeople to fall into the trap of a sense of security in the small rural town, and they hadn't all been receptive to my efforts to encourage them to button down a little tighter. It was unfortunate that events such as these minor break-ins had to occur to bring about the awareness of the need for tighter security.

I walked the perimeters of the buildings again to search for anything I might have missed that might be useful. Something about the back-to-back robberies felt desperate. Most theft occurred for one of two reasons. One, the criminal had selfish ambitions. Two, the criminal was taking some form of revenge on the victim. This didn't feel like either. Unfortunately, there was very little to go on aside from the small missing items. I decided it might be worthwhile to have a more prominent law enforcement presence in the town at night as a deterrent to the criminals.

Back in my office at the courthouse, I arranged for the night shift to make extra and intentional rounds through Main Street. Once I was satisfied with the schedule, I debated calling and checking on Jess. I didn't want to wake her if she'd finally found a comfortable position in which she could fall asleep. But she really had my nerves on edge this afternoon with the Braxton-Hicks thing. With zero experience with pregnant women, I was learning as things happened. I prayed daily that I would know what I needed to know when I needed to know it. Today had me wondering if I shouldn't start praying for more advanced knowledge so my heart wouldn't make a complete stop when the real contractions found Jess. I stared at the loud ticking clock on the wall, fingers drumming restlessly on my desk. After watching it in silence for two minutes, I decided I would duck out a couple of hours early and go home to check on Jess.

***

I locked my sidearm in the nightstand safe before sliding into the bed next to my sleeping wife. Jess roused enough to realize I was there.

"Hey, you. I thought you were too busy battling bad guys for naptime," she smiled sleepily.

Wrapping my arm around her, I breathed in deeply.

"You made it sound so irresistible, it was all I could think about."

With what appeared to take great effort, she turned to face me. As always, I was rendered speechless while admiring her. Her deep brown eyes were always a source of comfort for my heart knowing she could hear it without me ever having to say a word.

After several seconds she asked in a hushed voice, "Why did you really come home early?"

She ran her fingers through my hair and down the back of my neck making it hard for me to focus on her words.

"If you must know," I moved my hand to her waist. "I was worried about you."

She rested her hand on my cheek. "You are so good to me. I promise, I'm fine. Contractions are going to happen from now until this baby decides to make an appearance. I also promise that if anything that isn't supposed to happen starts happening, you will be the first to know." She rubbed her thumb back and forth across my cheek.

Taking her hand in mine, I kissed each of her fingers.

"This is all new to me. And I am here for it. But I can count on one hand the number of times I have ever been so nervous and excited about anything like I am right now. I'm terrified that somehow I will miss something or mess something up. The closer to time it gets for our baby to get here, the more anxious I get. And you're just as cool and laid back as you can be which makes me more anxious because I can't be cool or laid back. And that's not like me."

Jess intertwined our fingers.

"Mark, you have been more than wonderful these last eight months because that is who you are. If there was a book, you'd have followed it to the letter. I know we're moving into even more unfamiliar territory for you, but we're doing it together. I can only stay cool because you help me stay that way. It's been a team effort from the beginning, whether you know it or not."

I kissed her forehead and wrapped her up in my arms. She wiggled as close to me as she could and settled into the embrace.

I whispered into her hair, "I'm glad I'm on your team."

Chapter 5

Jess

When we pulled up to Cal's farmhouse, we noticed an extra car in the driveway. Mark shrugged and shook his head when I looked at him, silently asking if he knew about additional dinner guests. As we walked up the porch steps, voices and laughter poured through the screen door. Once inside, we were greeted with squeals and hugs from two very familiar faces.

"Deborah? What are you two doing here? This is – what a surprise!" I immediately wrapped Deborah tightly in a hug.

I turned to hug John who had just released Mark from a friendly slap on the back.

"So, it really was a surprise?" Deborah asked excitedly.

I looked at Mark, "Did you know?"

He shook his head smiling from ear to ear looking fully surprised, "I had no idea."

"Good! Oh, Jess, look at you. You are still the cutest pregnant person to ever have existed. How are you feeling?" Deborah asked as I followed her and Marí into the living room where we sat on the couches and talked while the men caught up on the front porch as we waited for dinner to finish in the oven.

The smiles and excitement carried us well into the evening. After dinner, the adults moved from the dining table to the living room and the girls went upstairs to play.

Mark turned to John.

"How long are you staying? I'd love to see about taking a day off so we can show you the town and introduce you to some folks."

John and Deborah gave each other a look that made both Mark and me pause.

Deborah picked up the answer.

"Well, if everything goes as planned, we should be in town for the next thirty-five to forty years. Maybe longer if the Lord allows."

My jaw dropped almost to the floor. A smile moved across Mark's face. Marí could barely contain her excitement while Cal sat and watched with amusement as the realization hit us.

"Are you serious?!" I finally said, my voice going higher with each word. "Really?! Don't joke like that. Really?" I continued as tears stung my eyes.

Deborah and John were beaming.

"Really," John said. "This place grew on us quickly after our first visit. We prayed about it for a long time, and it looks like God is calling us to start a church here. So, here we are."

Within seconds I grabbed Deborah and hugged her, holding onto her hands after leaning back. Tears were falling from both our eyes.

"We also heard it has one of the best Sheriff's around, so we knew it was a safe place to live," Deborah winked at Mark who chuckled.

"This is really great," Mark said. "I think a good church is something our town needs."

When a sleepy Hayley made her way downstairs rubbing her eyes, Mark picked her up and turned to speak to me.

"We should probably get this bug home and into bed."

I nodded and awkwardly scooted myself to the edge of the couch to make standing easier.

"Yes, and same for this mama."

Everyone said their goodbyes and made plans to see one another the next day.

———

After we tucked Hayley into her bed, Mark and I readied ourselves for bed.

"Can you believe John and Deborah? I am so excited for them to be here. And a church? Mark, a real church. It's so unexpected but it's so needed."

Mark pulled back the covers and moved in next to me, propping himself up with pillows.

"I can't believe they kept it a secret. More than that, I can't believe Marí kept it a secret."

We both laughed.

"We should add the new church to our prayer list," I said as I retrieved a well-loved notebook from my nightstand.

"That's a good idea. Can you imagine the difference a real church could make in a town like Owenston? I know Reverend Billings tries, but he's been struggling since his wife died last year. Our town needs a breath of fresh air."

I wrote in the notebook and handed it to Mark as I held in a yawn.

"You better start praying, sir. I'd like to be awake when you get to Amen."

We held hands as Mark prayed through the list on the pages in front of him. He prayed for me and the baby. He prayed for Hayley. He prayed for wisdom to help him work through the robbery case. Our list ranged from our friends to other townspeople we knew had needs. He prayed for the new church and its leaders as well as the community it would serve. As he said 'Amen', I squeezed his hand and yawned, again.

"Amen," I echoed.

My eyes stayed on my husband's as he handed me the notebook.

"This is my favorite time of day," I told him.

"Bedtime?" he teased, making me smile.

"Getting to spend time with just you, me, and God is my absolute favorite part of any day. It reminds me of everything God has blessed me with and how much I love you."

I snuggled down and wrapped Mark's arm around myself. He followed my lead.

Before he could get comfortable, Mark's work phone rang.

He kissed my shoulder and said, "I'll be right back."

Five minutes later, Mark reappeared in the room but was not getting back into bed. Instead, he was getting dressed as he explained there had been another break in attempt.

"Hey, be careful, out there," I said sleepily. "Get back as soon as you can."

He kissed my temple.

"I will. I love you."

Hand raised to his face, I opened my eyes to see him.

"I love you."

I let him go and fell into a deep sleep.

Chapter 6

Mark

"Sheriff," Deputy Higgins tipped his hat as I approached.

"Steve. What do we have?"

We stood in the back alley behind the Downtown Diner surveying the scene.

"I was makin' rounds and I saw a couple of shadows move across the way. I thought it might be a couple of cats but then I heard the trash cans crashing around so I came to check it out. I didn't see anything out of the ordinary except the cans under the window over there. Looks like someone tried stacking 'em and took off when they fell."

There was a small rectangular fanlight window above the back door and two metal trash cans on their sides. The lids had been knocked free allowing some trash to spill out on the ground around them.

"Steve, can you think of any body shape that could fit through a window of that size if they could reach it?"

The deputy stood and stared up at the window momentarily. "No, Sheriff. It would have to be a kid or somethin' to fit through that one."

Something caught my eye on the brick wall between the window and the ground. It was too high to reach from where I stood. After pulling nitrile gloves from my pocket and sliding them onto my hands, I set up one of the trash cans and put the lid back on it to use it as a step ladder. Deputy Higgins stepped in to steady the metal bin as I reached upward to retrieve a piece of red fabric from a screw that stuck out from the bricks. I turned the glove inside out and packed the fabric away for further inspection later.

Detaching the flashlight from my belt, I walked the alley to inspect the nearby areas. Nothing looked out of place aside from the trash. My gloveless hand dragged across the back of my neck as I glanced around. I walked back towards the deputy but stopped when I saw a single small orange mitten amidst the scattered trash. It was dirty, worn, and out of place in its location. With the still gloved hand I picked it up and wrapped it inside the glove as I removed it from my hand putting it with the fabric scrap.

"Did you find somethin', Sheriff?"

"I'm not sure. It might be something or it might be nothing. I'll take it to the office tomorrow so I can look at it more closely. I'm not sure there's much left for us to do here except keep an eye out. Are you good taking point on that?"

"You bet, Sheriff. Want me to call you if I see anything?"

Taking one more look around the area, I said, "If you need me, call me. I trust you to do what needs doing. Thanks for calling about this. Hopefully, we'll figure it all out before it goes on any longer."

Deputy Higgins reached out and we shook hands with an official nod. "Yes, sir. I'll write it up and leave it in your box for ya."

"Thanks, Steve. Have a good night," I waved as I turned and walked toward the truck.

"You, too, Sheriff."

It was after midnight when I got back home where I found Jess sitting in the living room on the couch. She was propped up with several pillows around her and a fluffy blanket over all of her except the hand holding a book.

"Hey, you," she whispered as she put down the book.

"Hey. Everything OK? I didn't expect to see you up."

She snorted. "I didn't plan to be up. I slept hard for about an hour and then woke up and couldn't get comfortable, so I thought I'd move in here. Then I was wide awake. Is everything OK with you?" she asked, flipping the blanket back and motioning for me to join her on the couch.

Instead, I moved the pillows to the other side of the couch and took their place behind Jess. She smiled and leaned herself against me, resting her head on my chest. Before answering, I took a minute to let her warmth radiate through me. The tightness in my shoulders melted as I wrapped an arm over her shoulder and across her chest, holding her to me. I closed my eyes, kissed the top of her head, and breathed her in wondering how this was my life and knowing it was more than I could ever deserve.

Jess never rushed me and always allowed me to process things at my own pace even though she was full of questions and need for answers. It was one of the many ways we balanced one another. We'd had to learn how to communicate with one another when we worked together in D.C. when she consulted on the cases I worked. It had not been easy in the beginning because she was a fire hydrant while I was a leaky faucet. She always had a craving for answers and knowledge that was difficult to harness, and it would lead her to frustration when I took my time giving answers or providing information because I refused to provide anything I wasn't willing to back up with complete evidence.

Fortunately, the longer we worked together the easier communicating with her became over the years. The friendship we forged in the wake of Bryan's death helped us learn to work together on a completely different level. It was that friendship that carved the path I found myself on that ultimately rerouted when I fell in love with her. It was a short path, but one that I will forever be grateful for because now there isn't a day that goes by where I don't thank God for the woman sitting on the couch in front of me.

"Yeah," I finally answered. "Steve thought he saw some commotion behind the diner, and I think he probably did but he didn't find anyone. It looked like someone tried to climb up on trash cans trying to get inside through the small window over the backdoor."

"Huh."

I could almost feel Jess's mind spin into motion.

"How would a normal sized person fit through that window? It's tiny, isn't it?"

"It is. I found a kid's mitten next to the trash cans. So now I'm thinking there really is at least one kid involved."

Jess was mindlessly rubbing her belly as she sat in silent thought.

"I hate that..." she trailed off.

We sat in silence for a few minutes.

"What if they're hungry?" Jess asked out of the blue.

Having almost fallen asleep, I jumped at her voice.

"Who?" I asked.

"Whoever is breaking into stores to steal cans of chili and trying to break into a diner. What if they're hungry?"

Shaking my head and rubbing my eyes with one hand, I joined the conversation.

"Well, they should probably ask someone for it and not try to steal it," I said trying to shake the fog that had already taken up space in my head.

"Yes, they should. But, what if for some reason they can't or won't? I have an idea. I'm going to talk to Deborah and John about it tomorrow. For right now, I think you need to go to bed."

She tried to move herself up from the couch but was only successful with my assistance. Once she was standing, she reached out a hand waiting for me to stand. Jess put her arms around me and whispered, "I'm glad you're home."

I leaned down and kissed her. "Me, too. Come on, let's see if I can help you sleep more comfortably."

Chapter 7

Mark

I was reading the deputy's report from the night before when the phone on my desk rang.

"Sheriff Collins," I answered after one ring.

"Sheriff Collins, this is Mandy Simmons, the counselor at the elementary school."

Running through my mental rolodex I tried to recall her face. I vaguely remembered meeting her at one of the activity days at the school.

"What can I do for you, Miss Simmons?"

"Well, I'm not sure. I have two students, they're brothers, who haven't been at school for about a week. And I've tried calling but it tells me the number is not in service. Anyway, I was wondering if you could send someone to do a well check and just make sure everything is OK."

The pen on my desk became a distraction for the restlessness building in my mind.

"Can you give me more information?" I asked.

"The boys have had a few rough years. Their dad was arrested a few years ago for abuse. Now, he's in prison for several other things.

Most recently, they told me their mom was having some health problems and honestly, I just have this feeling that tells me they need someone to check on them. The last time I saw them, there was clearly something they weren't telling me but neither would say a word."

The feeling she was referring to was one with which I was all too familiar as I'd had it when working certain kinds of cases in D.C.

"Can you give me names and an address? I'll go out there myself this morning."

There were abandoned toys, broken grills, buckets half-full of stagnant water, and a broken-down lawnmower strewn across the yard of a dilapidated trailer that I had to dodge as I pulled the truck into a dirt driveway. There was a pile of full black trash bags by the road being swarmed by flies. The steps leading to the front door were rickety and the handrail was useless. I knew by the smell already emanating from the residence itself, no one would answer, but I knocked anyway. The door pushed open with the tap of my knuckle.

Drawing my pistol, I took a deep breath and held it, and stepped inside. The floors were littered with empty food and drink packaging. There were dirty dishes piled on every surface. The trash can was overflowing.

As badly as I didn't want to breathe inside the house, I called out, "Hello? This is Sheriff Collins. Is anyone home?"

No response.

The silence was eerie and unsettling, almost oppressive.

Trying to breathe slowly and shallowly through my nose, I turned left and walked through the small kitchen and dining area into a bedroom. Someone was in the bed.

"Hello? Can you hear me?"

My stomach roiled. A woman I could only assume was Mrs. Brewer was lying on the bed, body limp and lifeless. The blood stained sheets around her along with the broken lamp and other miscellaneous items scattered across the floor indicated there had been a struggle that she'd ultimately lost.

Quickly moving through the rest of the house until I was satisfied the trailer was void of other people, I went back outside, vomited, then gulped the fresh air like water in the desert. It had been a long time since I had encountered a crime scene this gruesome. To think it had happened in my town, left a hollow sinking feeling in my core.

From the truck, I called Deputy Whitson then called the coroner's office. When the deputy, coroner, and coroner's assistant arrived, I explained the situation inside the home. Their faces went pale and grim as I spoke.

"Mike, I need to go to the school and talk to the counselor who requested the well check. I need you to hang out here and look around and see if there's evidence of the two boys being here recently. If you find anything, bag it, and bring it back to the station."

Then I turned to the coroner.

"Tim, Miss Simmons mentioned Mrs. Brewer had been sick recently, but she didn't say how. Give me a call when you get back to the morgue and have any updates for me if you don't mind."

With instructions given, I gave a nod and headed for the elementary school.

Chapter 8

Jess

Deborah, Marí, and I were sitting around the island in my kitchen while Hayley took a nap.

"He was half asleep when he got in last night so I decided I would run the idea by you two. He thinks there are kids involved in the break-ins which is sad if it's true. Regardless, I feel like the common thread is basic necessities. Food, batteries, soap. What resources do we have that are easily accessible that don't require direct acknowledgement of need? I can't think of any. The food bank requires an appointment and in-take. The church requires an application for benevolence. If someone was in need but for whatever reason they were too proud or maybe incapable of asking for help, they might resort to taking rather than asking. My idea is to place an easy access food pantry outside of the courthouse or even one of the local businesses that people could leave things in if they had extra, and people could take from when they had needs."

Both Marí and Deborah were immediately taken with the idea.

"I love that idea!" Deborah gushed.

Marí chimed in, "Cal has two or three of those mini refrigerators in the barn that he does not use, anymore. If there is electricity, even things that need to be kept cold could be donated."

"Marí, that is brilliant!"

I was energized by the others' excitement. These women exuded energy and joy and working with them to meet the needs of others reminded me what it had been like before moving to Kentucky. Serving in a community looked different in D.C. than it did in Owenston. In a large city, there were always very obvious needs. There were streets and sidewalks where the signs of homelessness were well-known. There were always non-profit organizations and churches struggling and failing to meet the needs at the same pace they arose. But there was always a willingness and excitement among our group for serving and meeting those needs.

In this small town, the one I now call home, it's a hugely different situation. Those who are lifelong residents of Owenston keep to themselves and by that, I mean they are wary of anyone who wasn't born and raised in this town or who don't have familial connections. If it had not been for Cal, who had lived in Owenston his whole life, the people certainly would not have embraced me being a newcomer as quickly as they had. I was convinced that my idea was a great way to introduce the community to John and Deborah as well as to acquaint them with the people of the town.

It was close to time for Marí's granddaughter Sadie to be home from school, so Marí stood to leave. Before she left for the farmhouse, Marí extended an invitation for my family to join them for dinner, again, if we were free. Not wanting to commit to anything since I hadn't talked to Mark, I promised to call later when I had. Deborah, however, did not move from her seat.

"I'm going to stay until Hayley gets up, if you don't mind, Marí."

"Oh, good! I'll drive her back down before time to eat," I offered.

Marí gave me a peck on the cheek. "OK, I will see you then."

Deborah and I sat in silence until we heard Marí start the truck. I watched Deborah who was swirling the cold coffee at the bottom of her cup. Her eyes had lost the spark that had been there moments before when we were talking about setting up the food boxes. I let it linger for another minute before I put a hand on Deborah's.

"Hey, what's on your mind?"

Deborah gave a half-hearted smile and sighed deeply but didn't speak.

"Come on, let's move to the couch. It's more comfortable." Still holding her hand, I led my friend to the sofa. "Now, talk to me."

Deborah took a breath and asked, "Is it OK to talk about Bryan?"

I automatically reached for the necklace that wasn't there remembering I'd left it in my jewelry box.

"Of course, it's OK," I said. "It will always be OK."

"I felt silly asking because I was sure that would be the answer. But we haven't talked about him in a long time, and I wanted to ask before I started."

It had been a long time since I'd talked about Bryan or what happened to him before we moved to Kentucky. I had processed everything in my own way and my own time and assumed everyone else had, too. While talking about Bryan was never off limits, it was not a regular topic of conversation. I always expected that one day I would need to be prepared to tell Hayley about her biological father, which is why I made it a priority to be open to talking about him. Having Deborah ask me if it was an acceptable topic made me realize that I could have done a better job checking in with her and making sure she had worked through her grief and giving her the space in which to do so if necessary.

My heart in my throat, I squeezed her hand. "I feel like that's my fault, and I'm so sorry. It's one of those weird lines I walk because I don't want anyone to feel like they can't talk about him or that they have to talk about him. Let's just put it out there right now, if either of us ever need or want to talk about Bryan, then we do it. No questions needed. Deal?"

Deborah smiled though she was on the verge of tears. "Deal."

I handed her the box of tissues from the end table next to the couch.

"Now, tell me what's going on in your heart and mind that's got you feeling like this."

"You know that John and I were never able to have kids. It's just what it was. When Bryan came into our lives, even as an adult he was an instant son to us. We felt like he had been meant for our family forever. And then he brought us you and you gave us Hayley. And now we have Mark and this miracle that awaits," Deborah put her hand on my stomach. "My world had been made brighter and happier and I thought the void in my heart would close up as time went on with all of these blessings."

Deborah wiped her eyes with a tissue as she thought about her next words.

"Then, last year, we had a man come and share with the church about the importance of orphan care and he told us how it was what God had done for us when he adopted us as his own children. This hit both John and me hard. Neither of us were ever drawn to adoption or foster care as an alternative because it wasn't something with which we were familiar. Honestly, when we were young, adoption was kind of taboo and was only talked about in hushed tones which gave it almost a shameful connotation. I hate that it took us all this time to learn that's not true. And we're not young like you and Mark, so we sat back and we provided support to the younger families that took it to heart and jumped at the call for foster parents and even adoption. It was beautiful to watch, and I was overjoyed every time a new child walked through the doors of the church. But that's really where it ended for us, and the joy never came home with us for long."

Deborah sighed longingly.

"John and I prayed about what God would have us do which led us to enrolling in foster parenting classes. They took months to finish and then there were home studies and interviews. When we finally completed all the requirements, we were excited. I was ready to say yes to the first social worker who called us. But it wasn't a social worker that called us. It was God. And now we're here. And I love that we are here, don't get me wrong. It's been two days and I have not felt this happy in two years. I just feel like we were about to start on a journey just to have the road change in front of us without warning, again."

I listened and watched as my friend poured out her heart. Her world had been just as wrecked as mine when Bryan died. And I didn't know the heartache that came with never having a child of my own. I wasn't sure that I had the words or the experience to offer sufficient comfort. But my heart went out to Deborah, just the same.

"I had no idea," I said. "I think it's wonderful that you took those steps. And you know, there are kids everywhere you go that need families. Once you and John are settled somewhere, you can try again. I don't know how the process works here, but I can't imagine it would be that different from state to state."

Deborah tried to smile and nodded. "You're right. I'm glad I finally said it all aloud. I've wanted to bring it up and ask you to pray for us, but it felt like the timing was wrong any time I thought about it."

This was quite the revelation to process and my desire to come up with a solution for Deborah was battling it out with my awareness that not everything needed an immediate solution. Instead, I offered something better.

"Please don't ever hesitate to ask me to pray for you. We already pray for you every night, but I like knowing what to pray when you have specific needs or requests."

Deborah pulled me in for a hug. "I am so thankful that God has brought us all back together."

"You and me, both," I said, squeezing Deborah a little tighter.

My phone buzzed loudly from the kitchen forcing me to wiggle off the couch. It was Mark.

"Hey, hottie," I answered.

"Hello to you, too. Are you free?" His voice was quiet and sounded strained.

"I was just sitting and talking to Deborah. What's up?"

He let out a breath. "I'll fill in the details later, but I'm probably going to get in late this evening. I hope to be home by the time Hayley goes to bed."

There was pain in his voice.

"Do you need anything?"

"Pray for me?"

His request tugged at my heart deeply and nothing would stop me from obliging.

"God, you are all knowing and all powerful. We trust you and we love you. Please hold Mark close to you in every circumstance and situation he is facing right now. Use him to bring glory to you and comfort to those he serves. I thank you for his life and his salvation. I thank you that you gave him to Hayley and me. He is yours above all else and I surrender him to you. I pray you would protect him and bring him home to me safely. Amen."

"Thank you. Today has been a very trying day. Tell Deborah I said hi."

"I will. I love you, Mark. Forever."

Some of the tension left his voice when he said, "I love you, Jess. Forever."

During my phone call, Hayley had wandered into the living room where she was showing her favorite ornaments on the Christmas tree to Deborah.

"Which one's your favorite, Mimi?" she asked in her sweet innocent voice.

Deborah looked at all the ornaments she'd been shown. She picked out a picture frame ornament that held a photograph of Hayley as a baby.

"This one is my favorite because that is my favorite Hayley-bug in the whole world." She squeezed the little girl and kissed her cheek.

I smiled at the scene in my living room.

"Mark is not going to be home for dinner so any time you're ready we can head over to the farmhouse and hang out there. But we can stay here as long as you'd like, too."

"Is something wrong at work?" Deborah asked.

"He didn't say but it sounded like something was not right. He said it had been a trying day."

Deborah nodded, "That sounds rough. The trying days are typically the most draining for John. They don't happen often, but when they do, they take their toll."

We admired the ornaments on the tree together a little longer before loading up and driving down to the farmhouse.

John and Cal were both enthusiastic about the food box idea when we presented it at dinner. It was simple and purposeful. I knew Mark would be, too, but I decided to wait and share the idea another time, after I had a better grasp on what was going on with him and the investigation.

"Mommy, can I spend the night with Sadie?" Hayley asked sweetly as she climbed into my ever-shrinking lap.

"You want to spend the night with Sadie?"

Hayley nodded, "Uh huh. Please?"

When Marí gave a slight nod and a wink of approval after I took a quick glance in her direction, I loudly whispered in Hayley's ear, "Tell you what, go ask Cal with your sweetest voice and if he says yes then you can stay."

There were few things more endearing than watching Cal with Hayley. Occasionally I'd catch mannerisms that reminded me of Bryan which made sense as Cal had helped raise him. Hayley's eyes got big as did her smile. She knew she had Cal wrapped around every single one of her little fingers. She hopped down and ran to Cal who was sitting in a chair still at the table. With her hands folded, Hayley tilted her head and batted her green eyes and in her most angelic voice asked, "Cal, can I please spend the night with Sadie?"

We three women held back our laughter and John just shook his head slowly knowing that Cal did not stand a chance.

"Sweetheart, you can spend all the nights with Sadie your mama will let you."

She jumped up and hugged him and said, "Thank you, Cal. You're the best!"

Then she turned and yelled, "He said I could spend the night!" as though no one else had heard the exchange.

When she and Sadie disappeared upstairs, the room filled with laughter.

John looked at Cal, "You understand that you will never win an argument with that one, right?"

We all laughed, again.

"I am well aware. Which is why I'm hoping her mom only sends her to me when she needs to hear yes." He looked over at me where I pretended not to understand his meaning.

Checking my watch, I realized it was getting late and hadn't heard from Mark. I called Hayley down to tell her goodnight and then made my rounds for hugs before making my way back to our house.

Once inside, I texted Mark -

Hayley is staying the night with Sadie. Just you and me when you get home. Mari sent cake.

This was the first time he'd been out this long and this late. I sent up another prayer as I made my way to the bathroom to brush my teeth and hair. My mind wandered to Mark's phone call as I finished getting ready for bed. Something had happened and I couldn't help but wonder if it had something to do with the break-ins. He hadn't sounded pleased as though there had been a positive outcome. When I heard the sound of a truck engine in the driveway, a sense of relief washed over me.

The familiar sounds of his homecoming made their way to me. I pictured him toeing his boots off and putting his hat on the hook next to the door. I heard the jangle of his keys on the counter. I had left him a note on the counter propped up on a plate with a piece of chocolate cake on it that read, You have two choices. I'd added a winking smiley face.

My heart picked up speed when I saw him in the doorway holding the notecard in his hand.

"I see you got my note," I said casually from the bed where I was pretending to inspect my fingernails. I was wearing one of Mark's flannel shirts mostly unbuttoned which seemed to be holding his attention.

One side of his mouth quirked upward but his eyes were void of emotion. "I did," he said and I noticed his voice was tired and sad. "But I only saw one choice in the kitchen. Where would I find my second?"

I didn't need to read him to know how deeply he was hurting. Motioning him over with a tilt of my head, I wordlessly patted the bed next to me. He climbed onto the bed fully dressed, and with his body stretched down the bed between my legs, he wrapped his arms around my waist and rested his head on my belly. I'd watched the tug-of-war raging within him play across his face which was all I needed to see before deciding his heart needed attention first. I ran my fingers through his hair, lightly grazing his scalp with my fingernails. We existed in the silence together, mutually giving and taking from one another without words for several minutes.

"It was awful, Jess. I don't even know if I want to tell you, so you don't have to even picture it," he said quietly.

I continued to play with his hair and trace his features.

"I'm here to listen or just support you however you need me to. You don't have to carry it by yourself."

Mark sat up and swung his legs off the bed, resting his elbows on his knees. After taking several deep breaths, he shared with me about the school counselor calling and agreeing to make a well check and described what he found when he'd arrived. There were clearly details that he had chosen to gloss over for which I was grateful.

What he did tell me was horrific enough. He'd spent most of the afternoon putting together a history of the family, asking around town about and looking for the boys, and waiting to hear back from the coroner.

"No one seemed to know much about the family. A few knew about the dad being in prison, but the family seemed to be on the fringes of the community. One neighbor suggested the mother had a boyfriend or at least a male companion that made infrequent visits but that was really the extent of the information I could get. And no one knows where the boys are. The older one is only eleven and the younger one is eight. They are either in danger or on their own out there and that's probably what makes this hardest of all."

There was pain and frustration on his face.

"Oh, Mark, I'm sorry. Thank you for sharing it with me." Immediately, a thought hit me. "Do you think the boys could be the ones breaking into stores?"

Mark sat up straight. "That did not even cross my mind until just now. I was so focused on finding the boys that I had pushed the break-ins out of my thoughts."

His eyes got big, and I could see him processing thoughts. His energy level went up several degrees.

"You don't go anywhere. I will be right back." He leaned over and kissed me hard and excitedly before he leapt from the bed. "Thank you!" he yelled over his shoulder as he left the room.

Mark

"Steve, I think I know why and who about the break-ins." I gave the deputy a quick rundown. "If you see anything, call me, OK?"

"You got it, Sheriff. I remember Brewer. I only dealt with him one time, but he was a mean one. Those kids deserve better."

"Thanks, Steve. And you're right. I hope we can find them so they can have a chance at better."

As soon as I ended the call, it was as though a huge weight had lifted from me though I still felt a sense of urgency for the little boys wherever they were. I prayed as I made my way back to the bedroom. *God, please let me find those boys and get them to safety. Keep them safe and provide for them until I can find them. And help me find the person responsible for this terrible situation and bring them to justice.*

When I walked back into our bedroom, Jess gave me a smile that sent heat through me from top to bottom. I held out a hand and when she took it, I pulled her from the bed.

"Can I help you?" she asked as she fell into my arms.

"I believe I had two choices and I'm not in the mood for chocolate cake. So, I choose option number two. However, I also need a shower."

Chapter 9

Jess

The smell of coffee and bacon pulled me from the best sleep I'd had in a long time. I couldn't help but smile as I replayed the previous night in my mind.

"Thank you for letting me sleep, my baby," I whispered as I gently caressed my tummy.

Mark's boyish grin when I emerged from our room told me he, too, had slept well. My heart raced and I still melted every time his eyes found mine.

"Good morning," he rumbled with a hint of mischief though there was still sadness and stress etching his face even though he tried to hide it.

He poured coffee into a mug and set it on the counter before moving to wrap his arms around me.

"And good morning to you," I purred.

As soon as the words were out of my mouth my entire body went rigid and breath caught in my throat. Mark's hold went from soft to tense.

"Jess?" He sounded panicked.

Putting a hand on his chest, I rested my head on him as I tried to control my breathing.

"Another contraction?"

I nodded.

Slowly, Mark moved around to stand behind me leaving me to lean and hold on to the counter. Before I could release the slow inhale of breath I had just taken, Mark was squeezing my hips and pressing his thumbs into my lower back. The sound of relief that escaped me was part moan and part growl. After my body relaxed, Mark' hands moved up and down my back gently several times before I turned wrapping my arms around his neck.

"OK?" he asked tentatively.

"Where did you learn that trick?" I asked.

"I talked to Marí. She's the only woman I felt comfortable enough asking who had actually birthed a child. She was more than happy to share far more than I was asking for, but it was probably better than trying to Google the answers I wanted."

Suppressing a giggle, I nodded. "I absolutely guarantee you made the right choice. And thank you. That means so much to me that you would do that. I know it had to be awkward."

I admired him silently before asking, "How many more reasons could I possibly find to love you even more?"

A slow smile took over his face. "I don't know but I sure hope you never stop searching." He held me tighter.

"I never will."

Our breakfast got cold sitting on the counter.

Finally sitting down to a rewarmed breakfast, I remembered I hadn't had the chance to tell Mark about the food boxes for downtown.

"Jess, that is genius." He checked his watch and thought for a moment. "I was already planning to go into town to do some follow up on yesterday's events. If I go early enough, I could run this by

Mayor Robbins and maybe we could present it at the Christmas Tree Lighting this evening."

A surge of excitement shot through me. "Do it! And call me as soon as you have a plan. I'll get John and Cal on it regardless so it will be ready to put into motion as soon as it's a go."

We only lingered at home a few minutes more before we were both ready to move into action for the day. As we pulled up to the farmhouse, Hayley and Sadie were laughing and playing outside with several of Carlos's children. When she saw us, Hayley took off toward the truck.

As soon as Mark had opened his door she was squealing, "Daddy!" and leaping into his arms.

He spun her around and kissed her cheek. Nothing existed outside of the two of them for that moment. I could see the weight of the last twenty-four hours evaporate if only for the moment. They caught one another up on the time they missed with one another, mostly Hayley did the talking while Mark listened. The bliss that flooded me at times like this was incomparable.

If Mark was my best friend, Hayley was his soulmate. From the day they met there had been a connection between Mark and Hayley. I knew that Bryan loved Hayley, and Hayley loved her father as much as an infant could through trust and compassionate caring. But there had never been the spark I imagined a daddy and his little girl having - the spark I never had with my own father and that I always hoped would be there for any children I might have.

The past being what it was, I knew that Bryan had been struggling mentally and emotionally, and by the time Hayley was born, he had all but become a different person. If I dwelled on it too long, it made me sad to think that Hayley would never know the true man who was her biological father. But this made me even more grateful that we both had Mark.

After placing a long kiss on his cheek, Hayley insisted she needed to get back to her game. She ran off to rejoin the children and Mark and I walked inside the house. Everyone greeted one another warmly and excitedly as was the nature of our friendships.

"Coffee?" Cal offered.

"None for me. I'm just here to say hello and drop off this pretty girl. I'm about to head to town to catch up on some things," Mark said.

Marí asked, "Will we see you for dinner tonight?"

Mark smiled at her, "Wouldn't miss it."

He squeezed my shoulders and kissed me on the temple. "I'll call you later. I love you and before I forget, thank you for last night and this morning," he whispered in my ear, facing away from the others.

My face was on fire as I turned and kissed his cheek. "Go, before I burst into flames," I whispered back with a full faced smile. "And I love you, too."

I watched as he walked out the door. There was definitely truth in the old adage, 'You hate to see them go but you love to watch them leave.' When I turned back to the room, all eyes were on me then were immediately seeking to focus elsewhere. I was slightly mortified but could not stop smiling.

John cleared his throat to break the silence. "So, did you have a chance to tell Mark about the food boxes?"

Thankful for the redirection, I enthusiastically said, "I did! He's going to talk to Mayor Robbins this afternoon to see if it's something we might be able to put in place this evening, if we're ready to pull the trigger."

There was a renewed sense of purpose and energy buzzing throughout the room.

Chapter 10

Jess

"Cal, do you have a few minutes before you get started on this project?" I asked before he moved into action.

He looked at John. "If you want to head on out to the barn and tell Carlos the plan, y'all can get started without me and I'll catch up."

John nodded and Cal put his arm out for me to join him. "Are you in good enough shape to take a walk?"

"Only if slow and steady sounds like a good pace for you," I said as I smiled up at him.

He chuckled. "I'll try and keep up."

We walked toward the pasture where the pregnant goats were lumbering along and munching on grass.

Resting a hand on my stomach, I laughed. "Bless them. I only have one to carry around with me. I don't envy poor Henrietta over there. Think it's triplets this year, too?"

Cal shrugged, "At least."

Staring at the animals my thoughts zeroed in on the baby growing inside me and how different our lives would look in just a matter of weeks.

"What's on your mind, darlin'? Don't get me wrong, I love takin' a leisurely stroll with a pretty lady, but you aren't the only one that knows things before someone says 'em." He turned to look at me. His eyes were kind and crinkled at the edges when he smiled. His smile always reached his eyes.

I prefaced my question with a disclaimer. "Please know that if I ever ask anything too personal or about something you don't want to talk about, you don't owe me an answer."

"Listen here, I will always answer your questions. It may not be what you want to hear, but I will always answer you, ya hear?"

I nodded, my heart overflowing with gratitude.

"What was it like raising another man's son? I know Bryan was older than Hayley is, but..." my words faded as my thoughts began blurring together.

Cal rubbed his whiskered face. "That something that's been botherin' you? Did Mark or Hayley say somethin' to make you ask this?"

Again, I reached for the necklace that wasn't there before fidgeting with the wooden fence post instead.

"No." I sighed and gently rubbed my belly. "It's just, with the baby coming, I've thought about a lot of things, especially recently, that I never considered until now. This baby is Mark's in every way. They will share DNA. We'll give him or her Mark's last name. And Hayley will be Hayley Grace Carsen. And I'm worried that it will change something between them. Maybe not right away, but maybe eventually."

Cal's eyes watered a little. "Bless your heart, Jess. I'm sorry you're even having to think about these things. I can assure you with one hundred percent confidence, Mark loves Hayley like she is his own and nothing will ever change that."

A heavy sigh escaped me as tears threatened to fall. I kept my voice quiet as I studied the ground. "I don't miss him as much as I once did."

When I looked at Cal, we both had tears rolling down our faces.

"I want to, but I can't. So much had happened before and so much more has happened since, that I have to force myself to think about him. When I do, I feel guilty. When I don't, I feel guilty. I want Hayley to know that her father was a good man who didn't leave like mine did. His leaving wasn't a choice. But we're all happy and we're a family."

Cal put his arm around my shoulders and pulled me into a hug. I hugged him back and sobbed. It had been a long time since I'd cried like this. Cal just held on and let me cry as he shed tears of his own.

It wasn't clear how long we stood there, but when my breathing returned to normal and the tears stopped, I felt different.

"Now," Cal said, "doesn't that feel better?"

A breathy laugh was all I could manage. Cal handed me his handkerchief which I used to dry my face.

"You can keep that," he said.

We both laughed quietly.

"Jess, Bryan loved you and Hayley, you know that. And I don't doubt for one second that you didn't love Bryan with all your heart. But Bryan isn't here. It's OK that you don't feel the same way you did about him. It would be wrong of you if you did because he's not your husband anymore. Mark is. When Hayley needs or wants to know about Bryan, you'll tell her exactly what she needs to know. But Mark is her daddy and there is no one on earth who would even question it when they see those two together. You don't need to stress yourself out about this. And if it really bothers you, talk to Mark about it. That boy would do anything for your happiness."

"You're right, as always. Thank you for always being willing to listen and give answers that I didn't know I needed."

He held out his arm to escort me back to the house. "Anytime, darlin'. Anytime."

Chapter 11

Mark

A knock at my office door had me looking up from the report I was outlining.

"Tim, what can I do for you?" I asked as the coroner poked his head around the door.

Stepping into my office, he closed the door behind him. His demeanor was somber as he tapped a tan folder against his palm.

"I've got the initial report on Mrs. Brewer," he said grimly then reached across and handed the file to me.

"What are we looking at?" I asked as I accepted the folder and flipped it open on my desk.

Immediately I was hit with the image of the cold, bruised, gray-tinged face of Eileen Brewer. Even though I'd known it was coming, I was still caught off guard and I took a sharp inhale through my nose before focusing on slowing my exhale. As I studied the photo, I could see the signs of violence that had been inflicted on the woman. Her face was bruised and her body showed signs of struggle and trauma. I felt a deep sense of empathy and sorrow for not only her but for the boys who were far too young to understand the gravity of the situation. Their mother was gone and at the hands of another person.

I knew that I had to remain objective and focused, but it was hard to do when faced with the stark reality of such violence. This was not the first time I had seen such brutality, but it never got any easier. It reminded me of the magnitude and seriousness of my job. Rather than read it for myself, I looked to Tim for the highlights knowing I'd read it once he left.

Tim sat in one of the chairs facing my desk. "Well, the preliminary autopsy report indicates that the victim died from multiple stab wounds to the chest and abdomen. Based on the stage of rigor mortis and body temperature, I estimate that she had been dead for approximately six to eight days before she was discovered," he explained.

"Six to eight days?" I asked not able to hide the shock from my voice. "Did you find any other relevant evidence?"

"Yes, actually. There was a bloody knife near the victim's bed and some fibers that could have come from the suspect's clothing on the victim's clothes. I also took swabs for DNA testing and ran some tests on the victim's blood and tissue samples to determine the presence of any drugs or toxins. Those came back negative."

"Good. Is there anything else?" I asked.

Tim continued, "There was unknown DNA under her fingernails that belonged to a man. It's all we've got right now until we get the full reports back."

I nodded as I processed his statement. "Thanks, Tim. This is a great start. I appreciate your hard work in this matter."

Standing, Tim gave me a quick nod. "Thanks, Sheriff. This is the worst I've seen from this area in a long time. And those boys -" his words caught in his throat. He swallowed hard. "I'll let you know when the rest of the results of the DNA come in."

"Thanks, again. If you can't reach me here, call my cell as soon as you know anything," I said, extending my hand to him.

After a firm shake, Tim left me alone in my office with the gruesome image hovering on my desk. I took a deep breath and tried to steady my nerves. There was justice waiting to be served and this investigation was just getting started. Someone was going to be held accountable for this, and I was going to find them to make sure of it.

Chapter 12

Jess

Marí, Deborah, and I worked in the kitchen together most of the day, taking breaks to feed and hug children, laugh, and in my case, take a short nap in Sadie's room. The nap was interrupted by the buzzing phone on the pillow next to me.

"Hey," I managed, trying not to sound as tired as I felt.

"Hey, sweetheart. Did I wake you?"

It was Mark. I braced myself for anything he might have called to share. The tone of his voice was quiet and low.

"Yeah, but that's OK. What's up?" I asked, blinking several times trying to focus.

"I just talked to Mayor Robbins."

He had my full attention.

"He loved the idea of the food boxes and he's ready to announce it this evening if the timing is right."

My excitement replaced the tiredness and worry I'd just been trying to shake.

"This is good. How's everything else? Any leads on the new case?"

Mark exhaled loudly and I could picture him rubbing the side of his face like he always did when he was trying to solve a puzzle.

"No. I think they're aware we know they are out there. And with all of the commotion in the square today, I'd be surprised if they turned up before dark."

Mark paused and I could hear his secretary's voice in the background.

"Listen, I have to go help Ms. Judy unravel some Christmas lights before she and Mason duke it out in the street."

The mental image of those two fighting over Christmas lights made me laugh.

"I'll see you around four. And Jess, I love you."

Those words made me smile every time but this felt heavier. It felt as though he was reaching through the phone for a tether.

"I love you, too," I said, hoping he could feel the pull I willed toward him, letting him know I was here - would always be here.

Scooting to the edge of the bed, I pulled myself together and went back downstairs where I shared the mayor's approval of our project.

"Great news," I said as I reached the bottom of the stairs. "Mayor Robbins said he loved the idea and was ready to move forward when the boxes were ready."

There was a small cheer from the room.

"That's great," Cal beamed. "Carlos is putting some lettering on the doors. We probably need to make a sign of some kind that explains what they are."

Deborah jumped in, "On it. Just point me in the direction of the supplies."

It had been so long since I had been in a position to serve others. For the last year it felt like I had been the poor soul that everyone needed to take care of as I navigated this new place both geographically and emotionally. I was young, widowed, a single mother, and hiding from the man who killed my husband. Then I married Mark who became the Sheriff. He served; I supported him. And if that was all I could ever do, I would do it freely and gladly. But it felt good to be the hands and feet in action, again.

By the time Mark pulled up a little before four, the other men had loaded two small refrigerators with clear doors onto Cal's truck. Carlos had done a perfect job lettering Blessing Box on each machine. One said "Cold" and the other read "Non-perishable". Deborah had created a sign that at the top read, "Have a Blessing? Leave a Blessing. Need a Blessing? Take a Blessing." She listed a few guidelines for using and leaving products in the refrigerators. Marí had created the same sign in Spanish.

"This looks great," Mark raved as he walked toward the truck where everyone had gathered.

I was practically bouncing with giddiness.

John hopped down from the truck and slapped Mark on the back. "It really is a great idea."

Deborah chimed in, "Two things. One, we should put the church's name on it, so the community knows who to contact if there are specific needs or questions. Two, the church doesn't have a name."

We all fell silent in thought. After several moments, an idea came to me. I looked to Cal.

"A couple of years ago, a kind soul told me that God had already redeemed me and if I would let him, he could redeem my circumstances. These boxes are just the beginning of redemption for so many circumstances, I can feel it. What if the church was an origin of that? Where do you go for redemption? A redeemer. Redeemer Church?"

A sound of agreement echoed in the group.

"It's perfect," John said with tears in his eyes before he suggested we pray over the boxes and what they represented.

Our group came together holding hands and wrapping arms around one another.

Chapter 13

Mark

The weight in my chest was heavy and the last thing on my mind was holiday spirit. But it was nearly impossible to hold on to that weight with Christmas songs ringing out through the square from a portable P.A. system that had been set up on the makeshift trailer turned stage in front of the old red brick courthouse. Lights twinkled on the fronts of buildings and around light poles. Heavy garlands, wreaths, and greenery bedecked storefronts and handrails. The large glass windows of the historic buildings and storefronts were festively decorated with Christmas scenes and holiday themed displays. The wide two-lane road that ran through the middle of town was blocked so traffic consisted only of pedestrians and a small train pulled by a jolly elf who looked very much like Ed Thomas who delivered the town's mail during the day. Children were dragging their parents from place to place to admire the Christmas magic as the parents tried to direct them toward the main stage. By 6:30 P.M., most of Owenston's residents had squeezed onto the front lawn of the courthouse.

Someone turned the music down to near silence.

"Friends and family of Owenston, welcome to the annual Christmas Tree Lighting!" Mayor Robbins boomed through a microphone.

The audience clapped and whooped excitedly.

"I am thrilled to be here with you tonight to kick off the Christmas season in our great city. As you know, we have experienced some good times and bad in the last few years. But I am hopeful that we are only looking at good things to come from here on out."

Another round of applause.

"Tonight, before we light up our beautiful tree, it is my pleasure to announce a new project that is being spearheaded by our new residents and friends who have come to Owenston to start a church."

This brought about some hushed conversations among the crowd.

"Pastor John Parker and his wife Deborah are here with us to help meet some of the needs we have in our community. Their church, Redeemer Church, will be opening right here in the old General Store on Christmas Eve. Tonight, however, I am pleased to tell you about the first project the church is sponsoring."

The mayor explained the blessing boxes which garnered a positive murmured response from the residents.

"Now, without further delay, let's countdown from ten and light up this impressive tree. At which point I invite you to help yourselves to cookies and hot chocolate, a visit with Santa and even a train ride with his elves!"

The crowd counted down from ten. As soon as the voices shouted, "One!" the tree lit up the entire square and "Joy to the World" blared from the speaker.

For a few moments, there was a silent awe quickly followed by cheers and clapping. The people milled about excitedly, kids joined the line to visit with Santa, and families visited with one another. Marí held Sadie's hand and Cal carried Hayley to see the massive

Christmas tree up close. Hand in hand, Jess and I followed behind with John and Deborah. Every face was wearing a smile that seemed endless. There was joy pulsing all around.

As we were meandering through the streets, something across the lawn caused me to slow to a stop. Jess stopped next to me trying to follow my gaze.

"What is it?" she asked.

"I'm not sure."

Letting go of her hand, I walked across to the line of children waiting to see Santa. I could feel Jess watching from her spot.

The line of kids with their parents was long but Bob Avery had been playing Santa long enough that he had the timing planned perfectly for each interaction, so the line moved relatively quickly. Without interrupting his process, I inventoried each family and as soon as I saw them, knew exactly who was bringing up the rear. The mismatched mittens, one dark orange and the other black gave it away. I'd bet that the red jacket being worn by the little boy had a missing piece of fabric in its outer lining.

Weaving through the crowd, I made my way back to where my family was admiring the handmade ornaments on the town's Christmas tree. The closer I got to them, the more solid the plan forming in my mind became and it was going to be a team effort to make it real. Once I was within an arm's length, I reached for Jess and pulled her toward me when my hand found hers.

The brightness of her eyes and the pure joy of her smile momentarily caused my mind to go blank and I found myself staring at her and asking myself how it was possible this was my life. Maybe it was the combination of emotions from the last week surrounding the case and the excitement of the Christmas festivities, but in this moment, I was overwhelmed by the love I had for the woman smiling at me.

My thoughts were interrupted when Jess squeezed my hand and said, "Hey! Where'd you go?"

Having been pulled back into the present, I explained my theory and shared the plan for keeping the boys from running away. Within five minutes, Santa was being delivered an envelope from one of his elves and given a secret message no one else could hear. I positioned myself close to the end of the line and watched as the boys waited their turn to meet Santa.

The older one with the mismatched mittens kept looking around as though he suspected a trap. The younger one kept his eyes on the man in red just a few feet in front of them. Both boys appeared thin and grimy but not for lack of trying. Their dirty shirts were tucked in, and it looked as though they had attempted to brush their hair.

Finally at the front of the line, the younger one prodded his older brother. "James, come on. It's our turn."

James rolled his eyes. "Colton, seriously, this is dumb. This isn't the real Santa. Come on."

Colton pulled his brother's arm and dragged him to Santa's chair. "I know he isn't the real Santa, but he knows the real Santa. Otherwise, he couldn't have his own suit."

Santa Bob's smile could not have been more genuine as he listened to their conversation. He interjected, "Your brother knows his stuff, James. You should consider listening to him more often."

Colton beamed.

"Now, tell me, Colton, what is it you want me to ask Santa to bring you for Christmas?"

Colton's face fell and his demeanor turned sad. James looked like a statue made of stone.

Colton's voice wavered as he said, "Mr. Santa, I have tried very hard to be good all year. And I know this is probably not something the real Santa can do, but I have to ask." His voice dropped to a whisper. "I wish we could have a home for Christmas. A real one. And maybe a family. And a dog. I've always wanted a dog. A big one with floppy ears."

James threw his arms down to his side. "Colton! That's stupid! Santa can't do that. No one can do that. We've talked about this. Come on. Let's go."

James started to pull Colton from where he was standing but Bob stopped him. "Now, James. It's not stupid to want any of those things."

He turned to Colton.

"I tell you what, I will talk to Santa for you. And I wanted to pass on something that Santa sent for you to have right now."

Colton's eyes lit up while James tried to hide his curiosity.

"What is it?" Colton was struggling to keep his feet on the ground.

Bob pulled out an envelope and handed it to Colton. "These are two tickets for free cheeseburgers from the diner over there. But there's a catch. You have to use them tonight or they will expire, and you won't be able to use them at all."

James's eyes flitted around as though he sensed danger. Colton jumped into Bob's arms and hugged him.

"Thank you! And tell Santa thank you, too, please. Thank you! Thank you!"

He waved the envelope at his brother. "James, come on! We have to go, right now."

James appeared skeptical at best and scoffed as he walked by Bob who smiled and waved and wished them a Merry Christmas.

Bob turned and we made eye contact as he gave a slight nod. Trying to keep my distance but stay within earshot, I followed the boys toward the diner.

James snatched the envelope from his brother. "Hey! Don't lose it! That was a gift."

With exasperation in his voice, James retorted, "Yeah, right. Nothing is free unless you take it. Let me see that."

He opened the envelope and inside were two business cards from the Downtown Diner. Having written it myself, I knew that on the back of one card was written, "One free cheeseburger for Colton Brewer" while the other read, "One free cheeseburger for James Brewer."

I watched the internal battle played out on the older boy's face.

Knowing everything I had uncovered over the week, there was a good chance he hadn't eaten real food in weeks. I'd also watched him take in his surroundings as though he didn't trust that he was safe. In the end, however, it was clear what his priorities were as his steps carried him closer to the diner.

Chapter 14

Mark

The boys walked up to the diner and were greeted by a smiling elf who closely resembled Mr. Mason from down the street.

"Good evening, gentlemen. What brings you to this fine establishment?"

Colton used every ounce of propriety his eight-year-old self could muster sending a pang of sadness through me knowing how quickly and unexpectedly he'd been forced to grow up.

"Sir, Santa gave us these and we would like to use them, please," he said, handing the cards to the elf.

Mr. Mason pretended to examine the cards thoroughly. "Very well. Right this way, please."

Grabbing the open door, I quietly stepped inside behind them. The excitement and anticipation on Colton's face was enough to bring tears to any eye. This was especially true for Jess and Deborah who I noticed happened to be watching from the kitchen of the diner.

Donning a cheerful Christmas sweater and a red Santa hat, Barb emerged from the kitchen.

"Well, hello, boys! You must be our special guests for this evening. Santa told us you might be stopping by. My name is Barb. If you need anything at all, just holler my name, alright?"

James nodded shyly. Colton bounced in his seat.

"Now, how do we feel about cheeseburgers and french fries?"

Colton nodded eagerly. "But, can I have one with no pickles, please?"

Barb smiled, "Of course you can, sweetie. And what about you?"

James looked at her as he tried to remain stoic. "I like pickles," he said quietly.

"Very good. I'll be back in a jiffy. Oh, and chocolate milkshakes to go with?"

Both boys gave barely visible nods as though they were unable to move.

"See! Santa sent this to us because he knows!" Colton told James.

"Shh! Let's not talk about that here."

Colton seemed to understand and nodded.

About that time Barb walked out with a tray carrying two plates overflowing with fries and large cheeseburgers and two chocolate milkshakes. When she set the plates on the table, the boys' expressions turned incredulous. Their eyes were almost the size of their plates.

"Thank you!" gushed Colton.

James swallowed hard. "Thank you," he whispered.

"You're welcome!" Barb said enthusiastically. "Now, remember, if you need anything, call for me."

James was about to take a bite out of his burger when Colton stopped him. "We didn't thank God for this."

"So?"

"James, this was a gift. We should be thankful. Put that down and pray."

"I don't want to."

"Fine. I will. Close your eyes."

Reluctantly, James put his food down and closed his eyes.

"Dear God, thank you for the gift of cheeseburgers Santa gave us. Please help the fake Santa talk to the real Santa and help the real Santa get us a family for Christmas. And take care of mama since she's there with you. Amen."

It was unfathomable how much strain James had been under for who knew how long, but it was clear that it was starting to affect him. Though, it would be no surprise to anyone if his life had already taken a toll on his young heart long before the death of his mother. With his father in prison and a younger brother he clearly took responsibility for, James Brewer had most likely been living with the weight on his shoulders for a long time. These thoughts were barreling through me as I watched the brothers.

Colton took his time with his food which resulted in him getting full before he could finish it. James had shoveled the entire hamburger into his body but had to slow down when he started on the fries. As both boys sat in a food coma of contentment, a familiar face walked into the diner.

"Miss Simmons!" Colton cried out.

James groaned and hung his head.

"Colton! Oh, Colton! James! You guys have had me worried sick!"

I stepped forward behind her from my concealed location. Colton's excitement waned.

"Uh oh," was all he could say.

"Hey, fellas," I said, trying to sound casual. "How are those milkshakes?"

James continued to avoid making eye contact with anyone.

Colton managed to say, "Good."

I gave him an approving nod before I cheerfully addressed the woman.

"Hello, Miss Simmons. How are you this evening?"

She smiled. "I'm fine, Sheriff. Thank you. I was just talking to my friends, James and Colton. Do you know them?"

With a shake of my head, I extended my hand.

"Colton, I'm Sheriff Collins."

The little boy tenuously shook my hand.

"James?" I acknowledged the older boy waiting for him to shake my hand as well.

There was no response. James crossed his arms and was tapping the table legs with his foot.

Retracting my hand, I continued talking.

"Well, it's nice to meet your friends, Miss Simmons. Do you mind if I talk with them myself for a minute?"

The woman excused herself and went to find Barb, Jess, and Deborah in the kitchen.

At the table with James and Colton, I leaned my forearms on the table and folded my hands in front of me. James had a look about him that screamed he was ready to bolt. I was fairly certain he wouldn't because Colton had started slowly eating his french fries one at a time, again.

"So, have you two had fun this evening?" I asked.

Colton's eyes gave his true feelings away when they lit up at the question.

James spat, "No. It's dumb and for little kids."

Colton clearly didn't like his brother's answer.

"Is not! Santa gave us a present. That's not dumb!"

Feigning surprise, I leaned back and said, "Woah, that's cool. Santa gave you a present before Christmas?"

It was obvious I was going to have a harder time with James, so I worked with what I had.

Colton shrugged as he took a drink of his milkshake. "I guess he knew we had been really good this year and that mama wasn't going to be able to get us anything. Ow!"

James had kicked Colton under the table.

Trying to make a connection with him, I looked at James who still wouldn't look at me.

"Is your mom, OK?"

James shot a warning look at Colton who appeared to be thinking through what to say next. The younger of the two boys sighed more heavily than an eight-year-old should ever feel the need to sigh. It felt as though it held years of secrets that he no longer wanted to hold onto.

"Mama went to be with Jesus."

This admission hit like a searing hot dagger through my chest.

"I'm sorry to hear that. What about your dad?"

With another shrug Colton said matter-of-factly, "He's in jail. Mama said he was never getting out because he hit her one too many times."

Another stabbing pain.

"So, who's taking care of you guys?"

James finally spoke. His voice was angry, "I am. I'm taking care of us and we're fine. Can we go home now?"

This kid was trying to mask years of fear and hurt with anger. It was a feeling I was too familiar with in my own life. There had been countless times in my personal and professional life when I had done the same thing. The day I walked into my brother's room as a fifteen-year-old boy and found my older brother, my hero, my role model a victim of a self-inflicted gunshot weighed on me so heavily for a long time that I allowed my resentment toward his actions to make me angry toward anyone who tried to tell me it wasn't the end of the world. That anger became a motivator in my life to the point I refused to allow myself to make close personal connections with other people. I did my job effectively, I kept my relationships casual and short, and I took care of myself.

These pent-up feelings very easily could have led me to my own destruction. Looking back, I was well on my way. If not for the relentless grace of God and his providence in the form of Jess and the Parkers, I can say without hesitation that my world would look vastly different right now. That's why I knew in this moment as I faced these children that I would do anything to make sure they felt safe, were taken care of, and provided for regardless of the lengths I had to go to in order for it to happen.

"Where's home?" I asked, keeping my voice calm as though speaking to a frightened animal.

James was trying to think of an answer.

I gave him time, but his answer never came.

"James, I know about your mom and your dad. I know that you haven't been home in several days."

James's face turned red, and his eyes filled with tears. Colton already had tears streaming down his face.

"Boys, I'm so sorry that you are going through all of this. It's my job to make sure people are taken care of and that's why I'm here with Miss Simmons. She wanted to see you and hug you and tell you how much she cares about you."

As though on cue, Miss Simmons came back into the dining room. When she came around the counter, Colton jumped up and hugged her tightly. She moved next to James and put a hand on his shoulder.

I continued talking. "And I have another friend who has a really big house with an extra room they would like you to stay in for a little while, if that's OK with you."

Colton's tear-streaked face turned hopeful.

James clearly wanted to object but as soon as he glanced at his brother, he relented. "Fine," he sighed.

There was a hint of relief in the word.

"Can I introduce you to my friend? I think he's outside."

I pushed my chair back from the table and stood as Barb came out of the kitchen with two foam to-go boxes.

"Thank you for stopping by fellas. I apparently made too many cheeseburgers and I don't want them going to waste. Do you think y'all could take care of them for me?"

Both boys took a box trying not to seem eager.

"Thank you, Barb," whispered James.

Colton put his box down and hugged Barb. "Thank you!"

She patted him on the back as her tears spilled over. She quickly wiped her eyes and stood up straight. "Alright, y'all go with Sheriff Collins and be good. I hope to see y'all again, soon, OK?"

Both boys nodded.

Chapter 15

Mark

While I introduced James and Colton to Cal and John, Carlos whistled for his children to find him. Carlos and his wife Ana's beautiful children ranged in age from six months to thirteen. They alternated boy, girl with the oldest being a boy. Marí and Deborah made plans to ride with Carlos and Ana to their home and borrow clothes that would hopefully fit James and Colton then Carlos would take them to the farmhouse before the rest of the family arrived.

I dropped Jess and Hayley off at our house before meeting the others at the farmhouse. When I arrived, the two women were waiting just inside the door and the brothers were stepping out of Cal's truck. James tried to remain unaffected while Colton practically bolted from the truck and up the front porch steps.

"You live here? Is this a hotel?" Colton asked in shock.

The adults chuckled and Deborah led him inside. James trudged slowly up the stairs as Cal waited to follow. James stopped at the door not trusting what might be waiting on the other side. Cal was standing behind him.

"It's all right, son. I promise you, what you find on the other side of that door will carry you through anything."

The boy's gaze remained fixed on the ground as he was unwilling to acknowledge the man speaking to him. Being the stalwart man I've ever only known him as, Cal placed a hand on James's shoulder, held open the door, and ushered James inside. I followed.

The boys were given orders to strip, leave their clothes outside the bathroom doors, and bathe at least twice. It was late when both boys emerged downstairs in clean long sleeve t-shirts and pajama pants. Colton was yawning and rubbing his eyes and James was trying to hold in a yawn.

"Do you boys need a snack or anything before getting to bed?" Deborah asked.

"No ma'am," said Colton. "I'm still full from all of those fries."

James shook his head but stared at his feet.

"Then let's go upstairs and I'll show you your room. I think you'll like it."

Marí had sent me upstairs to deliver two freshly cased pillows and I was making my way to exit the room when John and Deborah walked the boys up to the third floor. The door to the room opened upward like a trap door as the space was a finished attic that had been recently dusted and cleaned and straightened.

The room was surprisingly warm considering how cold it was outside making it feel less like an attic and more like a planned room. With the short amount of time they'd had, two twin mattresses had been placed across from each other on the floor. They were made up with sheets and cozy blankets. As soon as his head protruded through the doorway, Colton seemed to shake some of the tiredness he'd shown downstairs.

"Woah! This is cool! It looks like a clubhouse. James, it's like a clubhouse!" He claimed one of the mattresses for himself.

John chuckled. "That's what I said."

James looked around the room with displeasure.

"We're going to get real beds tomorrow, I promise. We weren't expecting company, so we scrambled for tonight," Deborah was apologetic, trying to provide James some kind of comfort.

Once again, Colton piped up, "That's OK. This is like camping on the ground. I've never been camping. Maybe I'll go camping one day. But this is good for now."

Deborah smiled. "It's late, so you two should try to sleep. If you need the bathroom, it's downstairs."

"Thank you, Mrs. Parker. You're really nice. So are you Mr. Parker," Colton said right before a yawn interrupted his train of thought.

John looked to James, "Need anything?"

The boy whispered and shook his head, "No, sir. Thank you."

"You're safe here. If you need anything, we'll take care of it," John said to both boys.

"Good night," Deborah whispered.

John, Deborah, and I made our way down the steps, and I pulled the door closed behind me. The three of us stared at one another wordlessly though it was clear we were each aware of the unspoken thoughts. There was a reason these boys had been dropped into our world. If there was a group of people who understood the meaning and importance of family, it was our diverse family that had been bonded together by more than blood and DNA but by a deep love for one another that had been solidified through the refining processes of our individual and collective grief and loss over the years.

Chapter 16

Mark

Jess was waiting for me on the couch when I left Hayley's room after tucking her into bed. She motioned for me to sit on the floor in front of her which I did only after leaning in for a kiss.

"I'm proud of you. What you did this evening was really great," she said as she ran her fingers through my hair.

As her fingernails lightly grazed my scalp, the tension I'd been holding onto receded and I let out a sigh of relief. It never failed that Jess knew exactly what I needed when I needed it. If I didn't know her as well as I did, I might think it had to do with her ability to read people simply by looking at them. I'll never forget the first time we met how she took one look at me and it was as though she had opened the door to my innermost thoughts and feelings.

Her ability to read facial expressions and body language of a person within moments of meeting them had been talked up by our mutual acquaintance at the university where she was working at the time. I'd been at the dead end of a case for longer than I had cared to admit and though highly skeptical, I was desperate and willing to consider alternative methods if it meant closing the case. The moment I walked through the door of her office, her eyes locked onto me, and I felt her gaze to my core. I had never felt as unnerved in my life as I did in that moment. We were complete strangers but, in that instance, Jess knew who I was in a way I had never let anyone know me.

She was already involved with her late husband at the time so when I asked her out, she'd turned me down. Looking back, I will always be grateful for that rejection, though my pride was slightly bruised for a while. What I didn't know then that I know now is God was laying the foundation for the future, where we are right now.

Jess ran her hands down my neck and over my shoulders where she began to work the tight muscles.

"I just hate I couldn't find them sooner. No kid should ever have to live in those circumstances for any length of time. But they were probably out there for weeks after having experienced things we probably don't want to imagine." My voice cracked as I said the last words.

Jess slid her arms down my chest and rested her chin on my shoulder. I let my head rest on hers.

"Hey. You didn't know. The important thing is you found them before anything worse happened. And they are safe, and you know they will be taken care of as long as they are with our family."

With a heavy sigh, I reached up and tangled my fingers through Jess's hair, mindlessly looping strands of it around my fingers.

"I guess I'll call child protective services Monday. I hate to add one more thing to the boys' list of traumas, but it's part of the process."

We sat in silence for a few moments before Jess pressed a kiss to my palm and sat up to continue massaging my neck and shoulders.

"Did you know Deborah and John are certified foster parents?"

This was actually news to me.

"Hm." I shook my head.

"Obviously, their certification is from D.C. so I don't know how that works. But, maybe..." Jess trailed off and I knew what she was thinking.

I rose up to my knees and turned to face her, putting my hands on her knees.

"Jess, I know what we would all like to see happen, but we can't get our hopes up. This system is a mess in every state and the process can fall apart more quickly than the reason it should come together."

Resting her hands on mine, Jess sighed, "I know. But could you imagine?"

The mere thought that so many hopes and desires could be fulfilled made me smile.

"It would be pretty amazing."

Chapter 17

Mark

Sunday mornings always started with a family breakfast at the farmhouse before church. The family kept expanding yet somehow, there was always plenty of room. The church in town closed soon after Reverend Billings' wife died. It had barely been hanging on to begin with and once there was no one to preach, people stopped coming.

Cal and I insisted at least our families would have a small worship service at the farmhouse. Eventually, Marí invited Carlos and his family to join us for the worship service. Now John and Deborah were part of it. The children far outnumbered the adults.

James and Colton were dressed and at the table with Cal and John, looking at an antique wooden box when Jess, Hayley, and I arrived for breakfast. Hayley ran to find Sadie who was still upstairs in her room. Jess went to the kitchen to help Deborah and Marí finish cooking. I joined the guys at the table.

"What are we looking at over here?" I asked.

"The boys found this in the attic this morning and Colton here thought it might be worth opening." Cal was inspecting the old cigar box.

It was locked. He looked at the underside of the box and found a small key taped in the corner.

"Aha," he said as he pulled a key from a concealed pocket and unlocked the box. We all stood around craning our necks, interested in what we would see inside.

"Oooh, cool!" Colton said excitedly.

Inside the box were thirty or so pristine arrowheads in a variety of earth tone colors. James started to reach in before looking at Cal who nodded at him. Colton followed suit. James turned the pointed arrow shaped rock over in his fingers, tracing the edges. He put it back in the box and picked up another to inspect.

Impressed at the find I said, "This is really neat. Did you know it was in the attic?"

Cal chuckled, "Honestly, there are probably more things I don't know about in that attic than things I do know about. I remember the box, but I didn't know it was still up there. This was Bryan's collection that he started when he was probably ten years old. He'd find them all the time, but they had to be in a certain condition before he'd add it to the box."

Colton looked at Cal eagerly, "Do you think there are more of these out there?" He used one of the arrowheads to point toward the door.

"I reckon there are plenty more out there. You just have to look for 'em."

"Can we go look for some?"

With his warm smile Cal gave a wink, "Sure thing, but after church."

Our group gathered in the living room, taking up more than all the available seating. Kids sat in laps and on the floor. Carlos played his guitar and led us in singing a song that declared the faithfulness of God followed by a couple of Christmas carols. Then I prayed before John gave a sermonette about Joseph and the providence of God.

"When we read about Joseph, we find that he lived through a series of events that might be really hard for a single person to endure. He was sold into slavery, falsely accused of bad behavior towards a woman, and spent a long time in jail for something he didn't do. Joseph learned that even through everything that happened to him personally, he was part of a larger purpose that God had set in motion. Because Joseph trusted God in all the hard times in his personal life, he was restored and blessed with the ability to take care of the very family who had meant him harm. Because God blessed Joseph, he was able to bless others. Let us remember this during this season of giving and receiving."

John closed his message with prayer and Carlos led the group in singing one more song. The atmosphere was sweet and warm and still. No one made an effort to move for several moments. Ana's baby broke the silence with a whimper signaling the moment had come to a close.

Chapter 18

Jess

Hayley, Sadie, and Carlos's two older girls went outside to play. Colton asked Cal if he would take them to look for arrowheads so Cal, Mark, John, Colton, and Carlos's two boys went out to search. James hung back on the front porch. Mark tried to convince James to join them, but he just shook his head. I followed the group out onto the porch and waved them off on their mission.

"You don't want to hunt for artifacts with them?" I asked James who was kicking at nothing.

"Nah. They're cool, but I'm tired."

I rubbed my cold hands together then stuck them in my coat pockets.

"I'm sorry. Maybe after lunch you'll feel better."

James shrugged.

The sound of giggling coming from around the house caught my attention. I turned to see Hayley petting a chicken whose head was sticking up from under her zipped jacket

"Hayley Grace Carsen, take that chicken back to the barn right now! I've told you; she does not get to play in the front yard."

Hayley's bottom lip stuck out in a pout. "But Henny likes the bugs in this yard better."

"Hayley." My tone said this was a warning.

"Yes ma'am." She turned and walked slowly back toward the barn.

I could hear her apologizing to the bird which made me chuckle and shake my head.

"That is her favorite chicken. And I've told her that the front yard is the perfect place for a hawk to swoop down and grab Henny because there wouldn't be any protection for her out here. She tries anyway."

This made James snicker.

We stood and watched Hayley until she was out of sight.

"I thought your last name was Collins," James said with more of a question in his tone than a statement.

"It is."

"Then why did you call her Hayley Grace Carsen?"

Nodding slowly in understanding, I said, "Oh. Well, because Hayley's last name is Carsen. Hayley's dad died when she was a baby. When I married Sheriff Collins, my last name changed, but hers did not."

James gave me a quizzical look then turned to stare at the ground.

"I thought Sheriff Collins was her dad. He acts like he's her dad." His voice was quiet.

His words squeezed my heart. I didn't know his entire story, but what I did know told me James and Colton hadn't had their dad in a long time. And the stories that I'd heard from the members of our community painted the man in such a light that even when he was home, he wasn't a particularly good father figure. And now he didn't even have his mother.

Hayley may not remember Bryan, but she will always know that he loved her and was a good father when she had him. And now she has Mark who has loved her pretty much from the day he met her.

She's at least had him wrapped around all of her fingers since the day he drove us away from the danger and to our safe haven here in Owenston.

"He is her daddy in every way except by birth. Family doesn't always look like we imagine it should."

We stood in silence watching the bare trees shake in the winter breeze.

"My dad left when I was younger than your brother. I never heard from or saw him after that. My mom raised me by herself and then I went off to college. She got sick while I was away and died soon after. I was on my own after that for so long. It wasn't until I met Hayley's father that I learned that I didn't have to be born into a family for it to be real. John and Deborah became like my parents. Marí and Cal are family to me, too, even though we aren't related. Sometimes, friends can even become our family."

James seemed to listen and consider my words for a minute before he asked, "Can I go catch up with the guys?"

"Sure, I'll walk around the house with you and see if we can find them, and also make sure Henny made it back to the barn." I gave him a wink and we parted ways.

Thoughts of the family I had been surrounded with flooded my mind and my soul. Hayley and the baby inside of me were the only two blood relatives I had remaining on earth, but I knew I loved and was loved in return by the family that I not only chose, but chose me as well.

Chapter 19

Mark

The afternoon melted into evening. After hours of fresh air and a full stomach from dinner, Hayley climbed into my lap while rubbing her eyes. That was enough to tell me it was time to head home for the evening. We said our goodbyes and loaded up into my truck.

Once Hayley was tucked into her bed, her eyes closed and her breathing deepened. I sat watching her in wonder for several minutes. I asked myself how it was possible for me to love a child that I had no biological connection to this much. Clearly, it's possible because just looking at her I knew I would do anything for her. And soon, there would be another innocent soul for me to love.

I never believed that I was capable of loving another person the way I love my family until I met Jess. When she and Hayley came into my life, it was as though my heart and soul expanded for the exclusive purpose of loving them unconditionally. I can already feel that same growth happening inside me for my unborn child. While our family may not be considered traditional, there is nothing about it I would change. Whether of my blood or of my heart, my love for them would never waver and would be forever.

When I left Hayley's room, I found Jess sitting at the island in the kitchen with an opened box of crackers in front of her. The smile she gave me was a shot of adrenaline straight to my heart as it always was.

"I love Sundays," Jess sighed as she swiveled on her barstool.

"Yeah? What do you love about Sundays?" I took a cracker from the box on the counter.

"It combines my two favorite things, God and family. What's there not to love?" She closed her eyes and inhaled deeply before opening her eyes. "When we're all together for worship, it's transformative," she breathed.

"Mm, that is a good word for it."

There were a few moments of silence in which I noticed a shift in Jess's presence.

"What's on your mind?" I asked, sliding my hand over hers.

"So many things," her eyes drifted to mine.

"Anything you want to talk about?"

She fidgeted in her seat before finally deciding to stand. I provided stability then pulled her to me, resting my hands on her hips.

"I was just thinking about James and Colton but especially James. He had to grow up so quickly and in such awful circumstances. It's going to take some time for him to trust anyone to do what he's been trying to do for his little brother and if they're whisked away to some kind of group home or foster care, it will be even harder for him."

Her voice cracked and tears began to roll down Jess's cheeks. She wiped them away and onto her jeans. My eyes started to burn.

"I know." My voice barely above a whisper. "I'm going to set forth a good case to CPS tomorrow suggesting the boys stay at the house with John and Deborah. Hopefully, mentioning their training and background will help. If it doesn't work, all we can do is pray that God's will be done."

My first stop was the farmhouse the next morning to pick up James and Colton on my way downtown to meet with a social worker. They were sitting at the kitchen table eating breakfast. Colton was chattering away about his plans to find more arrowheads of his own so he could build his own bow and arrows using his finds. With downcast eyes, James was poking at half-eaten eggs on his plate.

Sadie was the first up to greet me with a loud, "Mark!" She jumped for a hug, and I gladly squeezed her and set her back down.

"You are getting so tall, Sadie. It won't be long before you have to pick me up for hugs."

She laughed and went back to her breakfast at the table.

Marí kissed me on the cheek. "Coffee?"

I shook my head to decline. Deborah was right behind Marí with a hug for me.

"Will Jess be over later?" she asked.

"I'm not sure what they have planned for the day but I'm sure she will be at some point."

John was sitting next to Colton who was still talking up a storm. John was suppressing a smile when his eyes flicked upward to meet mine. The scene felt familiar, as though it had always been this way and that the two boys hadn't just found their way into the house last night.

Giving Cal a slap on the shoulder I asked, "Did everyone have a good night's rest?"

Cal took a long drink of coffee and was observing James. "I know I did. How about you, James?"

The boy shrugged one shoulder.

John paused his conversation with Colton and addressed James. "James, you were asked a question. It's impolite to just shrug."

Feeling all eyes on him, James's cheeks went pink. "Yes, sir," he mumbled.

His words were not directed specifically at the question nor John's admonition.

Not wanting to add pressure to the situation, I changed the subject.

"Good. Are you boys about ready to head downtown with me this morning? I have a friend looking forward to meeting you both at my office."

Colton jumped from his seat. "Do we get to ride in the truck with the lights on it?"

I chuckled. "Absolutely."

Colton took his plate to the kitchen sink and moved to give high fives to the men at the table and hugs to the women.

Deborah's eyes welled as she hugged him back. "Have a good day, Colton. We'll see you this afternoon, OK?"

He nodded with his little boy grin.

James moved slowly to take his plate to the kitchen and did not look up. Deborah tried to tell him goodbye the same as she had Colton, but he kept moving toward the coat rack and his backpack. We all knew he was grieving and angry, but it was clear it hurt her that he was trying to be unreachable.

When the two boys had walked out the front door, I turned back to the room.

"I'll talk to him. I can't imagine what he's feeling right now. I'll call when I know anything."

Deborah nodded as the tears finally made their way from her eyes.

"Thanks, Mark," John said for the both of them.

Chapter 20

Mark

Colton talked almost the entire way to the office, asking about every knob and button on the console. Thankfully, it wasn't a long drive, but my ears were exhausted by the time we arrived. My secretary was the only person present when we walked into the office area. She was a kind woman in her fifties who had lived in Owenston her entire life. If Sarah Hilton didn't know who, what, where, when, or why of the goings on in the town then something was amiss.

"Good morning, Sarah."

Her gray eyes matched the meticulously styled short silver hair on her head.

"Well, good morning, Sheriff. Did you bring us some new deputies this morning?" She smiled at Colton who seemed to be enamored with every object in the office.

"Mrs. Sarah, I would like you to meet James and Colton Brewer. These are some new friends of mine. We are expecting a visit from Helen Davis this morning. Will you let me know when she arrives?"

She nodded. "I sure will."

"Thank you."

Turning my attention to the children I said, "Boys, let's hang out in my office until Ms. Davis gets here."

They followed, Colton much more eagerly than his brother.

The social worker arrived right on time. She was a motherly woman who looked to be mid- to late-fifties.

I introduced her to the boys and as expected, Colton was eager to meet the woman and immediately asked, "Are you here to get us a family for Christmas?"

She tried to maintain her smile, but I saw the sadness behind it.

"I hope that is what I'm able to do," she responded sweetly.

James was less than enthusiastic about the visit. He was slouched in a chair and scrubbing the toe of his shoes against the carpet repeatedly. Helen asked him the same questions about school and his interests as she had Colton, but the answers were quite different. He was short, terse, and resistant to her inquiry.

"Excuse me, Ms. Davis. I'm sorry to interrupt, but I need to address James for a moment."

I turned my attention to James. "James, Mrs. Davis is here to help you. I would like for you to at least be more respectful. When she speaks to you or asks you a question, I expect you to answer her politely. I know you know how."

James raised his eyes without moving his head and mumbled, "Yes, sir."

Helen asked a few more conversational questions with James providing more polite answers but not anywhere near the substantial answers Colton freely gave. Afterwards, she glanced up and gave me a nod. This was the part I was dreading most as it was the hardest for everyone involved.

"Boys," I started, garnering each of their attention. "I need to ask you some questions that might be hard to answer, but in order for me to help you the best I can, I need you to be completely honest with me."

We stared at one another for a moment before Colton nodded. James only looked down at his lap. I chose to focus on Colton.

"I need to know if you can tell me what happened to your mom," I said gently.

Tears immediately sprang to Colton's eyes while James stood quickly and said, "We don't know. We were sleeping and the next morning she was dead. That's all."

James's defensiveness told me he knew a lot more than he was willing to say. Helen's expression said she knew it, too. It was like dealing with deeply wounded animals. If I prodded the wrong way, no one would benefit. I tried again, maintaining a quiet and controlled tone.

"Listen, I know it's scary to talk about what happened, but I need you to trust me. I'm here to help you and I can only do that if I know all the information I can."

Colton looked up with giant tears dripping down his face. He quickly cut his eyes to James who gave a small shake of his head. When Colton looked back at me, his lower lip quivered and barely audible he said, "We heard someone come in the front door. There was a lot of yelling and stuff breaking," he said, unable to hold in a sob.

Helen placed a gentle hand on his back and rubbed small circles. He caught his breath and said, "James told me to hide, so we got in the closet. When everything got quiet, we just stayed in the closet and fell asleep. When we woke up," he sniffled and gasped several times before he could go on. "James told me to stay put while he checked out the house. When he came back, he told me that mama was dead and I needed to get dressed so I did. We left and haven't gone back. He said he would keep me safe and take care of me."

My ears were ringing as I attempted to process what I was hearing. They had been there when their mother was murdered.

Hoping my voice would still work and not betray the multitude of emotions rushing through me, I took a slow breath in before saying, "Thank you for telling me, Colton. You are so brave for sharing what you remember."

His gaze went to the tissue in his hand that Helen had given him. I turned to James.

"Is there any chance you saw the person or recognized anything that might tell us who was in your house?"

James's eyes darted around the room before landing on mine. His nod was barely perceptible. I stood and moved to kneel in front of him and waited silently for him to speak. He was clearly waging a battle inside his own mind trying to weigh the costs and benefits of sharing what he knew.

"Mama had this boyfriend named Jake who would come around sometimes. He was mean to her sometimes and sometimes he was nice. He ignored us, which was fine with me. He yelled a lot. That's what I heard that night. He was yelling. I don't know what he was saying, but he was mad. Mama yelled back but when they got quiet -" this time James began to sob. "When it got quiet, I just thought he'd left. I didn't know he'd -"

I didn't need to hear anymore and the boys had said enough for the morning.

Placing a hand on his shoulder I said, "Thank you, James. It took a lot of courage for you to tell me that. Both of you are very strong and very brave. I'm going to make sure that the two of you are cared for and safe so you don't have to worry about that anymore, OK?"

They both nodded as they sniffled. Helen distributed more tissues and continued to rub Colton's back. I squeezed James's shoulder then returned to my desk.

After a few minutes of regrouping and calming, Helen asked if we could speak privately. I asked Sarah to give the boys a quick tour of some of the more interesting areas in the building, which she was more than happy to do.

Back in the office, I closed the door and took a seat behind my desk.

"Sheriff," Helen started. "These children have been through a lot in the last few years. It's probably the worst case I've seen in the last decade. What these boys need is a solid home with consistency, attention, and discipline. Right now, my strongest option is a group home in Frankfort. Foster homes are scarce as people aren't lining up around the corners to sign up."

My heart leapt into my throat. The closest group home was an hour from their school, friends, teachers, the only community they had ever known. Its residents were a combination of juvenile offenders and neglected kids.

"Mrs. Davis, what if I had a lead on some certified foster parents who just moved to the area who could provide all of the things you suggest are necessary and more?"

Her eyebrows raised in curiosity. "Where were they certified?"

Helen listened as I filled her in on John and Deborah's situation and experience.

"In your opinion, are John and Deborah able and willing to care for James and Colton during this transitional time in their lives?"

Without hesitation I looked directly at Helen and said, "They are, and they won't be doing it alone. There's something special about that farm and every person that lives there. I've never seen a more diverse, committed, loving family like this one. Even if and when the Parkers find a place of their own here in Owenston, they will still be part of our ever-growing family."

Helen sat and considered this for several moments.

"I tell you what, Sheriff. I will talk to my supervisor about the situation and see what kind of arrangements can be made for the future."

All I could do was hold my breath and pray there was more.

"In the meantime, because of your proximity to the residence and because you vouch for this family, I will allow the boys to stay under the pretense of fictive kinship. I will have to come out and do a home inspection to verify there is enough room and to survey the environment, but we'll set that up another day."

Warmth spread through my chest and I sent up a silent prayer thanking God for this answered prayer.

When our conversation ended, I stood to walk Mrs. Davis out of the office. In the reception area, Sarah had James and Colton labeling files and sorting papers on the floor next to her desk. Colton looked up beaming.

"Mrs. Sarah said we could earn our deputy badges if we helped her organize her files. Did we do it?"

He turned and looked at Sarah. She surveyed their efforts.

"You sure did."

Opening a desk drawer, she pulled out two Deputy Sheriff replica badges and set them on her desk.

With a look in my direction, she asked, "Sheriff, would you care to deputize these gentlemen?"

"Gladly," I smiled as I lifted one of the badges.

Colton looked as though he might burst from excitement as I pinned the cheap piece of metal to his shirt.

"Yes!" Colton shouted as he examined the badge on his shirt more closely.

"James?" I asked, holding the badge toward him.

Still not wanting to make full eye contact, James simply took the badge and nodded. It wasn't much but as he didn't outright refuse it, I'd consider it progress.

"Sarah, I'd like to call Miss Simmons to give her an update. Maybe these guys can help clean up in here before we go?"

Sarah smiled and looked at James and Colton. "What do you say, Deputy Brewer and Deputy Brewer?"

It was barely there but I would have sworn I saw a twitch at the corner of James's mouth at the title he'd been given. There was no doubt how Colton felt about it as he scrambled to his feet and agreed immediately.

"Yes, ma'am!"

The boys helped clear the office floor and as they finished, I was walking out of my office, hat in hand.

"Let's say we swing by the drive-thru and pick up lunch and head back to the farmhouse. I think we can find something for you to do other than go to school today."

There were cheers from the backseat. The reaction of those at the house had been even more emotional than I had expected. There were hugs and tears. James appeared overwhelmed but Colton melted into every embrace before they took off for the backyard.

Not wanting to be a downer but feeling the need to be a voice of calm I said, "OK, let's not get too far ahead of things. They are here for now and we'll take this one day at a time like we do everything. Do we have a lead on bed frames? I can pick them up on my way home this afternoon."

As I knew they would, the group of people I was surrounded by jumped into action and plans were rolling out as if these boys had been meant to be part of the family all along.

Chapter 21

Mark

By the time everyone was home from school and work, the farmhouse attic had been turned into a bedroom that any boy would have dreamed of having. There was a mysterious hideout feel to it and Colton seemed to live for it. James tried not to let on that he also thought it was a great space but anyone who took any amount of notice could see he liked it as much as his brother did. Deborah was more than happy to give Colton a full tour of the room, including the new-to-the-room wardrobe where he and his brother each had several new outfits hanging and the chest of drawers containing other essentials.

As we waited to be called for supper, James sat on the couch picking at invisible fuzz on the cushion. John lingered next to him.

"Is the room OK with you, James?"

With a small nod but not raising his head James replied, "Yes, sir."

"Good. We want you to feel comfortable here. If you feel something is missing, you'll let us know?"

"Yes, sir."

John patted the boy's shoulder and sighed.

"Anyone ready for supper?" Cal's voice called from the kitchen.

Suppertime was a family affair. Cal, Marí, and Sadie, Jess, Hayley, Deborah, John, James, Colton, and I all squeezed around the expanded table. Before the food was served, we all held hands and Cal led us in a prayer of thanks.

"Father, we thank you for our family that is here around our table and those who are around their own. We thank you for the blessings you have given us, even the ones we didn't ask for, but you gave anyway. Thank you for Jesus and his gift of salvation. Thank you for this food and bless the hands that made it. Amen."

There was a murmur of Amens from around the table, the loudest coming from Colton. Food was passed, conversations were had, and the air was filled with excitement. My heart was full as I observed the room in contentment when Jess reached over and squeezed my leg causing me to jump in surprise. I looked over to see my wife near tears with a smile that seemed endless.

Wrapping my hand around hers I squeezed it.

"How amazing does it feel to have been part of this?" she asked.

Unable to stop the smile from forming, I said, "Pretty amazing."

Once everyone had hit the stage of a full tummy stupor, Jess and I excused ourselves and took Hayley home for a bath and bedtime. Once she was tucked in, Hayley was practically asleep before we left her room.

Jess led me to the sofa, where we sat down facing one another. It was clear she had something on her mind and I was close to asking when she leaned over and retrieved a manila envelope before squirming to find a comfortable position, again. Once she was still, the look on her face was one of a kid on Christmas Day.

"I have something for you."

Her smile was contagious as I eyed the envelope.

"Before I give it to you, I want you to know that this was a very easy decision for me to come to on my own. But God has given me multiple confirmations through our family and events of this week that it's the right decision. You are the love of my life. There was a point at which I never thought I would say those words, again. I am so very thankful that God saw fit to allow it. You are a most wonderful husband to me and daddy to Hayley and I know this baby will love you as much as we already do," she rubbed her belly. "How you have navigated the nuances of our circumstances of the last couple of years is beyond words. I have never wondered if you loved Hayley as your own and it's obvious to everyone that she adores you. You are her daddy in every sense of the term, biology withstanding. And that's why I want to give you this."

She offered me the envelope. I stared at her in wonder as I unclasped the envelope's brad and opened the flap. Reaching in I pulled several sheets of official looking pages. My breath caught as I read the heading at the top of the first page.

Petition for Adoption of a Minor Child.

Tears immediately pooled in my eyes and fell.

"Jess." It was barely a whisper, but it was all I could muster as I stared at the page in front of me.

Collecting myself, I wiped my face with a hand, drying it on my pants. Sniffing and clearing my throat, I took a deep cleansing breath and laughed one time. I reached out and engulfed Jess with my arms.

"Jess, this is the most amazing gift you could have given me," I said hoarsely into her hair.

When we pulled apart, still swiping at our wet smiling faces, Jess asked, "Mark, will you adopt Hayley and unify our family in name?"

The emotions running through me – the love, the trust, the fulfillment – were all familiar yet foreign. I thought I had felt them all the first time I held Jess in my arms. Then I felt them again the day I asked Jess to marry me, but they had shifted, morphed somehow into something more. The day Jess and I waited those excruciating minutes in our bathroom waiting for the little piece of plastic to give us an answer, it all changed, again. Everything I thought I could feel for my family once again altered and intensified. The heart I thought was whole inside me was bolstered and reinforced to the point of becoming impervious. Surely it had been made as full as it could ever be. This moment right now, however, proved when it came to love, particularly the love of my family, I would never be sated.

At her request, my love and devotion and the longing inside me to be the man they needed me to be grew exponentially. And for Jess to take this step and make this request, I knew there was nothing I would not do for them.

"Nothing would make me happier."

Chapter 22

Jess

I woke to muffled voices outside. The sun had just started rising and light was peeking through the curtains. Dressing quickly, I walked quietly into the living room trying to get a look at the early morning visitors. Mark, fully dressed for work including his tan Stetson, was speaking in hushed tones on the porch with John and Cal. Something felt wrong. It was much earlier than his normal start time on a workday.

Sliding on my fuzzy boots and puffy jacket I opened the front door. The men all look toward me, their faces grim.

"Has something happened?" I asked, knowing by their expressions they were all worried and afraid.

John looked as though he might cry. Cal removed his hat and ran a hand through his hair. Mark met my eyes.

When he spoke, his words were strained. "It's James."

For a moment, my heart froze and the air I'd just inhaled was stuck in my lungs.

"He seems to have run away."

My hand flew to my mouth, and I let out a shaky breath.

"I'm going to go talk to Colton and help them search," he leaned over and gave me a quick kiss. I grabbed onto his coat.

"Call me when you find him or if I can do anything to help."

Mark nodded and the three men walked down the porch steps.

Before walking inside, I sent up a prayer.

God, show us where James is. Let him be safe. Help us to reach him.

As I worked through my morning routine and waited for Hayley to wake up, I prayed constantly for the search to be quick and productive. After one such prayer a thought struck. I called Mark. He answered after one ring,

"Hey."

"Have you found James?"

"No. And Colton doesn't remember hearing James leave the room. He's really upset this morning, and Deborah is beside herself."

"Check the barn."

There was a pause.

"What?"

"Check the barn. I don't know why, but I have this feeling that you need to check the barn."

"Jess, the morning chores have been done. If James had been in the barn, I think they would have found him."

"Maybe. But I was praying, and I felt the need to call you and tell you to check the barn. There are plenty of places that a kid could hide in that barn."

"You're right. I'll head over there and look. Keep praying."

Ten minutes went by, and Jess's phone buzzed with a message.

Found him... In the barn. I'm sorry I doubted you.

"Thank you, Lord!" The words rushed out of me in a single breath.

Mark

When I walked into Cal's farmhouse with James, Deborah jumped from her chair at the table and moved quickly to hug the child. Morosely, James accepted the affection but then pulled away and went to sit at the table. Colton, who had been at the table with Deborah and had clearly been crying, looked at James with fear and anger mingled with his sadness.

"Don't you ever do that, again!" his little brother chided. "I was scared you had left me, too."

He began to cry, again. James's cheeks flushed and he hung his head low.

His voice was barely loud enough for Colton's ears when he said, "I'm sorry, Colt. You know I'd never leave you." He put his hand on his little brother's.

Deborah and I watched the boys from the doorway.

"Where was he?" Deborah asked quietly.

"He was in the barn holding Henny. It looked like he was just talking to her."

Cal and John had gotten my message that James was back at the house and had made their way back from searching the pastures. Deborah latched on to John and the two walked slowly toward the table. Cal and I went back to the front porch and left the four to talk.

"I'm glad that was as easy as it was," I said as he looked over my shoulder back into the house. "I'm afraid John and Deborah may have their hands full with those two."

Cal grunted a laugh, "I have no doubt about that. They're good kids, though. And the Parkers are wise people. They'll find their rhythm soon enough."

I nodded then we both turned when the front door opened. James stepped onto the porch and looked at us.

"I'm sorry for causing you to worry this morning. I won't do it again." His eyes were watery.

Placing my hand on James's shoulder, I said, "We're just glad you are OK. We did worry, but that's because we care about you. Maybe just let someone know before you leave the house next time. Deal?"

James nodded.

Cal gave a nod. "I think it's time for breakfast. Let's go eat so you can get ready for school."

Turning to me he asked, "You gonna join us?"

"I think I'll go say good morning to my girls before heading to the office."

We shook hands and I made my way back home.

Jess

When he walked in the door, he hung his hat on the wall. Hayley was sitting at the island with a plate of eggs in front of her. When she spotted Mark she yelled, "Daddy!"

The look on his face was the same every time he heard the word leave her mouth. His heart was clearly hers for the taking.

"Hayley-bug!" He matched her energy and leaned down and kissed her cheek.

From the other side of the kitchen island, I smiled at him. "There's my hero. Coffee?"

He walked around to where I was standing and wrapped his arms around me.

"Yes, please. But first..." and he kissed me.

Hayley slapped her hands over her eyes. "Ew!"

We both laughed.

"Thank you for praying this morning," Mark said, as I moved to pour him a cup of coffee. "I don't want to know where I'd be without you always praying for me. Thank you."

I handed him his coffee and a plate of breakfast. He moved to sit next to Hayley who was happily shoveling her eggs into her mouth as she hummed a Christmas tune.

Mark leaned over and said, "Your mommy is really special, did you know that?" Without missing a beat, Hayley gave her head a strong nod and continued humming with her mouth full of eggs.

I couldn't help but smile at the sight across from me. Resting a hand on my belly I sent up a silent prayer thanking God for the family he had given me.

Chapter 23

Jess

Deborah, Marí, and I sat at the kitchen table of the farmhouse while John and Cal worked at the barn. The boys and Sadie were at school and Hayley was content playing with the toys in the living room. Deborah was telling us what Mark had said about James holding the chicken and talking to her.

"When I asked James why he'd gone out to the barn he said, 'I wanted to make sure Henny was safe'. I thought my heart would shatter into a million pieces. Do you think he feels unsafe here and he was putting his own feelings onto the chicken?"

Marí patted Deborah's hand and assured her, "He has no reason to feel unsafe here. I would wager that he's been accustomed to taking care of his brother all this time and now he doesn't have to, so he turned his attention to the chicken."

Deborah nodded sullenly.

"I think Marí is right. James was with me when I told Hayley that she couldn't bring Henny to the front yard because it wasn't safe. His precious heart needs to feel in control of something and the closest he could get was taking care of the bird. Maybe he needs a project or some easy chores that will let him have some responsibility without the burden. You know, there will be a lot of baby goats in the barn soon. I'm sure extra hands will be especially useful."

This seemed to raise Deborah's spirits slightly. "That's a really good idea, Jess. I'll talk to Cal at lunch and see what he can help us come up with for James."

Several minutes later, I was mid-sentence when my breath hitched and I had to take a moment to relax my body. This baby was running out of room and my body was letting me know more and more frequently. Deborah and Marí watched with looks of concern. Eyes closed I pushed the air from my lungs through my mouth before inhaling shakily through my nose.

Marí rose and helped me to my feet. "Maybe we should take a walk and stretch our legs."

I nodded in agreement and Deborah stood to join us.

"Come on, Hayley-bug. Let's go check on Henny," Deborah held out a hand toward her.

"Yeah! I bet she misses me," Hayley said before we all agreed with her.

John noticed us walking toward the barn first and waved as he put his phone back in his pocket.

"I was just about to come up to the house to tell you that the social worker wants to come by tomorrow morning." He spoke to Deborah as we approached. He then looked at Marí and then Cal. "Is that OK with you two? This is your home, and we want to respect that in every way."

Cal clapped John on the shoulder. "John, we've told you both, our home is your home for as long as you need it to be. Which reminds me, Marí and I would like to speak with y'all this evening when it's just the four of us. In the meantime, tell the social worker that tomorrow works fine, and we'll do whatever we need to do to appease her."

Deborah's eyes glistened with tears. "We just cannot say thank you, enough. Once we have things settled with the city about the church, we'll be able to make different living arrangements. Though I do think that both James and Colton will benefit from being here for any amount of time."

Marí linked her arm with Deborah's. "There is no reason for you to worry about moving anywhere else. We love having you and John here and would not want it any other way. So enough of this. Let's go make lunch and talk about a baby shower."

This put a spark in Deborah's eyes and a smile on my face.

Back inside, we worked to prepare lunch seamlessly, as we did often. Marí dressed a chicken while Deborah and I washed and sliced vegetables.

"Of course, we're going to have a baby shower! Why wouldn't we?" Deborah asked.

"Because we don't need anything. We've already set up the nursery and it's not my first time. I remember using fewer than half of the things that we were given when Hayley was born."

Deborah deflated but Marí did not. "We can at least host a lunch to celebrate. We can do it at the new church building. It will give us an excuse to get it ready faster."

Pausing the work I was doing peeling carrots I considered the idea.

"OK, how about this? We can have a baby shower, but any gifts will be given to the Pregnancy Resource Center. It can be a celebration of life."

Marí beamed and Deborah sighed, once again with teary eyes.

"We don't deserve you, Jess," Deborah said just above a whisper.

"Oh, I'm pretty sure I'm the one that doesn't deserve the two of you," I said. "But I am quite thankful God saw fit to put us all together."

Marí raised a fist in the air and gave a spirited, "Amen!"

Chapter 24

Mark

The social worker, Helen Davis, was scheduled to arrive at 9:00 A.M. Marí and Jess had taken the opportunity to make plans for a baby shower luncheon in town while Cal worked in the barn and in the field with Carlos. I was waiting with the Parkers. Deborah had been so nervous as she and John waited for the meeting to the point John had to convince her to sit down and held her hand to keep her from pacing once she finally sat. As she gripped his hand, John suggested they take a moment to pray for the meeting that was going to take place. The peace that settled over her afterward was evident.

Helen arrived at exactly the time she had said she would. She was pleasant, though as I had learned at our prior meeting her personality was very no-nonsense. Having been in the world of social work as long as she had, her skepticism had hardened her in a lot of ways.

"Mr. and Mrs. Parker, as you know, this is a very unconventional situation. I'm thankful for your willingness to open your hearts to James and Colton in this season of tragedy."

John and Deborah nodded as she spoke.

She continued gesturing in my direction, "Sheriff Collins has shared with me some of your story, and I must say, it feels very providential that the two of you ended up here when you did. I would like to hear from the two of you what you desire to see happen concerning James and Colton and the long-term plans you have, if there are any, for staying in Owenston."

Deborah looked to John and nodded, suggesting he be the spokesperson for the two of them.

"Mrs. Davis, it has been nothing short of God's intervention that we landed here in Owenston, Kentucky, of all places. We had every intention of retiring in D.C. and we prayed every day that we would get the phone call from our social worker there telling us we had a placement."

Deborah's eyes were watery.

John cleared his throat and continued, "One afternoon, we got a call, but it was not from our social worker. It was from your Sheriff's sweet wife, Jess, who is like our daughter. During our conversation, she lamented that there seemed to be a need for more outreach and ministry in the community, no offense meant toward Reverend Billings. Talking to her that day, we were reminded that not only did we have family that needed us as much as we needed them, but we were also equipped to serve a community in need. While we have not been part of the community for very long, we knew pretty immediately this is where we will call home from now until the end of our time on earth."

Helen's eyes were also misty as she considered the couple in front of her.

"As for James and Colton, we knew the moment Mark told us what he could about the situation, that we would do whatever we could to take care of them. We aren't strangers to loss and emptiness, Mrs. Davis, and I think that gives us an advantage as far as meeting the boys where they are and providing the right environment for them. They are already very dear to us, and we would very much like to continue to have the opportunity to care for them on a more permanent basis." John held Deborah's hand securely in his own.

The room stayed silent as Helen weighed her next words carefully. "There are several obstacles in this situation, as I'm sure you know. The first being the living situation."

She motioned around the house.

"This is a great home and the yard and barn full of animals are very nice. But the pond is unsecured and multiple families live in the dwelling among other things."

Deborah's face fell as she listened to the woman describe all of the reasons that might disqualify her and John from keeping James and Colton.

John offered, "We talked to Cal last night. He and Marí are going to put a new manufactured home on their property and allow us to live in it and rent it from them."

Helen nodded and made a note in the file on her lap. She studied the faces of the two people sitting across from her for several minutes. No one spoke until she had composed her thoughts.

"Mr. and Mrs. Parker, as I said before, this situation is unconventional. And right now, I don't have a foster family available in a sixty-mile radius. The boys have no known relatives able to care for them. And I have no desire to uproot them from their school as it is the only constant they have right now." She ran a hand over the file folder as though she was smoothing its already smooth surface. After another pause and a heavy sigh, she said, "It's my opinion that the best thing for James and Colton is to have them remain in your care."

Deborah gasped and a tear ran down her cheek. John dipped his head trying to keep his face neutral though his heart had written itself all over his face.

Helen raised a hand as she spoke. "This is not how I typically allow things to happen. There are procedures and standards required of me by the state. But, I also believe that there are opportunities placed in front of us to make choices based on what's right and not necessarily what a book of procedures prescribes."

Her eyes moved from John's to Deborah's to mine and back to the Parkers. "Sheriff Collins has already run perfunctory background checks and has agreed to make weekly reports or reports as needed as a condition of allowing the boys to remain in your care as we all work through the situation together. I need a timeline for your new living arrangements and then we'll set the necessary paperwork in motion for an official home study. In the meantime, I will talk with the judge and let them know of the situation and we'll go from there. Do you have any questions for me?"

"Just one," Deborah said with a shaky voice.

Helen inclined her head.

"Can I hug you?"

The social worker's face softened, and she stood to accept the embrace. It was hard to imagine how many children Helen had seen fall through too many cracks in the broken system. The way she refused to let James and Colton fall victim to that system spoke volumes of her heart and her character.

I waited inside as John and Deborah stood on the porch waiting for Helen to drive away before they embraced one another, each of them sobbing near uncontrollably. After several minutes, they returned inside to dry their faces and compose themselves.

Deborah blew her nose then said, "I need to call Jess and Marí."

John nodded and suggested he would take a walk to find Cal and Carlos, inviting me to join him.

Chapter 25

Jess

As I was waiting at the counter in the diner, the bell above the door chimed, and I turned to see who had entered thinking it might be Mark. Immediately, the hairs on my arms stood. Whether or not everyone sensed it, something definitely shifted in the air as the sound level in the room dropped to almost zero. It stayed that way until the sound of a fork hitting a plate broke the silence. Conversations resumed though they remained rather muted. My eyes never left the newcomer as he took a seat in an empty booth in a corner at the front of the building.

Anger. Anxiety. Apprehension.

Since I could remember I have been able to detect and interpret subconscious microexpressions and body language. This allowed me to break through lies and secrets quickly which came in handy when investigations were less than cut and dry. When my life turned upside down three years ago, landing Hayley, Marí, Sadie, and me in Owenston, I had been a successful consultant contracted with the FBI as well as other agencies that sought out my abilities. Some days the gift was a burden, though most days it was a blessing.

After moving to the farm, I'd relinquished the daily casework to my business partner, Dr. Thorne, in D.C. and agreed to consult on an as-needed basis. On the one hand it was nice to be able to turn off that part of my brain more often than not. There were very few reasons to scrutinize the members of our small community. Between everyone knowing everyone's business and the townsfolk being suspicious of newcomers, very little was hidden from plain sight. Aside from having little privacy, the drawback was little practice for my skills. Thankfully I did not use them often, but my senses felt slightly dulled when I did.

When I made initial reads in interviews for investigations, I scanned the eyes, lips, nostrils, and forehead for signatures. I also observed body language, the movement and position of the shoulders and hands. Even without verbal cues, I was rarely incorrect in my conclusions. And while I try not to make it a habit, in this case I had to assume that the read I had on this man was accurate.

Moving beyond his transsensatory image, I took in his physical appearance. He was tall, at least six feet, and broad shouldered. His arms were hidden in long sleeves of a flannel shirt but they filled the sleeves making me think based on the rest of him there was some kind of muscle hiding there. His eyes flicked over to me for a moment, and I shivered as I felt a chill run down my spine.

Suspicion. Hostility. Dominance.

I took a deep breath but I couldn't shake the feeling that there was something off about the man. His eyes said he was hiding a terrible secret, something that he didn't want anyone to know.

The door chimed again, and I was distracted by an incredibly attractive man walking in my direction. My heart swelled as I watched him stop by tables as people called out or reached for him. The man I watched smiled as he shook hands with the men and chatted with the older women who were most likely promising they were going to stop by his office with some baked goods they'd made with him in mind.

From the moment I met Mark I knew he was special. He was the reason I had started working with the FBI in the first place. We were colleagues for years before we became friends. That only happened when I needed his help working through evidence that would eventually provide answers to questions surrounding my late husband's murder. Thinking back to those days then seeing him now, the pride I felt just for knowing him was immense. It could never compare, however, to the love I had for him. My reminiscence and pondering were brought to an end when I found myself standing and looking up into my favorite pair of blue eyes.

"Hi," I said on an exhale. When it came to Mark, I never failed to be taken aback when he was near me.

"Hey, beautiful," he said before leaning in for a kiss.

Mark led us to the back corner where I scooted into the red vinyl cushioned booth and he followed me into the seat. Leaning into him I rested my head on his shoulder and he wrapped an arm around me and squeezed before letting me go.

Our relationship before getting married was anything but traditional. We went on approximately three dates the entire year we considered ourselves to be dating. We also lived over five hundred miles apart. Even though we were married eighteen months ago, I still had this need to be close to Mark any chance I got. Most people would say we were still in the honeymoon phase. I think it has more to do with making up for lost time and genuinely enjoying being with him.

Once we placed our order, I nudged my elbow into Mark's side to get his attention. He turned to face me but my eyes were back on the stranger who entered the diner before he arrived and was now solely focused on his coffee. With a nod I indicated Mark should follow my gaze, which he did.

"Who is that?" he asked.

I knew the question was not for me, but was instead a general ask. In a town the size of ours, strangers stood out.

"I don't know who he is, but I can tell you he kicked every one of my senses into gear."

Mark's focus quickly turned back to me. This time, his expression was serious. The townspeople hadn't been made privy to my abilities so we rarely if ever discussed them in public.

"Did you get a read on him?" he asked quietly.

"I read a lot of things on him. He's definitely hiding something. Even from here I can tell he's twitchy and anxious."

We continued to take turns staring in his direction in silence until our food was delivered to the table.

"Are you comfortable getting a read on him as I introduce myself?" Mark asked, concern and indecision clouding his features.

"Of course. Why wouldn't I be?"

He rested a hand on my leg and gently pressed his fingers into it. "I just don't want to add any unnecessary stress on you and the baby. I'm sure he's just someone passing through town, but if he's trouble, I don't want you pulled into it."

My hand rested on his. "Thank you. I promise I will maintain a safe distance from all trouble as far as I can help it," I said with a smile.

We let our conversation wander and found ourselves caught up in a conversation about our plans for Christmas when movement caught our attention. The man was inching out of his booth and dropping some cash on the table. Mark tossed cash onto our table as he stood. Holding his hand out for me, he assisted me to my feet, and we followed the man from a distance, waving at a few of the diner regulars on our way to the door.

The sound of us stepping out of the door and onto the sidewalk caused the man who had paused on the sidewalk just outside the door to notice us. He casually glanced at Mark who was in his standard khaki TACLITE pants and black Sheriff's Department polo, the logo hidden by his brown TACLITE Jacket that also touted an embroidered badge. His sidearm and actual badge were clipped to his belt, but his hands avoided them to maintain an unarresting demeanor. While he inspected Mark, I analyzed him. Reading his initial reaction was simple.

Pretense. Frustration. Wariness.

Attempting to appear genuinely surprised by his presence, Mark and I both plastered on our most welcoming smiles. With a protective arm around my waist, Mark positioned me behind him enough to feel as though he could become a barrier if necessary. I could feel the current of worry radiating from him which struck me as both odd and sweet. He definitively said he wanted me to keep my distance, but this level of concern was out of character for Mark. I made a mental note to assuage his fears later before zeroing back in on our objective.

In a voice I had heard him use with the members of our community, Mark switched on the neighborly charm as he extended a hand and addressed the man. "Hi. You look like you might be new to town. I'm Sheriff Mark Collins."

It wasn't lost on me that he did not introduce me, though our body language made it evident I was his. The man's eyes quickly twitched in suspicion before a mask slid into place. And Mark didn't need my special set of skills to notice it, either. He gave what was likely meant to be a smile but it failed to reach his eyes, and came across as forced. When he spoke, his tone echoed his expression — even, calm, and void of any emotion.

With only a slight hesitation he returned the gesture and said, "Jacob."

Not missing a beat, Mark asked, "Is there anything I can help you with today, Jacob?" He put emphasis on the solitary name that had been provided.

"Thank you, Sheriff, but I'm just passing through town," was his only reply.

"Okay. Well, you have a nice day Jacob. If you find yourself needing any assistance at all, just give my office a call."

The man gave a nod of his head and said, "I'll do that, Sheriff," before he walked across the street. The interaction had taken less than two minutes, but my nerves were on high alert. Mark and I stood and watched his departure until he was out of ear shot.

"I don't think you need me to tell you how suspect that meeting was," I said offhandedly before turning to face Mark who finally loosened his hold on me.

Pulling his gaze from the street and looking at me he huffed a laugh. "I'm pretty sure we both picked up on the fact he was hiding something. Did you pick up on anything dangerous?"

"He's definitely got 'threat' written all over him. Whether he's actually a threat or just likes to be intimidating, that's to be determined," I told him.

Mark wrapped my hand in his and we began walking toward my car. Quietly, he said, "James mentioned his mother had a boyfriend named Jake that he heard in their house the night she was killed. It feels a little too coincidental that we'd have a new guy named Jacob in town on the heels of everything. Do me a favor and keep this between us for now, O.K.?"

"Of course. And you'll keep me updated if you learn anything?" I asked.

At my car, I let go of Mark's hand and turned so I could wrap both arms around him as I looked up into the bright eyes that never failed to pull me in. I studied his face letting the familiar buzz of sensation from his touch roll through me. I can't help but relax when he's this close even after having my senses keyed up mere minutes ago.

"Of course," he said before resting his lips on my forehead.

"I know you have to get back to work but I could stay here all day," I sighed.

Pulling me closer, Mark enveloped me in a hug and held on for several seconds before letting go and running his hands down my arms until he intertwined our fingers.

"I'll see you at home," he promised before placing a gentle kiss on my lips.

We said our goodbyes and went our separate ways. On the ride home I replayed our encounter with Jacob and a strange feeling tugged at my thoughts, though I had no idea what it meant. In cases like this, the best way for me to find clarity was to let go of the thought and hope that it returned on its own with its own resolution. If it didn't return by the next day, I'd revisit it and try analyzing it from different perspectives.

The drawback to this process was that it took time and honestly, I never knew if time was going to work for or against me. All I could do now was pray that God would speed the process along in case there was something urgent that needed to be uncovered.

Chapter 26

Mark

Between my gut and everything Jess had said, I was aware that something was off with our new visitor. I had picked up on his alpha behavior on our first encounter. But our town and tight knit community did not attract random visitors. Owenston was not a tourist destination.

Behind my desk, I brought the computer on my desktop to life and began tapping the keys that would take me to the public records search. As I worked, I was reminded how long it had been since I had run any sort of criminal history check. When I left the FBI almost two years ago, I took a break, albeit a short break, from law enforcement. It was a nice reprieve, but I quickly learned my calling was to serve and protect, which is how I ended up running for and being elected Sheriff.

The action here is very different from what I experienced in D.C.. Until last week, the most complicated encounter I'd had here was with some parents of high school kids that had been caught vandalizing the field house at the stadium. Admittedly, as much as I didn't want there to be any kind of threat to our community, there was something exhilarating about being forced back into the fray even if it was benign in comparison to what I faced on the daily before moving to Kentucky.

Without any information aside from a first name, I leaned back in my chair and stared at the framed photo on my desk. It was a candid shot Deborah had taken one afternoon when all of the families had been together at the farm. Hayley was on my shoulders but had leaned down to kiss my head. Jess and I were looking at one another and laughing. Unbeknownst to us it was the first picture of us as a family of four. Jess and I learned three days later she was pregnant. This photo was the embodiment of my entire life. And every single day when I looked at it, I was reminded how exceptionally blessed I was and why I had consistently chosen the jobs I had. Serving my country, serving my city, serving my community all meant something to me before, but now, it meant even more.

My thoughts were interrupted by the phone on my desk ringing. I let my chair seat fall forward as I answered, "Sheriff Collins."

"Sheriff, it's Tim. We got a partial match on the print we found on the knife as well as several prints from the house. I'll bring the final report over this afternoon but I wanted to give you a name. Jacob Milton. I don't recognize it but hopefully it's a solid lead."

Thank you, Jesus!

"Tim, that is exactly what I needed at exactly this moment. Thank you. I'll be on the lookout for the report."

We hung up and my heart was hammering in my chest. There was nothing coincidental about the timing of that phone call and I knew it.

Entering the name Tim had given me into the search bar, I hit Enter and waited. Several minutes later, the results were in. There were a few violations listed such as assault and disorderly conduct. Both appeared to have occurred at a couple of different bars several years ago. Nothing stood out as cause for alarm but the fact that he had some recorded history of violence was tucked away for future reference. There was no mention of any connection to the next name I entered into the system - Eileen Brewer.

I wasn't sure what I was looking for exactly, but it wasn't long before I was reading a list of previous residences, relatives, and employment history. Since I was a kid, I'd been able to sort through information and make sense of puzzles faster than most people. It was how I was able to sort out the mess that was Jess's life when she was forced to run from her life in D.C. Information naturally catalogs itself in my brain and I remember it almost perfectly every time. It had come in handy on many occasions in my line of work.

I scanned the words on the page and stopped on a name listed as a sister-in-law for Eileen. Half an hour later I had learned that Kathleen Brewer Thompkins was the sister of James "Jimmy" Brewer, the boys' father who was currently serving a life sentence in prison for a laundry list of violent charges against him.

The questions started piling up in my mind, and I needed some answers. The one thing I knew for certain was that my number one priority was protecting James and Colton to the best of my ability from any more upheaval and harm. Those boys had been through enough. They deserved better. If having an aunt in the picture, even if she was their dad's sister, was what was best, it was an avenue to explore. Additionally, I wanted to find out if she knew anything about Jacob Milton.

My first call, however, was to the social worker, Helen Davis. She was both surprised and apologetic when I shared the information with her.

"Sheriff Collins, as you are probably aware, that while we try to prevent it, there are unfortunately times when things fall through the cracks. In this case, when Mr. Brewer's parental rights were terminated several years ago and the boys' mother was still alive, we had no reason to look into next of kin. When the mother passed, there was no information in the file that mentioned relatives from either side of the family. The boys made no mention of any relatives so we assumed there weren't any. But now that we know there is possibly an aunt out there –."

Her words hung in the air and I knew where she was going with them. A biological aunt that wanted custody would likely get it. My emotions were at war. The Parkers were my friends, and I knew that James and Colton would thrive in their home. I also knew that the system was in place for a reason and even if it was not always right, it was still in place for a reason. This process, what came next, was going to be a test of faith.

"So, tell me a little bit about what happens next. I'd like to prepare not only myself but also the boys and the Parkers."

For the next several minutes, Helen walked me through what would happen and what could happen. Since Ms. Thompkins had not made her connection to the Brewer boys obvious, Helen suggested it could be a mere coincidence. Nonetheless, there was nothing we needed to do at this point until that happened. Even so, the boys had been appointed a Guardian ad Litem who would be informed and who would in turn ask the boys about any relatives they may be aware of on the off chance they remembered something they had not mentioned previously. If there was a relative ready and willing to take the boys into their home, that process would begin, once again uprooting James and Colton from a home and a family that had already embraced them as one of its own.

The idea that any home apart from the one they were in could be remotely better was foreign to me. From the moment I met John and Deborah Parker I knew they were special. They were naturally loving, nurturing, and compassionate people. Being parents is something they had always wanted, and while the Parkers had not been given biological children, they loved every person they came into contact with as though they were one of their own. This was something I could attest to personally.

From the first time I called John in a panic one morning at 4:00 A.M. to ask him to walk me through the Bible, he made it clear that just like any father would, he would make himself available. And Deborah, she was always ready to provide open arms and warm embraces that brought more comfort than any kind words though she had plenty of those to offer, as well. They were a phenomenal couple and deep down in my heart, I knew they were exactly who the boys needed in their corner.

The night I laid eyes on the boys in the diner, I had to force myself to focus on the fact they were safe at that moment. I've had to run the same drill every time I've seen them. The lack of solidity in this situation, however, kept a sinking feeling in my gut that I was constantly having to battle. In my heart I knew that God had worked bigger miracles than securing a stable home for two boys. My entire life was proof of that. Even if I hadn't known it at the time, there was no reason I should still be here and I especially should not be living the life I'd been given.

I also knew that my wants and desires were sometimes out of sync with God's timetable and letting myself get ahead of Him would not work in anyone's favor. That's why I had to take the feelings of uncertainty and push them away intentionally and thoroughly. It would seem that would be easier said than done in light of our town's new guest.

As we wrapped up our call, Helen suggested that I speak with the Parkers but leave James and Colton out of the conversation for now. They would have a meeting with the court appointed advocate later and it would be best if they weren't able to dwell on it beforehand. Checking the time I realized I had places to be so as I packed up my things, I silently walked through the conversation I was going to have with John and Deborah, made a plan to call Kathleen first thing in the morning, then battled to find peace in my spirit to accept whatever came next.

Chapter 27

Jess

While the most consistent craving I'd had throughout this pregnancy were the french fries from the diner, there were rare occasions when a need arose for one of Barb's sweet maple bacon cinnamon rolls. Today was one of those occasions. It had been an emotionally charged week and my body or maybe this baby was demanding comfort in the form of warm spicy doughy goodness that had been drowned in sticky maple vanilla glaze and topped with candied maple smoked bacon. Since I conveniently passed through downtown on my way home from my doctor's office, I justified my stop as a mere convenience, and gave in to this overwhelming need for sugar.

As I sat on the red vinyl barstool trying not to inhale every bite as though it was my last, the chime of the door sounded. Out of habit, I glanced over ready to dole out greetings to a town member all while secretly hoping it wasn't Mark coming in to catch me indulging in my second confectionery splurge of the hour. It wasn't that I couldn't eat two cinnamon rolls, but his paranoia after having read far too many books and articles about pregnancy had made it a little more difficult for me to enjoy these kinds of indulgences. It was endearing that he was concerned for both me and the baby, but no matter how many times I assured him an occasional treat was not going to immediately plunge me into danger of risks or complications, he would sweetly and gently remind me of said potential risks and complications. Because he was under enough stress between work and the holidays in addition to the pregnancy, I only felt mildly remorseful for harboring my guilty pleasure.

It was not Mark who walked into the diner, yet my relief was fleeting. Instead, our new town visitor was walking through the door. My senses went on high alert and kicked into action. With one scan of his face and posture, I found myself tensing. He looked like a predator as he scanned the room looking for a seat. I wiped my hands and fired off a text to Mark. After what he told me last night about Tim's call concerning the new evidence they'd found, I was not necessarily going to hang around and make a new friend.

When Hayley and I first moved to Owenston and we met new people, the inevitable question would arise about my career. While I tried to gloss over details, that was not always possible. So when it came out that I had worked for the FBI, I was immediately seen as some kind of strong female law enforcement icon. It was hard to convince some of the older ladies that the truth of the matter was that a lot of my job was done behind two-way glass and behind a desk or computer monitor. I would occasionally sit in the interrogation rooms and court rooms but those instances were rare and I was always a silent observer while actual law enforcement was in the room with me, typically leading the charge.

Field work was a foreign concept to me, so when it came to making contact with actual criminals or accused persons, I was at a huge disadvantage. Could I defend myself? I think I could if the situation required it of me, but sitting at the counter in the diner eight months pregnant was not the ideal situation in which to find out.

When I realized that the man who had introduced himself to Mark and me as Jacob decided to seat himself two barstools down from me, I acknowledged him with a tight smile and attempted to focus on the cinnamon roll that now felt more like paste in my mouth.

He ordered his meal then turned on his barstool to face me.

"Mrs. Collins, was it?" he asked.

My skin prickled, every hair on my arms rising. I took a drink of the water sitting in front of me hoping to clear my features before acknowledging him.

Before I could answer, a familiar pair of blue eyes met mine from the doorway. He had clearly made a quick trek from his office to the diner, which was not a far walk but was obviously a very quick jogging distance. I made it a point to look over the stranger's shoulder and waited for Mark to approach before making any kind of contact.

I was always happy to see him but in the moment, I was also relieved that he was here.

"Hey, love. Fancy seeing you here," I said beaming up at him.

Mark sidled up next to me and casually wrapped his left arm around me, pulling me in to kiss my temple. I could feel the warmth radiating from his physical exertion but his breathing was perfectly even. He didn't let go of me and coolly rested his right hand on his hip where his firearm was holstered.

"I heard Barb had just pulled out a tray of cinnamon rolls, and those are hard to resist," he teased as he nodded toward my empty plate.

"I'll have your cinnamon roll out in just a sec, Sheriff," Barb said as she breezed by to refill a customer's coffee.

Barb was the best.

It was then that Mark acknowledged our onlooker who had turned his attention back to his coffee while occasionally cutting his eyes to us.

"Jacob, nice to see you, again," Mark said casually with a jut of his chin.

"Sheriff," he responded with a less than genuine smile, something impendent in his eyes, and a drawn out tone that sounded sardonic.

Mark took the seat that had been separating me from Jacob,

keeping his body turned toward the man, looking casual though I knew his posture to be anything but. He was coiled, bracing himself as he inventoried the situation. Having seen Mark in action on more than one occasion over the years, I could see the pieces of the puzzle surrounding us falling into place. He had a plan for any and every potential scenario forming in his mind. His presence alone was comforting, but knowing I was safe in his presence, made it easy for me to relax.

"So, Jacob, what brings you to Owenston?"

Without missing a beat he jerked his thumb toward the door and replied, "Having some work done on my rig."

That was definitely information that lined up with Jacob Milton based on what Mark shared from the results of his search the the man was a big rig truck driver. I studied his body language and posture while his focus was on Mark.

Brazen. Smug. Assuming.

It was interesting that while his posture said one thing, his eyes were constantly searching which contradicted the message that he had a handle on his own situation. He watched Mark intently, eyes flickering to the holster on his belt on more than one occasion.

I had tuned out their conversation in favor of observation until I heard Mark say, "Barb, make sure his order goes on our ticket."

With her trademark smile in place she gave a nod and said, "Sure, thing, Sheriff."

This had an interesting effect on our visitor. Immediately he had tensed but almost as quickly relaxed stretching both hands toward the counter and leaning back in an exaggerated stretch. The smugness he had exuded earlier amplified and was reflected in his eyes. He felt comfortable.

"Thank you, Sheriff. I appreciate the hospitality your town has given so generously," he said with a nod packed with false modesty.

"We don't get a lot of visitors in town and I thought it would be a nice way to say we're glad you're here," Mark offered. "If you need anything while you're in town, my office is just over there," he pointed through the window toward the large brick building that was next to the courthouse.

To an outsider, Mark was acting the gracious host, but I heard the intent in his words. He was telling Jacob, "I'm right here." And I could tell the message was received.

Clearing his throat, Jacob stood, pulled out his wallet and dropped a few dollar bills onto the counter. "Thanks, again, Sheriff. Maybe I'll get to repay your generosity soon," he said in a slow drawl. His eyes darted to me and with a crooked smile he gave a quick nod, "Mrs. Collins."

The smile I gave in return was tight lipped. I didn't respond otherwise. As soon as he was out the door, my entire body relaxed for the first time since he'd walked into the diner. Mark watched the man until he was no longer visible from where we sat then swiveled to face me.

He clearly read my relief and rested a hand on my cheek which I gladly pressed my face into, taking in its warmth. He silently studied me for a few more moments.

"You, OK?"

"This does not sit well with me," I said, still trying to process everything. "It cannot be coincidence that Jacob shows up so soon after Mrs. Brewer's passing and the boys being found in their current situation."

Drawing circles on the back of my hand with his thumb, I felt Mark processing everything, too, but mostly focused on me. It felt less like the warm vibrations we typically share and more like a hive of nervous bees stirring to life. I squeezed his hand in response.

"Jess, I don't want you anywhere near that man. I'm glad you sent the message so I could be here. My gut tells me he's who we're after but I don't want you involved in this investigation, OK?"

His words were commanding though his tone was gentle. But he didn't need to worry about me inserting myself into the investigation. My focus was on our family, the baby, and supporting him as best I could without being directly involved.

"And whether it's coincidence or not, we will do everything we can to take care of James and Colton. I spoke with Helen this morning and right now, the boys are going to stay exactly where they are, with John and Deborah. I'm going to reach out to Mrs. Brewer's sister-in-law and see if she can be of any help. In the meantime, I don't want you going anywhere alone. I know the town is protective of their own, so if you feel threatened at all, you make it known to anyone until I can get there."

He was right about our community. When I first landed in Owenston, my world had been abruptly turned on its axis, and I was wary of people in general. The first time I ventured into town without Cal, I felt the stares and the whispers but I also felt safe. It didn't take long after for the people to accept me as one of their own, but I knew it had more to do with my connection to the farm than who I was apart from it.

Mark, however, had zero waiting period when he came to town. He obviously had the same connections I'd had but there were also the obvious draws to him. His smile alone captivated any audience he conjured. The older ladies stood no chance at resistance which in turn meant the men of the town kept their attention on him, too. He was also charming and always willing to lend a hand if he saw a need. It would have been easy for me to find myself jealous of his quick acceptance into the community, but instead I simply felt blessed to be part of a city who could easily determine the value of one of its members.

Does the small town gossip get old? It does, but I cannot remember a single time it was ever malicious in its intent. And it's this line of thinking that makes me ask my next question.

"So, has anyone said anything to you about there being a new person in town? Surely, someone has said something at some point."

"Surprisingly, no. I had considered asking Sarah if she had any kind of insider information. She always seems to have a pulse on the town," Mark answered.

We walked several more minutes catching up on the rest of our mornings including how the doctor told me we were currently in a holding pattern for this baby. There had been no change but that really meant nothing at this point in the game. Things could change and progress just as rapidly as they could sit still.

As we crossed the last intersection that was near my car, Mark's phone buzzed with a notification. He checked it as I retrieved my keys and unlocked the door.

He turned the phone to face me and said, "Looks like word is spreading about the newcomer."

On the screen was a message from Sarah asking Mark to stop by her desk on his way in because she had some questions about an unfamiliar person that had been spotted at the diner.

I just smiled and shook my head in amusement. "Looks like your afternoon just geared up to be more interesting."

Leaning down and pressing a kiss to my lips Mark smiled. "There's never a dull moment in this town."

We said our goodbyes and went our separate ways. On the drive home I prayed that God would not only give all of us a peace of mind but that he would give the situation a quick resolution. I knew better than most how important it was to hand over the anxiety that came with the unknown. The situations in which I had no control tested this knowledge thoroughly. I couldn't handle letting this situation overwhelm me. There were already too many factors in my life that threatened my peace of mind on a daily basis that I had to surrender to the Giver of Peace. This one was simply joining the list.

Chapter 28

Mark

On the one hand, I knew it would be beneficial to speak with my administrative assistant, Sarah. She'd been in Owenston her entire life and genuinely had a pulse on the town as a whole. Very few things can happen that slip under her radar. On the other hand, there have been times when I've needed to listen, then sort out for myself the important information that I was looking for in the first place. In this case, it looked like we were going to need to combine forces to reach any certain conclusion.

"Sue Ellen Turner called just before I messaged you to tell me that there was a man at the diner that she thought looked menacing but a little familiar," Sarah was explaining. "She even sent me this photo from her phone but she still uses one of those older flip phones with a fickle camera and it may as well have been one of those blurred out photos they sometimes show on the news when they don't want the face to be seen."

She turned her phone so I could see the picture and she was right. There was nothing useful about the image I was seeing on the screen. I nodded patiently as she tucked her phone back into her desk drawer.

"So I asked her if she had asked anyone about the man or if anyone had offered up any information but she said no one knew anything about him. She even said Barbie had a tough time getting him to talk about anything specific and you know if Barbie can't crack a person with her heart of gold, then there's not a lot of hope for anyone else."

I scratched the stubble I'd let grow on my jaw and took in a deep breath before slowly letting it out. Maybe if Sue Ellen had noticed Jacob, it would not be long before someone actually recognized him. While I couldn't imagine anything bad coming of that scenario, I would like to be ahead of the rumor mill and maybe control some of the information before it took on a life of its own.

"Mrs. Sarah, does the name Jacob Milton mean anything to you?" I asked, trying to sound conversational.

With a furrowed brow, the woman appeared to be working through her memory bank. It did not take long before recognition dawned on her.

"Jacob Milton? Do you mean Jake Milton?"

My blood went to ice. James had said his mother's boyfriend's name was Jake.

"Who is Jake Milton?" I asked.

"Well, Jake was one of the boys that used to run around terrorizing the town with Jimmy Brewer and his brother before he died in that tragic accident. The year his parents were killed in a car accident he went to live in the group home north of here. Before that, he and Jimmy got into trouble everywhere they went, though neither of them ever really got the punishments they deserved. But once he left town, I never heard anything more about him."

It was hard not to tune her out but there were still a lot of unanswered questions floating around in my mind. I wasn't sure that Sarah would be the best one to continue my line of questioning with but I knew that I could ask her to keep anything we discussed under wraps and it would go into a Fort Knox kind of vault.

In hopes of keeping her from launching her own investigation, I gave her what I knew to be true. "It appears that our newcomer is named Jacob and has yet to provide his last name. He gave me a story about his rig needing work as to why he's in town. And honestly, I have no reason to push him to give any additional information. That being said, I have two favors to ask of you, if you are willing."

Sarah's eyebrows lifted and with a hand over her heart she said, "Of course, Sheriff. What can I do to help?"

"First of all, I think it would be best to keep anything we've talked about between us for now. If people start speculating or talking on their own, let's not give anything away, just yet. That being said, if you learn anything just from listening around town, I would really appreciate it if you would pass it on so I can be aware of what is happening in our community."

A sweet smile brightened her face as she gave a single nod. "You got it, Sheriff. I'll keep my listening ears on and you'll be the first to know if I learn anything."

Thanking her, I returned to my office where I considered calling Jess. Instead, I needed to call Kathleen Brewer. I hoped she would offer up some kind of answers that would open another avenue of this investigation.

Around the ever expanding table in the farmhouse kitchen, I silently listened and smiled at the conversations happening around me. I watched the faces and the smiles letting the moment stitch back together some of the small fissures the heaviness of the last two weeks had caused inside me.

When I was in D.C., before Jess was anything more than a coworker, I could work the most gruesome of cases and never once find myself emotionally invested. Becoming attached to the victims or giving more than the canned response of 'I'm sorry for your loss' was never an issue for me. I did my job. I followed the leads wherever they took me, I found the answers I was looking for, and I wrapped it up neatly at the end of the day inside a tan manila folder so I could start solving the next case. I worked completely detached from anything but the facts. Which was the exact opposite of how I watched Jess function on the cases we worked together.

Even though she was not one to show her hand to the suspects and even victims she worked with and she kept her emotions hidden away in the process, she would occasionally voice her empathy. She had a compassion that would break through her guards on especially hard cases and she let it show without apology. It was something I neither understood nor attempted to embrace. That is, until I learned how and why she worked the way she did. And even then, I struggled for a while to comprehend her ability to both compartmentalize and empathize with people. It wasn't until I had my own life-changing experience that the same shift happened for me.

For months as Jess and I navigated life after the investigation of Bryan's death, she would casually mention her faith and her hope for a happy future even in the face of the heartbreak she's faced.

I will never forget the first time she outright asked if I believed in God. We were on our way to Kentucky after a violent threat that had been made against Jess. The ride had been quiet. We all seemed to be in some mode of processing the events of the day. Then out of the blue, Jess turned to me and asked if I believed in God.

Immediately, I had gone on the defensive and years of pent up anger and emotions that I had never properly dealt with surrounding my childhood, the death of my older brother, things I had witnessed in combat and in my job bubbled up to the surface. And for whatever reason, I could not stop myself from unloading some of those thoughts on Jess. And rather than bristle at me, she simply thanked me for trusting her with my story. That had not been my first glimpse of her compassion directed at me, but it was the one that struck the sharpest chord inside me.

From that day forward for months I toed the line of wanting to push against the idea that there was hope in the face of all the ugliness I saw daily. Then there were days where I desperately though secretly wanted everything Jess would tell me about the God she trusted to be true. It was not until one night after I had spent an hour in John and Deborah Parker's living room being presented with reason after reason hope was real that I came face-to-face with a hope of my very own. Every wall I had ever erected around my heart, trying to deny that there was a God and life was only going to be as good as it had been, crumbled in light of the truths that I had been made aware of that evening.

It was not a complete one-eighty change for me overnight. In fact, it was almost a full year after that night that something inside me seemed to click into place, and I realized that I had changed drastically. I was no longer cynical and angry. Instead, I saw people in their places of hurt, sorrow, loss, bad decisions, wrong choices, and hopelessness, and I hurt for them. It was in those moments of watching an accused murderer confess to his crimes or a convicted kidnapper get his sentence or a neglected child get rescued that my desire for justice mingled with a desire to see the guilty individuals find the same grace and forgiveness and hope that I had found.

There were still days in that job that even with knowing my future was secured and full of promise that I struggled with wanting to exact my own forms of justice, and it was those days I felt the weakest. These last two weeks were reminiscent of that. My heart and mind felt weighed down and I was struggling to hold on to the good. It was sitting here with my family, the family that opened their arms and hearts even when I rejected the best thing they had to offer me, that reminded me I was not dealing with this crisis on my own. Being here was a reminder that God had not only given me a new outlook, but he had graciously provided a physical representation of hope, love, joy, and peace through the mere existence of these people he had surrounded me with when I needed them most.

In that moment, I knew whatever came of the circumstances in which we found ourselves, hope was waiting for us on the other side.

Chapter 29

Jess

It was hard to believe that Christmas was just around the corner. It was just over a week away which meant my due date was just a couple of weeks away. There was so much going on for our family, both immediate and extended, that I was finding myself exhausted by the end of each day. We bowed out immediately after dinner with everyone because Mark had seen my chin slip off my hand when I dozed off as I was listening to Colton excitedly tell us about his most recent school project. Marí had also seen it happen and shooed us out when I offered to help clear the table. I was grateful as I had only offered half-heartedly, and I really only felt a little guilty until Mark offered to put Hayley to bed and allowed me to sink into my own bed well before the normal hour I'd fall asleep most nights.

There was no telling what time it was when a tiny sob followed by a sniffle woke me from beside my face. It only took a second for me to come to full awake and slide out of bed to scoop a crying Hayley into my arms along with her favorite blanket. Not wanting to wake Mark, I gently shushed her and stroked her hair as I walked her into the living room. I probably should not have carried her as it was definitely a lot harder than it was even a year ago. But, my baby needed her mommy and I was going to make it work.

We rocked gently on the couch in the dark living room and I was immediately transported back to the seemingly endless nights when this had almost become routine. She and I had drawn comfort from one another then as we let our hearts crumble and repair in those dark hours. One day I will tell her how much those moments meant to me, and she will be able to understand the depths to which I would go to make sure her heart was always taken care of, but tonight, she was hurting for some reason and she needed me to be her comfort.

When her sniffles subsided I leaned back trying to determine if Hayley had fallen asleep or had merely stopped crying. Trying to hide her face from me, she buried her nose into my chest and attempted to snuggle down into me. This was not an easy feat as there was a very round baby bump to curl herself around. Nonetheless, I let her and I squeezed her tighter, bringing her as close to me as I could.

Knowing she was still awake, I quietly asked, "Sweetheart, what's the matter? Did you have a bad dream?"

Without saying a word, Hayley nodded her face against me making a mess of both my shirt and I'm certain her face and hair.

"Do you want to talk about it," I asked.

Her ragged inhale immediately made my eyes fill with tears. She didn't answer but she was clearly hurting deeply from the dream that had awoken her. I didn't rush her to speak. Instead I gently rubbed circles across her back and smoothed her hair the best I could. After a while she turned her head and took a deep breath before sitting upright.

Her face was red and tear streaked and in need of washing. Her hair was matted and damp where it had been wedged between her face and my shirt. I tried to smooth it down the best I could and used my shirt to dry and clean her face as much as possible. Then I held her face in my hands and kissed her forehead.

"You don't have to talk about it if you don't want to. But I will listen when you need me to, OK?"

Hayley stared down at my belly then gripped her blanket tighter in both hands. After a long sniffle, she brushed her hair back from her face and raised her eyes to mine.

"I dreamed that you got a new baby and made me sleep in the barn with Henny."

Her voice was barely a whisper but her words were like a knife to my heart. A thousand thoughts flitted through my mind as my heart began to race. Questions that wanted to demand answers propelled themselves into my brain such as *Why would you ever think this? Did someone say something to make you think this would happen? Who do I need to talk to about this?* Of course I couldn't voice any of this aloud and would never verbalize them to her. Instead, I wrapped her tightly in my arms and held her as the tears finally left my eyes.

"Oh, Hayley, sweetheart, that is a terrible dream. You know that would never happen don't you?" I asked, trying to keep my voice steady. "Your daddy and I love you so much and would be sad if you were anywhere but right here with us at bedtime or any time."

She pulled back, her eyes downcast again and she gave a small shrug with one shoulder before barely nodding twice.

I continued, "This baby is not coming to take your place. This baby is coming because we have so much love to give that God thought our family would be the perfect place for him or her. He knew that you would make the world's best big sister, and I agree with him. You helped pick out all of the new blankets and stuffies and I know you're already planning on teaching him or her how to take care of Henny. There will never be a time when you are not wanted here, do you understand that?"

Her watery eyes had brightened, if only a little, when she looked up at me again and nodded. She swiped at some of the rogue hairs that were falling back into her face and sniffled once more.

Hayley's voice was stronger when she spoke again. "Yes, ma'am."

My heart was ready to burst with love for my babies as I held both of them here with me in this moment. I hugged Hayley and this time she wrapped her arms around my neck and hugged me back. We stayed that way for several minutes.

"Are you ready to go back to bed?" I asked.

She nodded, this time her face was pressed against my neck. I scooted to the edge of the couch but there was no way I could stand holding her.

"Hey, bug? I think I'll need you to walk back to your room. But I'll come tuck you in after you go wash your face, OK?"

She smiled. "Your belly is too big," she said before covering up a giggle.

Seeing her smile made me smile. "I know. I look like a balloon, don't I?" I whispered.

"You don't look like a balloon. You look like a pretty mommy."

The tears were back but this time it was just my heart leaking from my eyes. It was full, and I knew I didn't deserve everything I'd been given back in the last two years. But I was thankful - so very thankful.

Once I had Hayley tucked in, she closed her eyes and drifted off in seconds. I, however, was wide awake. There were still so many thoughts and images swirling in my head that my already tired brain was struggling to catch up but the one thought that stood out the most was that from now until this baby came, I needed to make sure Hayley was assured daily how precious she was to both Mark and me. There needed to be zero room for doubt in her little heart or mind.

Resolved that I was going to lie in bed waiting for my alarm to go off, I crawled back in after a trip to the bathroom. As I tried to gently ease back into my spot under the covers, an arm came around me and pulled me backwards.

"Everything O.K.?" a sleepy husky voice asked into the back of my neck.

A chill shuddered over me before I relaxed into the warm hold.

"Hayley had a bad dream," I whispered. "She's fine. You can go back to sleep."

Mark must have heard how awake I sounded even though I'd tried to disguise it in a whisper. He leaned up on his elbow, so I turned my head to face him. There was barely enough light in the room to see much but the ambient light from the moon filtering in through the windows showed me enough. The concern on his face tugged on my heartstrings. I rolled onto my back so I could see him more clearly.

"What?" I asked, unable to make any kind of deduction in the dark.

Running a finger down my nose and over my lips and stopping at my chin he leaned down and lightly kissed the tip of my nose.

"I just hate that you're awake. I know you haven't been sleeping well, and you've been exhausted by the end of the day for the last week. And now you're awake at 3:00 A.M. What can I do to help?"

This man.

Tears stung my eyes and I started to question my emotional stability. I reached up and rested my hand on his cheek and he leaned into it before turning and pressing a kiss to my palm then pressing his face into my hand. Gently, I stroke his cheek with my thumb. All I could do was stare up into the face of the man who has repeatedly picked me up and helped me find my footing in the face of danger, sadness, anxiety, and now exhaustion.

Knowing he needed to be given some kind of job, an assignment, in order to feel connected to the situation, I smiled. "How late can you let me sleep in this morning?"

I felt the smile more than I could see it. "As late as you need to sleep," he said softly. "I'll get Hayley situated, and we'll go hang out at the farmhouse in the morning. You can take as much time as you need to rest."

"Hmm," I sighed before pulling his face to mine. "I don't deserve you," I whispered.

"And I don't deserve you. Yet, here we are, living the dream together."

His lips pressed to mine and lingered for several quiet moments.

Mark helped me reposition and wrapped me up in his arms. With a gentle kiss to my shoulder he murmured, "Sweet dreams, Jess."

Very little time passed between his words and my slumber. The next thing I knew, I was waking up in a sunlit room feeling much more energized than I had in several days.

Chapter 30

Mark

When I left Jess in bed, she finally looked restful. She barely moved once she fell back asleep and it made it extremely hard for me to want to leave her. But I heard movement in the living room so I knew that was my cue to get up.

Sure enough, I was met with bleary green eyes and a head full of messy hair when I walked out of the bedroom and immediately my heart felt full. Hayley walked towards me, rubbing her eyes with the back of her hand while she gripped her blanket in the other.

When she was within reaching distance, she raised her arms and as I always did when she reached for me, I picked her up and held her close. She buried her head in my shirt and her free hand went to my face and lightly rubbed the stubble forming on my jaw, a habit she formed the day we met. I closed my eyes and smiled, breathing in the scent of her fruity kids shampoo and enjoying the quiet moment meant just for us.

There had never been a moment in my life where I thought I would raise a child, much less another man's child. If I'm being honest, until a few years ago, a committed relationship was not even on my radar. Now, I can't imagine my life any other way.

As I'm standing there, I quietly say, "Mommy told me you had a bad dream last night."

She nodded, her head still pressed against me.

"Did your dreams get better after you snuggled with mommy?"

She nodded again.

"Good. How do you feel about pancakes for breakfast before we go play with Sadie, James, and Colton?"

This got her attention and her head popped up revealing a now bright-eyed smiling face. Her head nod became more vigorous.

"OK, go get dressed, and I'll make pancakes. But we're going to do everything as quiet as we can so we don't wake mommy. Think you can do that?" I asked as I set her feet on the ground.

Giving me her mischievous grin she nodded again, slowly, put a finger to her lips, and tiptoed toward her bedroom. My phone buzzed on the counter as I chuckled watching her sneak away. I had a message from John.

Any chance you and Jess would be available to watch the boys while Deborah and I wrap Christmas presents?

There was a combination of joy and dread inside me as I read the message. It gave me so much joy to think those boys could have found a family and filled in a missing puzzle piece at the same time. I knew, however, that until it was finalized, nothing was secure. I had to hope the Parkers remembered the same thing at least somewhere in the back of their minds. Regardless, I admired them for their willingness and excitement to love these kids unconditionally at first sight.

I texted John back suggesting I would arrange to leave Hayley with Marí so she could play with Sadie and I would take the boys into town for a "guys day". I had no idea what that might look like, but it sounded like the start of a good plan. John agreed so I set the plan in motion, starting with pancakes for my little girl.

Hayley was more than happy at the idea of having Sadie, Marí, and Cal all to herself. There was a bond between the four of them that was unique and special. I could only hope that one day Hayley would understand how blessed she was to have such a diverse group of people to love and support her.

Marí was there from the darkest of the days Jess and Hayley experienced. She took care of both of my girls before they were mine and walked through the valley of the shadow of death holding Jess's hand every step of the way. Even though she was older, Sadie played a huge role by acting as a surrogate big sister to Hayley. She was a built-in playmate and distraction which made the adults' jobs easier most days. Cal came into the picture shortly after Bryan's death. And not just because she was Bryan's daughter, though that was a contributing factor, but Cal loved Hayley from the moment he'd laid eyes on her.

Cal had never had a permanent family of his own until the day I delivered Jess and the rest of the crew to his doorstep. He had stepped in when Bryan's father died and had taken care of Bryan's mother as she battled ALS until her death. Bryan had been like a son to him and though he never said it aloud to me, I know he took that loss hardest of all. It had been ugly and unexpected. In the end, as he told us all in numerous ways and on numerous occasions, God redeemed his losses and restored to him ten-fold even when he didn't deserve it. It's always his favorite reminder to give when things look bleak.

These were the thoughts that occupied my mind as I cleaned up the kitchen after breakfast. I was pulled from these thoughts when Hayley announced she was ready to go. When I looked up, I discovered she was wearing what looked like two sweaters with her sweatpants and a pair of pink fuzzy boots. She had her backpack on one shoulder and her hair was a wild rat's nest on top of her head.

Trying to conceal the laugh building inside me I said, "It does appear that you are ready to go somewhere. Do you think I could help you brush your hair and put it back in a ponytail before we go?" I was trying to be gentle and not hurt her feelings.

Hayley had reached an age at which she was adamant about being independent and sometimes it was to the detriment of fashion sense. Jess and I agreed there were harder battles we'd decide to fight when we came to them. I was afraid, however, the hair might be a little too far gone to let it stay in its current state. Jess would probably kill me if I let Hayley leave the house in all of the spectacular glory in which she'd appeared.

With a heavy sigh Hayley dropped her chin practically to her chest and muttered, "Fine."

Barely able to stifle a laugh because she was far too adorable to scold her sass, I nodded toward her room. "Go get your brush and meet me back on the couch. I'll make it quick and then we'll go."

Situated on the couch, I detangled the fuzz wrapped around the elastic band in Hayley's hair without incident. As I used my fingers to make the hair a little easier to brush, Hayley surprised me by saying, "I like it when you brush my hair. It feels like you're being careful, and I like that."

I had never once imagined I would be sitting on a couch brushing a little girl's hair or even knowing how to do it, yet here I was. The emotions that crashed over me in that moment were intense and I could not give a single reason why, other than this girl owned my heart and I lived to make her feel safe and loved.

Clearing my throat so I could speak through the thickness building there I said, "I like brushing your hair. And I will always be careful with you because you are my little girl and I love you."

With one last twist of the ponytail holder and a swipe of the brush, I handed the brush to Hayley and said, "Alright, now I think you're ready to go."

She hopped up and turned around and wrapped her arms around my neck. "Thank you, daddy. I love you, too." With that, she kissed my cheek and skipped off to her room to return the brush.

When she came back, we loaded up her stuff and headed for the farmhouse.

Chapter 31

Mark

Being a girl dad had woefully under-prepared me for keeping up with two young boys. Hayley and I have our moments of high energy activities but she is just as content for us to have a quiet tea party or play in her room with her toys. And even if we do find ourselves playing outside and running around, it's never as full contact as the morning had been with James and Colton. Adding to our morning excitement, I am almost positive Colton only stopped talking long enough to hear any answers or responses meant for him before he was immediately back at it. Physically and mentally exhausted after spending hours running around the park, tossing a football, and listening to a constant stream of chatter, I decided it was time for a break.

Colton was explaining how he had recently learned that lizards' tails can be removed and they would grow back as we parked and were making our way down the sidewalk toward the diner. We were mere steps from the door when Jacob stepped out onto the sidewalk and froze when he spotted us. The boys mirrored the action, eyes wide, faces going pale. My immediate reaction was to position myself between him and the boys.

Trying to maintain a casual air between us I took a step forward and smiled, knowing it wasn't reaching beyond my mouth and with a nod greeted him. "Jacob."

His eyes were not focused on me but were instead moving between James and Colton. They shifted uncomfortably and stared at the ground.

"Boys, why don't you two go inside and find us a table. Tell Miss Barb I'll be inside in just a minute."

The boys both jostled their way through the door, Jacob's eyes not leaving them until they were out of view and being seated in a booth toward the back of the diner. Then he turned to face me. A mask slid into place hiding any genuine feelings he may have had.

Sliding his hands into his pockets he gave a nod, "Sheriff Collins."

"Jacob. I guess this is becoming a habit for us, meeting here."

"It would seem so. Those your boys in there?" He asked, gesturing with a tilt of his head.

"They are not. Just my charges for the day," I answered coolly. Unwilling to allow his focus to remain on the boys I turned the conversation back to him. "How long are you in town for, Jacob?"

"It's hard to say. However long it takes, I reckon."

"Alright. Well, it was good to see you, Mr. -" I trailed off. "What was your last name, again?"

His grin was cocky as though he knew I hadn't forgotten anything. "Miller," he said.

"Good to see you, Mr. Miller. I'm sure we'll run into each other again, soon."

With that, I dismissed him and entered the diner where I found James and Colton whispering in a booth. As I took my seat they went silent. Colton stared at the table while James considered speaking, swallowing several times before he did.

"Do you know him?" James finally asked, his voice barely a whisper.

Folding my hands, I leaned forward over the table and shook my head. "Not really. Do you?"

James quickly scanned the room as though he sensed a threat looming, his bottom lip falling victim to his teeth. His voice was shaky when he spoke again.

"That's Jake." James's eyes met mine then quickly fell to the table where he fidgeted with an empty straw wrapper, twisting it into a tight spiral.

This was exactly the confirmation I had been looking for and while I should be experiencing a victory, I was instead overcome with a sense of dread and concern. Jacob "Jake" Milton had not only recognized the boys, the boys had recognized him. And he'd lied about his last name.

My mind briefly drifted to the phone conversation I'd had with Kathleen Brewer. She hadn't known the circumstances of Eileen's death, but had seen the obituary in the paper. According to her, she had only visited her brother's home twice, both times had been right after one of the boys had been born. Otherwise, her contact had been relegated to occasional phone calls with her brother until their last one - the day he went to prison. He had cut all contact with his family that day.

Aside from her concern and condolences for the boys, Kathleen was happy to know that James and Colton were being cared for and offered her assistance in any way if it was needed. That led me to asking her about Jake Milton. She had gotten quiet when she heard the name for so long I thought the call had been disconnected.

Then she quietly asked, "Does Jake have something to do with Eileen's passing?"

I assured her I didn't know anything for certain and that I had just recently learned he had been friends with her brother. She paused again for a long time as though she weighed her words before speaking.

"Sheriff, Jake Milton was never the guy you wanted to make angry. He and Jimmy stirred up a lot of trouble when they were younger and for all the trouble Jimmy started on his own, the kind Jake got into was a lot worse. He had a horrible temper and it fueled a lot of his behavior. I'm honestly surprised it hasn't landed him in a lot more trouble. If he was hanging around Eileen I wouldn't hesitate looking into him more."

Not wanting to push her, I'd thanked her and promised I would be in touch if I needed to speak to her again or if I had updates she needed to know.

I returned my attention to James and Colton who were quietly talking about lizards once again and munching on their fries. They pulled me into their conversation and I was happy to join in if it meant they were able to think about anything other than the experiences they'd had in the last few weeks. I was even able to jump in and tell them about some of the lizards I'd encountered in Afghanistan and how I'd find them hanging out in my boots - sometimes by their own choice and sometimes by the choices of my tent-mates.

As we sat there, a couple of the men from the town stopped by our table, James and Colton taking the opportunity to entertain them with some of their stories from the farm. Even though they had not been there long, it was obvious to anyone who spoke to them that they had started to think of the farm as a place where they belonged. It was a special place. My hope was that it felt like home. I knew the moment I stepped foot on that property that it was a place anyone could feel at peace and at home. And I knew deep down that I was going to fight for these boys to be able to make it theirs, protecting and keeping them safe in the process.

Chapter 32

Mark

As it was Saturday, everyone would most likely be at the farmhouse getting ready for dinner by the time James, Colton, and I pulled down the long driveway. The ride home was the quietest Colton had been since the kid had come onto the scene. The silence was welcomed but also heightened the restlessness inside me.

I kept waiting for the boys to ask questions or say anything about Jake but their attention had remained focused elsewhere. As far as I could tell, they had zero curiosity about the situation I had been replaying in my mind on a loop.

Putting the truck in park, I turned to the boys and said, "Hey, guys, thanks for hanging out with me today."

With his reserved smile James gave a quick nod and, never to be without a reply, Colton said, "Thanks, Sheriff Collins! It was a really great day."

My only desire at that moment was to make sure every day they had was a really great day. The reality was, however, I could never promise that. Instead, I nodded and said, "It really was, Colton."

The mood inside the farmhouse when we walked in was the

usual warm excitement that seemed to be infused into the house itself and amplified by the people inside its walls. The volume and activity increased noticeably as Colton began a recap of the day. James sat at the table next to him quietly but with a look of contentment resting on his features - a clear improvement from his typical scowl.

Jess walked up beside me as I stared at the scene. Her presence surprised me. I wasn't sure if it was because I had been lost in thought about the conversation I was going to have with the adults this evening or if she had walked in from another part of the room. Regardless, she had seen me and my face had sent her an urgent message without my knowing. It wasn't often I forgot she didn't need my words to know what I was thinking, but somehow that's exactly what had just happened.

She wrapped her arms around my neck and stood on her tiptoes, my arms immediately enveloped her around her waist. "Whatever happened today, we can talk about it now if you need to," she whispered in my ear before moving to plant a kiss on my lips. She rested her feet back on the ground and leaned back to observe my reaction.

My focus had been redirected solely onto her as it always was when she was near me. "I love you, and thank you. Something did happen today, but it's something that I need to talk to all of the adults about, which means it will have to wait until after dinner."

She smiled and slid her hands over my shoulders and rested them on my biceps. "OK," she said with a nod. "I missed you today. You look a little ragged. Did the boys wear you out?"

This made me chuckle. "You have no idea. I might need to start getting in some two-a-days with my workouts just in case this one's a boy," I moved a hand and rested it on her belly. "They have a completely different energy than Hayley and Sadie."

Her laugh was a light my soul had been missing since my run-in with Jake. Releasing her grip on my arms, she took my hand in hers and led me to the kitchen. It took a couple beats before I felt ready to dive into the conversation knowing the one that was to come. Once I got there, however, the anxiety that had been building melted. As we ate and talked, I was reminded again how much I loved this place and these people and how much we needed each other.

———

After her bad dream, Jess and I decided it would be beneficial to talk to Hayley about the new baby and some of the things that were going to change in the near future. Once she was in her pajamas and ready for bed, the three of us piled into her twin size daybed as we had done countless times before, only this time Jess made it a point to stay near the edge. She learned the hard way not long ago that it took a lot of effort to get from the back to the front of the bed.

Hayley created a small nest of pillows, blankets, and stuffed animals around herself then offered each of us a pillow and stuffed animal. When we were all situated and comfortable, Jess started the conversation.

"Hayley-bug, your daddy and I wanted to talk to you about some things that are happening soon. But first, do you want to tell us if you've had any more bad dreams?"

She fidgeted with one of her favorite stuffed puppies and danced it on top of one of the pillows. "Nope, no more bad dreams. I did dream that I rode a unicorn."

Jess and I both chuckled. "A unicorn? That sounds like fun," I mused.

Hayley nodded, "It was. I wish unicorns were real."

When it came to this kid, smiling was non-optional. It just happened and it was magical. I'd go so far as to say it was almost as magical as riding a unicorn sounded.

I reached out and adjusted her puppy's ear that had flipped over and said, "So, are you excited to be a big sister, soon?"

Her eyes grew big as did her smile. "Yes! I'm going to help mommy and the baby can sleep in here with me. I'll even share Puppy."

Jess reached out and brushed a few strands of hair from Hayley's face. "You can definitely help me, but I think the baby will sleep in the room next door for a little while. He or she will be so small that they might get lost in the pile of stuffies you keep on your bed."

"Okay. But I'll still share Puppy. Puppy is the best," she said, turning the dog in circles as though it was cartwheeling.

"There's something else we wanted to talk to you about," I said.

She stopped and looked at me with a serious face.

I continued, "When this baby is born," I rested my hand on Jess's belly, "we'll give it a name and the last name will be Collins like mine and mommy's. We were wondering if you would be okay with changing your last name to Collins, too, so we would all match."

A slow grin spread across her face turning into a beaming smile. She launched herself at me and loudly said, "Yes!"

The three of us smiled and snuggled briefly before Hayley sat back allowing her thoughts to become words.

"Can we name the baby Hayley like me if it's a girl so we can match?"

Jess and I laughed, and it felt good to be here and present just being together and laughing.

"I think that might get confusing if we had two Hayleys. Maybe we should come up with a list of names and we can all choose our favorite and it will make it easier to decide when the baby is born," Jess suggested.

And that's what we did. For the next half hour, we made a list of names, most of which would never actually become an option, but Hayley enjoyed being a part of the process. When she suggested Twinkle Star, we decided it was time to call it a night.

Chapter 33

Mark

I was at my desk, Helen Davis sitting across from me. In my gut a solid stone of disquiet weighed heavily. Because Jake had clearly recognized James and Colton, I felt the urgent need to bring Helen into the loop about my suspicions. It felt like a good idea to have as many people looking out for the boys as possible.

"I know it doesn't need to be said, but let's keep this information as locked down as we can for now. We'll tell the boys what they need to know and when they need to know it. There's no need to upset them," she told me.

I made my way around the desk to walk Ms. Davis to the door. "Thank you, Helen. You are handling this situation beautifully. I hope I can remain as objective as you through the process. I only want what is best for James and Colton."

She smiled softly and patted my arm. "You and I both do, Sheriff."

I felt my shoulders sag under the weight of the meeting and I leaned against the doorframe.

Sarah eyed me from her desk before suggesting, "Sheriff, why don't you head home for lunch. I think you could use some down time. Your schedule is clear the rest of the day. I can manage things until then, and I'll call you if I can't."

Trying to muster at least a half smile, I thanked Sarah for the suggestion and told her I would let her know my plans when I made them. Then I returned to my office, closed the door, and hit my knees to beg God to intervene and secure the boys' safety. He was the Great Defender and Protector. A while passed before I was back on my feet, my heart feeling lighter though my spirit still heavy with the pressure of the unknown.

Before I could decide what my next move would be, my cell phone vibrated with a message from Tim Stephens.

Final DNA results are in - inconclusive. Results in your email.

Sure enough, as I clicked and scrolled through the report, there was nothing other than fingerprints belonging to Jacob Milton tying him to Eileen Brewer. It wasn't enough in the way of physical evidence, and I wasn't ready to risk having the boys make any kind of official statement. They hadn't actually seen the person who had been in their home; therefore, I was not bringing them into it. I wouldn't until I had to. But I really needed a reason to bring Jacob in for questioning without putting a target on anyone.

Frustrated, I rested my elbows on my desk and squeezed my head on both sides with my fingers in an attempt to relieve the building pressure. Releasing on heavy breath I decided I needed to clear my mind and there was only one place that was guaranteed to happen. I grabbed my coat and hat and headed out the door to let Sarah know where she could reach me if she needed me. Then, I headed home.

Chapter 34

Jess

When Mark walked in too late for lunch but too early for his work day to be over, a pit formed in my stomach. Normally, he would call before he came home unexpectedly but the look on his face told me there was not much about his homecoming that was normal. He looked tired and dejected. There was also some worry and sadness he was not trying to mask.

Hayley had dozed off in my lap on the couch so I had sat there and enjoyed the quiet with a book. One look at Mark told me he needed me more than she did at that moment. I gently maneuvered her head out of my lap and onto the pillow on the sofa and headed straight for Mark. He had just slipped his boots off at the door when my arms wrapped around him. His arms draped over my shoulders and he rested his head on mine. We stood in silence for several minutes. The emotions rolled off him and over me as we wordlessly processed whatever he was carrying together.

His work phone buzzed on his hip pulling us from the quiet moment. He released one arm and checked the message, sighing as he stared at the screen. Questions were building inside me but my curiosity would have to take a backseat to the needs of the man standing here with me. Instead, I waited for him to tell me what he needed from me. His eyes closed in a resigned frustration, and he let out a heavy sigh.

Mark put his phone back in its holder and slid the hand into mine. We silently walked toward the back door then out onto the back deck. He flipped the switch for the gas fireplace before sitting on the outdoor sofa and pulling me down next to him.

"Is it too cold for this?" he asked as he pressed his lips to the top of my head.

I shook my head as we both stared into the flames. Unlike me, Mark always had to work through as many answers and scenarios to his quandary before he would talk about it. My ability to give quick initial assessments and his pragmatic thinking process is what made us such a good team, a balanced team. And even though we aren't working cases together anymore, we still made a really good and balanced team. While I waited for him to process his thoughts I found my own drifting to the past.

Two and a Half Years Ago

My phone buzzed in my pocket just as I was leaving Hayley's room. I tugged the door closed behind me until it latched then pulled my phone out. I was already smiling because I knew whose name I'd see before I looked at the screen.

"Hey," I half-whispered as I walked quietly down the stairs. Mari and Cal were at the table doing a puzzle so I gave a little nod as I walked out onto the front porch.

"Hi," the deep voice said, the smile evident in his tone. "You're whispering. Did I interrupt something?"

"No, I was just leaving Hayley's room when you called. She was a little restless this evening, so it took her a while to get to sleep."

"Is she okay?" There was an edge of concern in his words.

My heart melted. "She's fine. Some days are just harder than others, you know?"

"Mhm."

There was a longer pause which wasn't unusual except this one felt different.

"Mark?"

"I'm here. I was just thinking."

"Yeah? Care to share with the class?" I asked, half-teasing but also feeling as though something big was hanging between us.

"Maybe. But first, how was your day? Was today a hard day for you, too, or just Hayley-bug?"

His nickname for her made my cheeks ache from the smile it put on my face.

I thought about it for a moment before answering. It had been six months since Bryan had been taken from me, six months since the life I'd known had crashed down around me in flames. It had been two months since the building blocks of a new life had started forming into a new shape when Mark confessed his true feelings for me, and I'd come to realize just how deeply I felt for him. Time was a funny thing.

The year before Bryan's murder had been one of the longest years of my life. Days passed by in slow motion as the tears and frustrations pummeled me like machine gun fire. The six months after his death, had whipped by like a speeding train. And the tears became less frequent, and the heartache lessened. My mind was clearer than it had been in a long time, and I was able to focus on reclaiming the joy I had lost. Today, even with the struggles of adjustment I'd faced with Hayley, I felt at peace with where we'd landed.

"It was a good day," I finally answered.

"Good." He sounded relieved.

"Mark, you are either really distracted or you have something you need to say and aren't saying it." We had talked on the phone enough times that I knew this wasn't just a case of him being distracted, but I wanted to give him the opening he needed.

He sighed and I could picture him running a hand down his whiskered face. He was probably still at the office, so he'd be reclined in his desk chair staring at the ceiling. We'd spent many hours in his office with him just like this while I sat in a chair on the other side of his desk going through notes in a file or reading email on my phone.

Several more beats of silence went by before he finally said, "Jess, I could really use your eyes, but I don't want to put you in this position."

"You need my help on a case? Why didn't you just ask?"

He hesitated. "Because it's not just any case. It's the case."

Everything inside me and around me seemed to freeze in time as he emphasized "the case". We sat in silence for several minutes.

I finally mustered the words, "What do you need me to do?"

There was another hesitant silence.

"Jess," my name from his lips was full of emotion. He must have really needed my help because he clearly didn't want to ask for it. It sounded as though it pained him.

"Mark. If you need my help, I want to help," I said, almost believing my own words.

He took a deep breath before letting it whoosh out and saying, "You know I'm breaking at least twelve rules by even asking."

The corner of my lips twitched. If there was one thing I knew about Mark, it was that he followed the rules to the letter.

It was just above a whisper, but I managed to say, "Let me help."

Taking on a case was nothing new. I'd been working and consulting virtually for years, especially after Hayley was born. Now, my office was just five hundred miles away from my base of operations. The idea of getting involved with Bryan's case felt different. I was aware that it was different, but I also had to remind myself that I had been given the gifts I had for a reason. And I also wanted justice for Bryan.

The sound of Mark shifting on the other end of the phone had me picturing him leaning forward from his chair and resting his elbows on his desk, one hand massaging just above his eyebrow because that was a thing he did. He never made snap decisions and he was clearly still debating this one. And when he was torn about a decision, he'd rub a small scar that was hardly noticeable until he rubbed it absentmind-

edly and drew attention to it. While I appreciated that he was taking into account the breadth of impact this decision could have on me, I also needed him to know that I had a lot riding on the resolution of this case.

When he finally spoke, he had shifted into full-on Special Agent mode sparking something inside me. Since I started noticing him, I'd always found him attractive, but FBI Mark was something else.

"So, we know the victim was a government employee who had initially been working on a classified project. He had connections to our suspect but, from everything we've gathered those ties were loose at best with the exception of a couple meetings they had in the last three and a half years. Nothing shows that anything came from those meetings though testimony revealed the suspect did offer the victim employment which he turned down."

Hearing all of this again made my insides shiver with trepidation. I knew I had to do this, but it was already harder than I imagined. My entire body was vibrating with nervous tension.

Mark paused, then asked, "Jess, are you still there?"

That's when I realized I hadn't taken a real breath since he'd started talking. I took a sharp inhale and shook my shoulders.

"Yeah, I was just listening." My words were hollow, and we both knew it.

"Jess, you don't have to do this."

My voice quavered, "Yes, I do."

With that being my only statement, Mark continued.

"What we were able to deduce with the help of our victim's thorough personal investigation and the trail he left for us, was that our suspect was working with an unidentified source to gain access to sensitive information. This is where you come in, Jess. We think the suspect is working with someone inside the CIA, and we have our suspicions narrowed down, but have you ever interrogated someone from the CIA? It's like talking to a brick wall."

His words hung between us as I took in the magnitude of what he *was saying. This was an inside job, meaning Pete was likely a fall guy in over his head, and we were going to go toe-to-toe with the CIA.*

"What do you need me to do?" I asked, feeling less confident than I had been feeling.

"We have multiple recorded interviews with the suspect in which the agent questioning him casually drops the names of some of the CIA agents we're looking into. I'd like you to watch the interviews and see if there are any reactions to the names we didn't pick up on."

I couldn't help the amused huff that escaped as I thought about the first time Mark and I met. It was in an office at the university where I worked, and that meeting led to me watching videos of interrogations that led to the exoneration of an ex-NFL player who had been accused of murder.

"You know, if I do this, the FBI is going to owe me a favor," I said, grinning as I remembered the deal we made after that initial case. He'd suggested that as my services had been done as more of a personal favor to him, my compensation would in turn be a favor from him. Never in a million years would I have imagined how big of a favor I would be asking of him almost four years later.

I could tell he remembered, too. "I'll do anything you ask of me," his voice was quiet but firm, sending a warm buzzing sensation through me I hadn't felt in a long time.

The tone of our conversation shifted after that, turning to topics like our plans for the rest of the week and we ended with a schedule to video conference about the case. I spent the next several hours tossing and turning in my bed, unable to fall asleep with the thoughts of seeing Pete's face again and having to study it up close and personally. And then I'd hear Mark's low rumble of "I'll do anything you ask of me," and my heart would race at supersonic speed. I missed him, and I loved him, and I hated that he was even having to ask for my help. But, I reminded myself that we were a good team, and we had been brought together for a reason.

Lost in my thoughts I was startled when Mark started to speak.

"The only evidence we have is circumstantial at best, hearsay at worst. And none of it is conclusive," his voice was quiet and sad, tinged with anger.

I repositioned so I could see his face. His eyes were sad and a bit angry, too.

"And the way he keeps hanging around is unnerving. Why hang around after doing something so awful unless he has some other reason to stay? And if he has another reason to be here, I need to figure it out before it costs someone else their life."

There was underlying anger in his tone. It was rare that Mark became emotional when it came to cases of any kind. The last time he reacted like this was the day he and I found ourselves being targeted by a hidden shooter who happened to be the same man who killed Bryan. There is a reason law enforcement is not allowed to work cases involving family or other closely tied victims. At the time, however, he and I had only been colleagues. This is hitting even closer to home for him since it impacts all of us.

"And I have to talk to John and Deborah but not let James or Colton know anything is wrong. They've been through enough."

I reached a hand up to his face and ran my thumb over his cheek. He pressed his face into my palm. "We don't know what's going to happen, but we'll all get through it like we always do - together," I told him.

He wrapped his hand around mine before pulling it to his lips and kissing it. "I love you," he said, his words confident, less defeated. "You're right. I just don't want to see the boys or the Parkers hurt again. And I definitely don't want to put you, Hayley, or the baby in danger."

Mark hadn't known John and Deborah well until the aftermath of Bryan's death had died down significantly. But the bond they formed was almost instant. John had taken him under his wing and walked with him through the questions Mark had about God and the Bible. They became fast friends and Deborah had made it a point to have Mark over for dinner at least once a week. Not that Bryan would ever be replaced, but Mark had filled a void in their lives and it had clearly been mutual for him. They became family to him, and now his family was potentially facing heartache again.

"How can I help you?" I asked.

"Come with me when I talk to them. I think Deborah will need you there."

"OK."

We sat on the couch for another half hour simply being together when Mark's phone buzzed again. I maneuvered myself to standing and held out a hand to him which he took even though my assistance was merely for show.

Before checking his phone, Mark pulled me into an embrace so warm that I considered staying outside in the cold longer just to snuggle into him again.

"Jess, I know I tell you this all the time, but I am so thankful for you. Just sitting here was everything I needed, and I don't know how you do it but you knew. Thank you." He sounded better, more focused, less tense.

I squeezed him around his middle, pressing my face into his chest and closely as I could get. "I'm still on your team. I will always be on your team. Team Collins, forever."

His chuckle reverberated through him and into me, making me smile. "Team Collins, forever. I like it. Sounds like a good family motto."

With one last hug I released him and we made our way back into the house, turning off the fireplace before we went back inside where we found a groggy Hayley waking up from her nap. One look at her daddy and she was wide awake and leaping into his arms. The rest of the tension he had been holding onto melted away immediately as he stood there swinging our little girl in circles and laughing as she giggled.

Because I knew the rest of the evening would be stressful, I was glad to see this reprieve even if it was short-lived. We don't know what tomorrow looks like on any given day, but we know what we have right now and there is always something to be grateful for. It's those things, those moments like this one, that serve as anchors to the tangible blessings we hold onto and recall when our world feels vulnerable or threatened.

Chapter 35

Mark

The afternoon break was exactly what I needed to regroup and recalibrate my thoughts. Jess, Hayley, and I sat in the living room playing one of Hayley's board games laughing and indulging in cookies before dinner. Unfortunately, it had been too short of a respite. Though I had tried to push it to the back of my mind during our family time, I had gotten a message from Helen letting me know that she thought it would be a good idea to bring Kathleen into the loop as a contingency resource. The need to talk to John and Deborah became exponentially urgent.

Jess won the final round of our game, and after the final cheers and smiles, I kissed them both and excused myself to our home office. Rather than sitting behind the desk, I opted for the old leather chair in the corner. The chair had been with me since I left the Marines. It was the only piece of furniture I had other than a bed for a long time. It had seen more than its fair share of life, good and bad and it was always there when I needed it. It was also the only thing aside from my clothes and important documents that came with me from my life in D.C. There was nothing inherently special about the chair. It was, however, a good reminder of everything my life had been, hadn't been, and how far I've come.

Running my hand over the worn leather I smiled and sent up a prayer thanking God for everything I had that I definitely did not deserve. I retrieved my phone and stared at it trying to think of the best way to let the Parkers know we needed to meet without causing them too much worry. With my elbows resting on my knees, I bowed my head and asked God to give me the right words at the right moment. Not even a minute later the doorbell rang.

The office was on the opposite end of the house from the living room but I could hear and recognized the familiar voices immediately. I put my phone back in its holder and stood. Looking at the ceiling I nodded. There was no need to send a message of any kind because the very people I needed to see, to speak to, were in my living room.

Colton beelined for me as soon as he caught sight of me entering the room. As had become our tradition, I raised my hand high enough for a high five that he had to jump for it. We were still at a 30% success rate but he was determined. I walked over to James and held out a fist and he returned the gesture as we bumped our knuckles together. Both boys headed straight for the kitchen after our greetings where Jess was unwrapping what looked like a plate of some kind of bread that was making the room smell like cinnamon.

Deborah had Hayley in her arms getting a full recap of our board game adventure that sounded far more dramatic when she told the story than I remembered it being. Jess and I exchanged looks and shrugged, both of us smiling at the excitement with which she told the story. I approached John who looked like a man on the verge of bursting with pride. The scene almost did me in. My heart was trying to escape my chest, or so it felt as hard as it was pounding behind my ribs.

With a beaming smile and a nod John said, "Mark, good to see you, son."

Forcing myself to smile knowing it had to be lacking I said, "You, too. What brings your crew over this way?"

"Deborah thought we needed to bring over some cinnamon bread to say thank you for keeping the boys busy Saturday," he said gesturing to where Jess and Deborah were standing with the kids and plates of the bread for all of us.

The smell alone had me salivating, but I wasn't sure if I could even enjoy it knowing the conversation I was close to starting. I accepted the dish anyway and took a bite of bread. It tasted as good as it smelled, but the bread seemed to become sand in my mouth. Jess caught my stare and knew the debate warring inside me. She barely tilted her head and I knew she was asking if now was the time. With a quick dip of my chin and whatever she saw on my face, Jess understood that it needed to be now.

"Hey, kiddos, why don't you three go play outside for a little while so you'll be hungry for dinner when it's time," Jess suggested as the children all shoveled the last bites of cinnamon bread into their mouths.

Colton tried to agree enthusiastically around his mouthful, and Deborah reminded him to wait to speak when his whole mouth was free to do so. Hayley practically dragged James toward the door asking him if he had seen the chickens that laid the blue eggs. When the room only accommodated adults, the silence was a good indicator that something was not right.

Deborah looked to Jess who was looking at me so her gaze turned to me. John also rounded to me with a look of concern, maybe some confusion. I cleared my throat and set my plate on the island.

"Let's go sit in the living room."

The mood in the room shifted. It was obvious that something was wrong. Deborah looked back to Jess in search of anything that would explain what was happening. Jess reached for Deborah's hand and walked with her to the couch, guiding her to sit in the middle. John and Jess took either side. I remained standing.

Staring at the carpet, I rubbed a finger over my eyebrow and silently prayed, *God, give me the words.*

After exhaling a deep breath, I looked up and found three sets of eyes fixed on me. Locking mine onto Jess's allowed me to find the footing I'd been looking for. I could only glance at Deborah because the expression she wore was one that said she knew what I had to say was going to hurt, and hurting her or John was the last thing I wanted to do. Instead, I spoke to John.

"I'm not sure if you've heard that we've had a mysterious visitor in town. At the rate the news travels, I have a feeling everyone knows there's been a man hanging out around the diner most days."

John and Deborah both nod.

"It's not great news. And please understand that everything I'm going to share with you needs to stay right here until the need arises otherwise."

Deborah visibly stiffened. John sat up straighter and said, "We'll consider it clergy privilege."

I nodded and continued, "The man calls himself Jacob Miller but we believe his name is Jacob Milton. He goes by Jake. The boys identified him at the diner the other day as their mom's boyfriend."

I let the information sink in hoping they would be ready to hear the rest when I could finally muster the words. A couple of minutes that felt like hours went by as the room held its breath waiting.

"James identified him as having been in their home the night their mother was killed."

Tears began falling from Deborah's eyes, and Jess squeezed her friend's hand to reassure her. John swallowed loudly, and one of his knees started bouncing nervously. They both appeared to have words they either couldn't or wouldn't say. This next part was going to be even harder for them, and I wanted nothing more than to wave my hand to brush it off and make it go away. But it wouldn't be fair to my friends, and I am still responsible to do the job I've been given.

Running a hand through my hair I sighed and began talking before attempting to make eye contact. "Right now, I believe the boys are safe here. But, we need to take precautions when we're out in public for the time being. Jacob knows the boys have been with me and probably assumes that means they're also connected to Jess. And she has already been encouraged to avoid being out and about alone right now." I said all of this to John because I knew he would feel the immensity of the words but also be able to carry Deborah through them. And as I knew he would be, he was immediately moving closer to her side.

"So are the boys in danger?" Deborah asked as her shaking hand gripped her husband's tighter.

Running a hand through my hair I blew out a breath. "I honestly don't know, Deborah. Neither Jess nor I have a good feeling about Jacob. He has a propensity for anger and violence as I've learned from others who have known him prior to now. If he was responsible for Eileen's death, then yes, he is absolutely a danger and probably not just to the boys."

After a few moments, Jess squeezed Deborah's hand and released it before standing and coming to me. She didn't say anything but instead wrapped her arms around me and reminded me that we were in this together.

For several minutes the room remained quiet aside from the occasional sniffle until John cleared his throat pulling our attention to him. Positioning himself on the couch next to his wife, he held her hand while looking at me.

"What do we tell the boys?" he asked, voice quiet.

Jess moved to stand beside me keeping an arm around me so I could face John and Deborah. "We don't tell them anything right now. We form a silent battalion around them and do everything we can to keep them safe. This brings me to my next bit of information."

The Parkers looked at each other before John nodded for me to continue.

"The boys have an aunt named Kathleen who lives in the neighboring county."

Deborah gasped and tears fell faster. I held up a hand.

"She doesn't want to take the boys from you. In fact, she was grateful that they had a place to go."

There was a bit of relief that eased the tension that had been growing in the room.

"Helen did suggest, however, that we bring Kathleen into the picture as a contingency resource in case we need a place for the boys to go if things get too dangerous or even overwhelming for us here."

We all remained silent for several minutes as the Parkers processed everything I had just told them. Was there a specific threat to them? Not that I could point a finger at, but I felt it. My instincts were rarely wrong in cases like this.

"I need to return Helen's message. Do you have any questions before I go take care of that?"

When the Parkers both gave subtle shakes of their heads, I squeezed Jess's hand then made my way back to the office and closed the door. The ache in my chest was deep, my heart felt as though it was cracking in half, and I knew I needed to reacquaint myself with the ability to emotionally detach myself as I had always done in all my prior cases. That would be easier said than done in this situation because this was my family.

Even James and Colton had wedged themselves into my heart and this felt like a betrayal. They had done nothing but weather the horrible circumstances they had found themselves in for practically their entire lives as best they knew how, and now people they had grown to trust were trying desperately not to upend their world all over again. I hoped that we were successful in preventing just that.

Telling the Parkers had been hard and we were all emotionally charged in some ways and drained in others after the fact. John was torn between fear and frustration while trying to comfort his wife. Deborah was clearly worried and hadn't spoken a word but instead had shed a river of tears. Jess and I had a few whispered conversations, mostly words of support for one another though I may have expressed some mild irritation with the process we were facing and all the unknowns before us.

It was close to dinnertime and that meant wrangling the kids and making our way to the farmhouse. Jess suggested John and Deborah get a head start to both gather themselves and to give Marí and Cal a heads up on the situation. A short while later, we loaded the kids into the pickup trying to conceal any sign of crisis or danger. Fortunately, Colton had taken up his mantle and kept the three of them entertained for the short ride. Once again, I was faced with the reality we were about to encounter. These boys had been part of our family for less than a month and the idea of their absence was a blow to my heart.

There was an obvious pall over the dinner table even with the attempts to keep the mood light. As the evening went on, I could feel the tension building inside me. I could almost feel what was coming, and I wasn't sure if I was ready for it, which was a foreign concept in my mind. I had been sent to battlefields with armor and ammunition and zero visibility and had felt better prepared than I did at the table.

A little while after dinner, John and Deborah took the boys upstairs to get ready for bed and when they returned downstairs Deborah was somber but John looked determined.

"What can we do?" he asked, as he led Deborah to the sofa and he remained standing, hands on his hips. He looked ready to form a battle plan right then and there.

The boys had become part of their family, and now they were being threatened.

Marí had come downstairs after putting Sadie to bed and taken the seat next to Deborah while Jess held a sleeping Hayley in the armchair, covering her ear as though she might overhear us in her sleep. Cal stood like a sentinel, arms crossed over his chest, awaiting orders.

The sight bolstered my resolve and gave me the courage to form a plan.

"Here's what I think needs to happen. Ladies," I addressed the women in the room. "I don't want any of you alone in public for the time being. Right now, Jess is the only one of you that has been connected to me, thus to the boys. But, because I know Deborah sometimes takes the boys to school and other activities, there is an increased possibility that connection could easily be made. If you can't take John with you, try to take Cal or myself, even Carlos if he's available. I'll speak to him tomorrow about it and for Ana's sake. Marí, the same goes for you. I know it's an inconvenience, but until we know there is no threat, we take as many precautions as we can."

Heads bobbed in agreement around the room.

"I don't want to put so many restrictions on things that the kids get scared or start questioning things. But, we should consider everything thoroughly before agreeing to go places and do things in public. We can try to keep everything as normal as possible while also being aware."

There weren't many words exchanged among the group before Jess and I headed to our own home just up the driveway that had been extended to practically connect our property to Cal's. But as we made the short silent trek, Jess held my hand and I could feel her watching me. When I put the truck in park I turned to face her.

"I feel you staring," I said, unable to hide the curiosity in my voice.

"Something wrong with me staring at the hero of my dreams?" she asked.

I breathed a laugh. "Hero, huh? I don't feel like a hero. I feel like I'm stuck."

She squeezed my hand then before letting go she said, "Stuck or not, you're my hero. And I'll be here to help you get unstuck when you need me."

Chapter 36

Mark

I was on my way to grab a cup of coffee when I saw Jacob Milton sitting in a beat up Ford truck outside Ms. Judy's store. I took a detour and walked down the sidewalk to his truck. I tapped the window with my knuckle and he looked up from the phone in his hands.

When the window came down I said, "Hey, Jacob," I said with a friendly smile.

Jacob's grin made him look more like a snake than a friend. "Hey, Sheriff. Good to see you."

"I was just headed to the diner for some coffee. Care to join me?"

He seemed to consider my question with some hesitation.

Before he could decline I suggested, "I think you should join me."

Pocketing his phone, he rolled up his window and opened the door. His narrowed eyes stayed on me, constantly assessing the situation. It felt as though we were two fighters circling one another in a ring, waiting to see who was going to strike first.

We walked in silence to the diner where I nodded to Barb who followed us to the booth nearest the back. The silence continued until there were two white cups of black coffee steaming in front of us.

I decided to cut to the chase. "Listen, Jacob. I know you were involved with Eileen Brewer. She's been missing for a few days now, and I think you might know something about it."

Jacob's face paled only slightly, and there was a flicker of something that resembled fear in his eyes before a mask slipped into place. "I knew Eileen," he said slowly.

I kept my voice calm and steady. "You knew her? Because I have reason to believe that you'd been spending a lot of time with her lately."

Jacob stared me down, trying to look intimidating. "I haven't seen Eileen in a long time."

I knew what he was trying to do, but I didn't want to push him too hard. I pressed my back into the booth's vinyl cushion as I surveyed him. "I have it on good authority that you and Eileen had been seeing each other for a while."

He scratched the dark stubble on his cheek before running a hand down his face. "We may have seen each other a few times, but like I said, I haven't seen Eileen in a while."

"Why is that?" I asked.

With a quick tilt of his head and a smirk that told me we were going no farther down this path, Jacob knocked on the tabletop twice before sliding out of the booth. "Thanks for the coffee, Sheriff," he said as he walked away, coffee untouched.

Watching him walk out the door, I had a mix of emotions bombarding me. Jacob was slippery and smug, and I knew that it was going to be hard to get anything useful out of him without something to back up my reasons for questioning him. But I also knew that I couldn't give up. Justice for Eileen and her sons depended on it.

Chapter 37

Jess

It had been just over three weeks from the time Mark had started investigating the break-ins at the stores in town. So much had happened since then that it felt a lot longer. The Parkers had moved to town, we had initiated the Blessing Boxes Ministry, Carlos, Cal, and several of Carlos's friends had remodeled the General Store building, I had petitioned the court to allow Mark to adopt Hayley, the boys had come to the farm, and Mari and Deborah had planned a community baby shower. Somewhere in there we had managed to put a small pile of wrapped Christmas presents under our tree. If I thought about it for too long, I would become exhausted all over again. And for the time being, I had to be as awake and attentive as I could be, as today was the baby shower.

When my friends had insisted on some sort of celebration, as much as I appreciated the thought, Mark and I had been so excited that we decked out the nursery four months into the pregnancy. Thinking back, I laughed as I remembered how my face had hurt so badly by the end of the day we had spent shopping because I had not been able to stop smiling one time. Watching Mark go heart-eyed over baby onesies and cribs had been the most intoxicating thing I had ever seen. Remembering the man he had been before almost became impossible.

He had always been kind and patient and even during the hardest cases I had rarely seen him lose his temper. But he had typically been emotionally detached and aloof. Then he met Jesus, and it was as though he'd emerged from a shroud and a new Mark was born. I thought that had been my favorite version of Mark, but I had been wrong. Seeing him as a daddy to Hayley and then finding out we were expecting took the man to a completely different level of emotional availability and expression. It was overwhelming to try and imagine what would happen the day they put our baby in his arms.

I parked up the street from the building and it took a moment for me to realize the sign on the General Store building read Redeemer Church. The joy already swelling in my heart overflowed and became tears leaking from my eyes as I took it in and thought about all of the good that was going to come from this place. I stayed in the car long enough to dry my face and check my reflection before making the short walk up the sidewalk.

Yellow, green, and purple balloons were attached to either side of the double wooden doorway with a drape of matching streamers loosely hanging between them. I smiled at the poster resting on an easel on the stoop. Two young women were pictured with radiant smiles on their faces. Above the photos the sign read *Celebrating Moms to Be* and below the images were the women's names. I studied their faces and choked back tears amazed at how brave these young ladies had to be to make the choice to become single mothers.

Instead of a baby shower for me, we opted to celebrate the soon-to-be mothers who had sought help from the local Pregnancy Resource Center. The women we were celebrating were soon to discover that raising a child takes a village, but what's more, they were going to know even sooner just how large their village actually was. If I hadn't been able to vouch for it myself, it would have been very apparent to anyone who walked through the doors of the new church building.

As I pushed open the door and stepped inside, the sound of laughter and chatter filled the air. The room was filled with tables and chairs, Baby-themed decorations adorned the tables while more streamers and balloons hung from the wooden rafters. Women of all ages from our community dressed in their Sunday best were gathered together smiling and admiring the guests of honor. In the corner, there was a refreshment table with plates of cookies, cupcakes, and punch, and a table with gifts wrapped in paper covered in baby animals, fluffy clouds, and nursery rhyme themes.

I was welcomed with hugs and congratulations, and I made my way to a table where my closest friends were standing and arranging Petits Fours on a tray. We chatted and sipped punch, admiring the decorations and the energy in the room. As I looked around, I saw the village I relied on so heavily in our beginnings here, united in their support of these young mothers-to-be.

After a while, the celebration began in earnest, with speeches, games, and laughter filling the room. I was struck by the outpouring of love and support these young women were receiving, and I was reminded once again of the power of community. I could come up with story after story about how practically every woman in this room had supported me personally in some way since moving here. It was no surprise to me that they had shown up to love these women who were currently strangers.

About a month after settling into the farmhouse, Hayley and I were still struggling to find a sense of normal when we first arrived in Owenston. Marí and Cal were indescribably present and available any time I needed them at home. But it was our town that stepped in when they couldn't be there.

One afternoon on a day Cal had taken Marí and Sadie with him down to Lexington to talk to a man about some horses, Hayley woke up halfway through her nap covered in vomit. I got her cleaned up but within minutes she was covered again, and the process repeated itself many times. We had been fortunate in our few years together to avoid the stomach plague, thus, I was woefully unprepared.

Desperate and alone, I made a call to Mason's Pharmacy and explained my situation to the pharmacist on duty hoping he would give me some idea of how to take care of the situation with what I had at home. Twenty minutes later, a knock on the door brought me face-to-face with Mr. Mason's wife, Hannah, carrying a bag filled with electrolyte drinks for kids, crackers, a coloring book and a pack of crayons, and an assortment of chocolates she made sure to say were for me.

As the party happening around me wound down, and the women began to gather their gifts and make their way home, I felt a sense of joy and fulfillment. It was a beautiful reminder of the good that can be done when people come together, and of the significant role that a supportive community can play in the lives of those in need. I was grateful to have been a part of such a special celebration, and I knew that these young mothers-to-be would never forget the kindness and love that had been shown to them on this special day.

Mark, Carlos, Cal, and John arrived shortly after the last guest had made their exit to take down the tables, helped clean, and set the chairs up in rows across the room for the upcoming Christmas Eve service. Without the baby shower decorations, the room was plain. The walls made of wood paneling and the smooth wooden floors, worn from the decades of use, were simple and rustic.

I sat in one chair with my legs spread across another chair trying to keep my eyes open as the events of the day had taken their toll on me. My back was tired from standing and my feet and ankles were swollen from having worn cute but impractical shoes for most of the day. Hayley crawled into my lap, and we giggled together over the green icing she had on her forehead from one of the leftover cupcakes Deborah had given her. A few minutes later, Hayley was still and asleep on me. I ran my fingers through her silky hair and watched the room transform into a proper meeting place.

The feelings of anticipation and contentment vanished immediately and were replaced by a sudden jolt of pain that scorched through my abdomen. The gasp it elicited was loud enough to draw attention and within seconds Mark was next to me. The look of terror on his face mirrored the feeling bubbling inside me. Deborah was there lifting Hayley from my arms.

"Jess, I need you to talk to me," Mark said in a low voice that sounded calm but was anything but.

Taking in a shaky breath, I tried to push myself into a more comfortable position, but the pain returned causing me to reach out and grab Mark's arm and squeeze. My eyes were closed as I attempted to control the sensations wracking my body. Mark had turned away and spoken to someone then returned his attention to me. Everything happening around me became a blur and like static on an old radio station not in use. When I was finally able to take a breath, I opened my eyes and locked them onto Mark's.

"Hey," he whispered.

"Hey," my voice shook. "I think we need to go to the hospital."

He raised his hand to cup my face and attempted to give a comforting smile. "Cal went to get the truck. I'm going to carry you out and get us there, OK?"

I gave something between a nod and a shudder trying to steady my breathing.

Mark slid an arm under my legs and behind my back and scooped me up and walked as quickly as he could to the truck without jostling me. By the time he slid into the driver's seat, the pain was back, and I was unable to hold in the guttural sound that had been trying to escape. It took every ounce of control I had left not to leave the seat. Mark reached out his hand and took mine, gently squeezing. I squeezed back but it was not gentle.

The hospital was thirty minutes away on a normal day. With his flashing lights on, Mark made the drive in twenty. Having called ahead, when he pulled in and parked under the Emergency Department portico there was a doctor and a nurse waiting for us with a wheelchair. The nurse gave him instructions to find me after he parked the truck then whisked me away to an exam room.

One nurse wrapped a blood pressure cuff around my arm and asked questions about my pregnancy and the pain I was experiencing while another strapped a fetal monitor to my abdomen. There were beeps and clicks accompanied by murmurs of voices. A woman in purple scrubs walked in followed by Mark. At his appearance I immediately relaxed to the extent that I could.

"I'm Dr. Lofton," the woman said as she picked up the chart sitting on the foot of the bed I was occupying. "I hear you are having some pretty serious pain and it looks like the cause is fairly strong and consistent contractions."

I nodded, and managed to say, "That seems to be the case."

Dr. Lofton nodded. Her expression was neutral as she produced a pair of gloves and had them snapped onto her hands instantly. It was rare a person could school their features so smoothly but doctors, especially the good ones, did so easily. It was a technique used in a lot of high-pressure professions to foster calm environments for patients, clients, victims, or even suspects. Regardless, her eyes were kind, and her concern was genuine which made it easier to settle my nerves and focus on what was happening and what I needed to do.

"Mrs. Collins, I'm going to do a quick exam to determine what our next steps should be. You are right at thirty-seven weeks, correct?" she asked as she began her examination.

"Yes, thirty-seven weeks today, actually," I answered as I attempted to control my breaths.

She pulled back and snapped her gloves from her hands and tossed them into a trashcan. "That's good," she said as she picked up the chart and made a note. "Thirty-seven weeks means we're dealing with what is likely a healthy baby. Complications after this point are less likely to do with underdevelopment."

Mark was standing at the head of the bed holding my hand in

both of his. The breath he let out was one of relief. His posture relaxed slightly.

The doctor continued, "Fortunately, it looks like you're only dealing with contractions and not any other signs of labor. I want to set you up in a room for observation, get you on some IV fluids, and continue to monitor you and baby for a few hours. Once we slow things down we'll talk about the next steps.

Another contraction hit, sending an intense wave of pressure through me causing me to grip the side of the bed with one hand and Mark's hand with the other. Gritting my teeth, I inhaled through my nose praying the pain would stop as I nodded in agreement with the doctor's plan. Mark's grip tightened on me as we both awaited my relief.

Once the IV was in place, the last of the staff cleared out and left us reeling in what became an intense silence. The feelings were overwhelming as they vibrated through our hands, still clinging to one another. Mark had pulled a chair from against the wall next to the bed. He rested his forehead on our clasped hands, and I could hear him whispering a prayer.

Forcing myself to relax, I laid my head back onto the flat pillow and closed my eyes. Tears began rolling down my cheeks forming small streams dripping onto my chest and shoulders. Unable to stifle my sniffling, Mark raised his head then stood and motioned for me to make room in the bed. Working around the IV line and monitor wires, he climbed into the small bed next to me and wrapped an arm around me as best he could.

We both laughed through the snot and tears at the awkward position in which we had put ourselves. He brushed my hair with his hand then pulled me to him so he could press his lips to my forehead, my nose, and then my lips. I gripped his hand that rested on my face and closed my eyes. We laid there quietly for what felt like hours. I must have fallen asleep because the next time I opened my eyes, it was dark outside and I was in the room by myself.

Mark's voice was low and quiet outside the door. It sounded like he was on the phone, most likely updating our family. My thoughts became a replay of the days' events and while this was not how I expected the day to end, I was reminded to be grateful because in the end, our daughter was taken care of, our baby was safe and healthy, and I hadn't had to face any of it on my own.

Chapter 38

Mark

My phone started vibrating shortly after Jess had fallen asleep. I had laid next to her in the small hospital bed unable to relax as the fear of everything that had happened continued to pummel me. The phone call had initially been a welcomed distraction when I thought it was our family calling to check on us. It quickly became a more pressing issue that went to war with the situation I had just faced with my wife and unborn baby.

It was Cal who had called and as soon as I answered, I knew what was coming.

"Mark, we might have a problem," Cal had said, his voice serious.

He explained that as they were leaving the church, he caught sight of a man he didn't recognize watching the group from across the street. There was little doubt in my mind exactly who had been watching them. Cal knew everyone in the town as he'd lived there his entire life. If he didn't recognize the man, I'd place a hefty wager that the man was Jacob Milton.

I'd asked if they'd seen any indication that they had been followed home. It would have been obvious seeing as the closest neighbor lived several hundred acres away from the farm so any traffic not related to our family stood out. Fortunately there had been no sign they'd been followed. However, they had all been identified as individuals with direct connection to James and Colton.

The more I had thought about it, the more convinced I'd become that Jake figured out that the boys had been home the night he had shown up. If they knew something, he didn't want it getting out. I wasn't quite sure why this had resulted in him hanging around town as opposed to leaving town, but I was positive his eyes were on James and Colton. That meant he was likely going to zero in on anyone connected to them, especially if it seemed like there was any kind of suspicion cast on him.

My suggestion to Cal had been that everyone remain vigilant and I'd take care of things. After a quick update on Jess, we disconnected the call and I immediately called my night shift deputy, Steve Higgins, and instructed him to keep an eye on Jacob from a distance as much as possible.

"You got it, Sheriff," was all he'd said. It was comforting to know that even having been in my position for a short time, my people trusted me. They knew I would do anything for them, thus they were willing to take my directions without question.

My next call went to Helen Davis. As I paced the hallway outside of Jess's room I tried to keep my voice quiet as I explained what was happening. Before I could ask, she suggested it was probably a good idea to consider sending the boys to stay with Kathleen until we knew any threat was contained.

In my gut I knew it was the right move, and I also knew it would be temporary. But the thought of sending the boys away from the Parkers broke my heart. Helen and I made a plan to talk to the boys and introduce them to Kathleen and just as I was ending the call, a nurse approached our room with Jess's discharge papers.

I followed her into the room where she said, "Alright, who's ready to go home?"

Chapter 39

Mark

I drove the boys to my office where we met Helen and Kathleen. The ride was silent. Even Colton, who typically insisted on touching most of the knobs and buttons on the dash, was subdued. Three small suitcases containing all of the boys' belongings rattled in the bed of the truck.

The women were waiting for us in the lobby, and both stood when we walked inside. Tears of sadness laced with apprehension were visible in their eyes. The boys froze in front of me as they were faced with two strangers who held their futures of uncertainty within their hands. James attempted to flee the scene but only made it a few steps before I had my arms wrapped around his middle and his face pressed into my chest. His silent sobs shook his lean frame. I swallowed hard to hold back the tears of my own, threatening to join his. Colton stared at the tile floor and his sniffles echoed in the stillness of the room. I could feel the fear radiating from them.

This was a test of my self-control. I knew my reaction would set the tone for that of the boys. If I remained calm, there was a higher likelihood they, too, would at least refrain from additional outbursts or escape attempts.

Guiding both James and Colton by a shoulder, I led us all into my office. There were beanbag chairs in one corner that the boys immediately fell into as the women took a seat in the armchairs. The mood was somber and as much as I didn't want to let the boys go, prolonging things was going to make it that much harder.

The three of us stared silently at one another until Helen spoke. Her attention was on James and Colton who barely raised their eyes to meet hers before looking away from her.

"I know this is hard for all of us. We want to do everything we can to keep you boys safe, and right now, Sheriff Collins and I think that means staying with your Aunt Kathleen. It's just for a little while, until we know that there isn't any danger here."

Colton's gaze shot up to meet Helen's then mine. "No! I don't want to go!" His breathing was ragged with the emotions threatening to overpower his little body.

Speaking softly, I said, "Colton, let's listen to Mrs. Davis, OK? She's here to help us."

Tears were flowing down his cheeks and his brow was furrowed but he nodded one time then swiped at his cheeks with the back of his arm. James reached over and gripped his brother's shoulder with the hand not currently balled into a fist next to him.

Her voice gentle, Kathleen volunteered, "I know we haven't officially met, but I am here for both of you. I have a room that will be perfect, and I have three cats who love attention. I know this is all a big change for you, but I promise I will do my best to make sure you are taken care of. And I'm not trying to take you away from the Parkers. From what I've heard, they are wonderful people. We all just want you safe."

The boys seemed to relax a little bit, but still looked as uncertain as I felt.

Colton's chin wobbled when he asked, "When can we go back to the farm and the Parkers? They're so nice and Henrietta is going to have her babies and Cal said we could be there for it." There was a desperation to his words as he tried to hold on to what had become familiar and stable.

The silent tension in the room seemed to expand and thicken with every second that ticked on the clock. A headache was forming behind my eyes, whether it was from staunching tears or my anger at the man who had put us all in the position, it was hard to tell. James was growing restless in his seat and the look on his face said he was angry.

Knowing that this was not the last time I'd see them made this next part easier for me. My thoughts felt selfish but I had become invested in these boys' lives before I'd even met them. They had been young, scared, and lost like I had been, and I had been much older when I faced my darkness.

My thoughts strayed to the fifteen-year-old boy who had felt like everything he knew was real and true had been ripped away and replaced with an emptiness. Sure, I'd had both parents, but my dad was rarely home, he claimed it was because of work, and when he was, he was detached and aloof. My mother became a shell of herself the day my brother died. We all became abandoned vessels lost at sea unable and maybe a little unwilling to take command of our own lives causing us to drift apart and away from one another until one day there was nothing left tethering us together.

Until I had found Jess and my new family, the ones who opened their arms and hearts to me selflessly and unconditionally, people who pointed me to Jesus and never failed to forgive me when I failed, I hadn't known what it was to be found. It gave me hope, a sense of belonging, a new identity. And I knew that James and Colton had experienced the same from the moment I'd found them in line to meet Santa. I couldn't let them lose this second chance at a family that loved them and cared for them.

I helped get the boys and their stuff to Kathleen's car and somewhere in the process Colton had practically climbed me and was clinging to me as though I was the only thing keeping him afloat. He was sniffling and releasing the intermittent sob. James, on the other hand, was stoic, anger clearly boiling beneath the surface. While I wanted to give Colton the comfort he needed, James needed my attention, and even then, I wasn't sure it would be enough to cool the heat rolling off him.

Setting Colton's feet back on the ground, I knelt in front of him and held his shoulders waiting for him to look at me. When he did, I said, "You have so many people who love you and will miss you. But they also want what's best for you and James. Right now, this is what's best, and this is what needs to happen. But I want you to know you can always reach me if you need me. I will always be here for you and your brother. And I'm going to fight harder than I have ever fought to catch the bad guy sooner than later. OK?"

He nodded then swiped under his nose with his shirt sleeve. I stood and ruffled his hair before stepping toward James. James made a half turn trying to block me by giving me his back. I put a hand on his shoulder and spoke to the top of his head, letting him have control over this situation.

"James, I'm not going to lie to you. This hurts my heart like I know it does yours. Right now, we may not like it or understand it, but it's the choice we've been given. How you handle this choice will impact more than just you. Do you understand that?"

He gave a single nod.

I continued speaking hoping only he could hear me because my words were only meant for him. "Colton is going to look up to you whether you want him to or not because you're his big brother. He needs you to be there for him because right now he doesn't think anyone else will be so you can't run away, OK? You need to stick together and be the best and amazing kids I know you are. Can you do that for me?"

James gave two quick nods then spun and slammed himself into me, wrapping both arms around me tight enough to take my breath away for a moment. I hugged him back knowing that he'd be faced with some pretty big emotions in the near future, and I didn't know what that meant for him. What I did know is that I was about to go to war for these boys to bring them back home.

Chapter 40

Jess

The mood on and around the farm was wrong. A sadness lingered as we all felt as though we were grieving. As expected, John and Deborah took the separation from the boys hard. Cal had worked with them to get a beautiful, manufactured home squared away on a parcel of the property. For Christmas they had planned to surprise the boys with their own rooms on Christmas Eve after the church service. The day James and Colton spent with Mark, the Parkers had spent the time turning the rooms into private hideouts for the boys. Deborah confessed to having a tough time being on that end of the home because it felt deserted even though the boys had yet to step foot into it.

What surprised me most was how hard Mark had taken the situation. He had been quiet and a little withdrawn the last few days with a constant simmer of anger underneath his surface. His focus had been laser sharp as he made a plan to get to the bottom of everything.

While he hadn't been vocal, it was clear he needed more support than he'd let on as his need for physical closeness had ramped up quite a bit. He was constantly reaching for my hand or sitting as closely to me as he could get. At night, I'd hold him and wait for him to relax before I fell asleep. My heart broke for him.

We had both been awake for hours and his head rested in my lap as we sat on the couch. His breathing slow and steady, I gently ran my fingers through his hair as I considered how this quickly became unfamiliar territory for Mark – getting emotionally involved in what was only supposed to be a case. And though he hadn't outright said it, I'd place a hefty bet that it triggered a childhood trauma for him.

We talked a lot about our families before we got married because I had my own history that had major impacts on who I'd become. I had an alcoholic father who walked out when I was young, and my mother raised me on her own. It had been the two of us until she died of cancer not long after Christmas during my first year in college. Then it was just me until I met my college roommate, Stacy, who had been my best friend and was the reason I even met Bryan. Stacy died from a stroke before she turned thirty, but I still had Bryan, for a little while at least. Three years later, he was gone, too. At the rate I lost people I cared about, it surprised me how little residual trauma I had. Honestly, I attributed it to the fact God always had someone there waiting for me when I needed them most. It's not that I didn't grieve or wasn't sad. There are still days that I find myself grieving my losses and I'm certain that will always be true. But I've never had to make my journey alone.

Mark, on the other hand, spent a great deal of time as a loner. He told me about his brother's death the same day he brought Hayley, Marí, Sadie, and me to Kentucky. It had gutted me and surprised me that even after all the years of working alongside him, I still hadn't really known him. After Bryan's death, our relationship grew into more over time, and we talked about his family and how he'd never felt secure or rooted to anything or anyone from the time he was fifteen. Everything changed and the world moved on without him, including his parents.

It's fair to suggest that Mark only came to know the safety and security of family in the last few years. It could probably even be narrowed down to that fateful day when he saw Cal embrace two women and their two little girls he didn't really know because he knew they needed a family to care for them. He still speaks of that experience with a sort of reverence.

My thoughts stuttered as the beautiful man in my lap turned from his back to his side and pressed his lips to the round belly that had almost taken up most of the real estate. His arm snaked behind my back, Mark mumbled something into my abdomen.

With a laugh I scratched his scalp and asked, "What?"

Groaning, he mumbled a little more clearly, "What time is it?"

"It's almost 7:30. If you're going to make the drive and be home before dinner, you should probably get up," I said, still playing with Mark's hair.

With everything moving at what felt like a snail's pace, Mark decided he was going to make a visit to the one person who had connections to both Eileen Brewer and Jake Milton. Unfortunately, it required him to make a two and a half hour drive to the federal prison in Manchester where Jimmy Brewer was spending the rest of his days.

"You make a less than compelling case the more you do that," he said, referring to my fingernails roaming over his scalp.

I ran my hand down his face and held it against his cheek. He rolled onto his back holding my hand in place with his own.

"We can pick this back up when you get home," I said, smiling down at him.

He closed his eyes and released a deep sigh. "You're right."

Breathing a laugh, I stared at his mussed hair, made unruly by my fingers. "You might want to go deal with this in the mirror," I said, scruffing his hair even more.

His eyes were tired, but his smile was almost boyish when he grabbed my hand and kissed my palm, closing my fingers around the spot he kissed before sitting up and facing me.

Mark studied my face, and I didn't need any kind of ability to read his.

Exhaustion. Stress. Love.

"You were made for me, Jess Collins. You are all I could ever want or need on this earth. Everything else is an added bonus."

He swept me up from my seat and wrapped me in his arms and pressed his lips to mine. The sadness, the uncertainty, the reservation seemed to melt away in the moment, so I embraced it.

A sense of relief rested over us and all signs of worry had been erased from Mark's face for the time being. I knew his concerns were far from removed completely, but the more frequently he could experience the calm and assurance that came from moments like this one, the easier it would be for him to grasp onto the truth that God was not going to let these circumstances go to waste. As hard as it has been to find the good, we had to remind ourselves that God had a plan and we were being given front row seats to see it in action.

Chapter 41

Mark

I spent the entire drive running through every shred of evidence that had come across my desk since I had discovered Eileen Brewer's body in that bed surrounded by destruction and chaos. My thoughts then drifted to the inmate I was going to see - Jimmy Brewer. The man had been locked up for multiple charges, including homicide. According to his file and many of the townsfolk, he had been a troublemaker since he was a teenager, and prison had only made him more dangerous. He had several incident reports in his ever growing record.

Finally, after what seemed like an eternity, I arrived at the federal prison where Jimmy was being held. After a few security checks, I was led to a small room where Jimmy was already sitting at a table, his hands cuffed in front of him. He looked up as I entered and scowled.

I took the seat across from him sitting on the edge of the chair. Folding my hands, I leaned forward and rested on my forearms as I studied the gruff bear of a man in front of me.

"Who are you and what do you want?" Jimmy asked.

"Mark Collins. I'm the Sheriff over in Owens County. I want to talk to you about your wife."

Jimmy's expression softened though only slightly. "What about her?" His tone betrayed his threatening body language. It was then I realized he didn't know about Eileen.

"Are you aware that Eileen was found dead last week?" I asked, trying to find a balance between compassionate and deliberate with my words.

His jaw twitched as though his back teeth were grinding against one another and he blinked several times, likely trying to mask any emotion. Jimmy's nostrils flared with every deep and controlled breath he took. We sat there and stared at one another for a full minute before he gave half a shake of his head.

"How?" he practically growled.

Without giving too much away, I quietly said, "We believe she was murdered."

Jimmy's eyes flared and his features became full of anger. "Who?" he demanded as his hands became fists on the table in front of him.

I took a deep breath and slowly released it. "I don't know. But I wanted to ask you what you knew about Jake Milton."

The face of wrath became one of pale stone. Jimmy's breathing became near silent compared to his previous seething.

"Jake Milton? You think Jake had something to do with Eileen's death?" he asked slowly and in a way that sent a chill down my spine. If ever there was a voice of death, Jimmy Brewer's in this moment would be it.

Trying not to let my uneasiness show, I merely said, "I don't know who killed your wife. But I was hoping you could tell me about Jake."

His eyes narrowed on me and we endured another bout of silence before he said, "Jake always had a thing for Eileen. Even in high school. Then after I married her, he'd come around once in a while and joke about her leaving me for him. I told him more than once to stay away, but he wouldn't listen until one day I made sure he got the message. I didn't see him again."

I slowly nodded as I listened. There was my connection but I needed a motive. Jake may have been hanging around, even seeing Eileen on the regular, but why would he want to kill her? Everything pointed to a crime of passion - the crime scene, the boys' account of Jake storming into the house yelling, the stab wounds. But something had to trigger it.

"Do you have any idea why Jake or anyone would kill Eileen?" I asked.

For the first time, Jimmy's facade fractured ever so slightly as evidenced by the crack in his voice when he whispered, "No." But that fracture quickly healed itself when he followed up with, "I swear if I find out it was Jake, I'll make him pay."

After a few moments of studying him, I stood up to leave. "Thank you for your time, Jimmy. If you think of anything else, please let me know."

His stare had gone cold and distant, unfocused on anything. I could see the anger and frustration building and festering.

As I reached the door, I heard Jimmy's voice behind me.

"Hey, sheriff," Jimmy called out.

I turned around to face him. "Yes?"

"Just remember what I said. If I find out it was Jake who killed my wife, I'll make sure he pays. And you won't be able to stop me."

I didn't respond, just nodded and left the room. As I made my way back to the truck, I couldn't shake the feeling of unease that had settled in the pit of my stomach. I needed to find the real killer and bring them to justice before Jimmy had the chance to take matters into his own hands. Eileen and her boys deserved justice, and I wasn't going to rest until he had found it, hopefully before Jimmy could do anything first.

Chapter 42

Mark

The heat was pumping through the truck but I felt cold all the way through. Jimmy's words kept playing over and over in my head leaving me feeling hollow. He had nothing to lose inside those prison walls for a long time to come which meant he could take risks and play the odds if he so chose.

A glance at the clock said if traffic cooperated, I could be home for lunch. That sounded exactly like what I needed. The next two and a half hours were a combination of work calls and silent prayers as I begged God for an opening, a tiny crack even, that would send the case to the closed pile. The drive home seemed to go by exceptionally fast and as I turned into the drive that would take me past the farmhouse and toward my home.

Expecting a vehicle other than Jess's in our driveway, I was surprised to see a solitary car sitting there. There had been no cars at the farmhouse so I'd assumed Marí was with Jess. If Marí wasn't here and no one else's vehicle was here, that meant Jess was alone. I put the truck in park and for a moment I was tempted to be angry because we had all agreed Jess wouldn't be left alone in case she needed help or something happened to her.

Before I could get too upset, I noticed from a distance there was a vaguely familiar pick-up truck parked in front of John and Deborah's place that sat a couple acres behind the farmhouse, and only few acres from ours. My heart began to pound and I could hear the blood rushing behind my ears. Throwing the truck in reverse, I quickly backed out of the space in which I had just parked then slammed the gear into drive and peeled out of the drive.

Dust and rocks kicked up behind me and crunched on the unpaved path. Sure enough, the rusty Ford truck I had recently seen Jacob Milton in was parked next to Deborah's SUV. I hit the brakes, shoved the gear selector into park, and unholstered my gun in one motion. Chambering a round, I opened the door as quietly as possible but opted not to close it in hopes of keeping my presence as concealed as possible. It was possible my tires on the rocks gave me away well before now but I'd take any advantage I could.

God, whatever is waiting for me inside that house, go before me, stay beside me, and have my back. Clear my mind and protect my family.

Slowly, I crept up around the front of the truck and up the three short steps. I wrapped one hand around the door knob as the other held my gun aimed in my line of sight. I was a mere second from turning the knob when I heard a distinctly male voice inside.

Muffled through the door I heard, "I'd hate to see something happen to the Sheriff's pretty little wife so tell me."

My heart rate spiked as adrenaline began pulsing through me. Was Jess inside? This was my worst nightmare coming to reality. Since the voices were close to the front door, I made the assumption whomever was in the house was in the living room right inside. I released the knob and gingerly stepped backward until I was down the steps. With a quick survey of the yard, I took off around through the yard and around to the back door that came in through the kitchen and dining area.

Standing to the side to keep myself hidden, I tried to peer through the frosted glass of the door. The view was too obscured so I sent up another silent prayer as I gripped the knob. While I was going to have a talk with Deborah about leaving doors unlocked, I found myself very grateful that her actions had been a blessing in this moment. Slowly, I turned the knob, gun at the ready. With a deep breath, I gradually pushed the door open.

Not wanting to draw any attention in my direction unless absolutely necessary, I squeezed through the door not even bothering to close it behind me. The view before me had me frozen in my tracks. On the other side of the room directly before me was a man's back. A glint of light from the window reflected off an object in his hand. He had a knife. I tightened the grip on my gun. But that wasn't what stopped me from moving.

His form was blocking the person but the voice belonged to Deborah. I wasn't fully aware of what she said aside from it being laced with fear because sitting next to Deborah in my full view was my very pregnant wife. Jess was staring up at the man whose profile clearly belonged to Jacob Milton.

Jess knew I was there because I saw the quick movement of the finger she raised that was resting on her knee. She was signaling for me to wait which she confirmed with a quick glance toward me then back at Milton. My mind and my heart were racing quickly enough that had I not started focusing on my breathing, I easily could have passed out.

A desert full of hidden would-be assassins strapped with bombs had nothing on seeing my wife and unborn child being held and threatened by a lunatic. Trying to breathe silently while also sending enough oxygen to my brain was becoming a distraction. I needed to focus because what needed to happen next was precarious.

"I saw them with you. You know where they are and you're going to tell me," Jacob rumbled.

Before I could take a step forward, Jess gave me one more look with a steady wink before grabbing her abdomen and crying out. Even knowing it wasn't real threatened to send me into a panic, but before I could get distracted, Jacob turned his head to look at Jess but was then caught off guard when he caught sight of me. Jacob whirled and started to raise his knife.

"Drop the knife, Milton!" I yelled.

He hesitated.

"Drop it or I will drop you." My words were laced with more venom than I had ever heard from myself.

Gradually, he lowered his hand and released the knife. It landed with a dull thud on the carpet.

"Now, walk toward me, slowly."

When he was halfway across the room I said, "Stop. Turn around."

He did as I said.

"On your knees, hands behind your head."

I took cautious steps toward him as he obeyed, my aim never wavering from him. When I was close enough, I leaned down and used one hand to cross one of his ankles over his other before grabbing his wrist and yanking it down. In fluid motion I holstered my gun then retrieved the cuffs on my belt, slapping the metal band around the man's wrist. I pulled his free arm behind his back to join his hands together.

Pulling him to a standing position I forced him to take a seat at the dining room table where I stood and kept watch while I made a call to Deputy Whitson. Within minutes we could hear sirens approaching. Crunching gravel followed by multiple footsteps preceded a flurry of activity including additional officers entering the house.

As soon as Milton was in secure custody, I instantly moved toward Jess who was still sitting on the couch comforting a terrified Deborah. As though on cue, John raced through the front door, and was kneeling in front of Deborah who collapsed onto his shoulder.

Jess reached a hand for me and I helped her to stand. The moment she was on her feet, my arms were around her and my face was buried in her shoulder. It was impossible to differentiate between the sobs as we were both shaking and crying together. There had never been another time I could recall being as scared as I had been the moment I walked through the door and saw Jess sitting on that couch in front of a man wielding a knife.

Needing to see her, I loosened my grasp on her and leaned back.

"Are you hurt?" I asked, examining her face.

Shaking her head, she sniffed loudly and wiped her face with one hand.

"Are you sure? Is the baby OK?" I was trying hard not to panic as the thoughts of what could have been rushed through my mind.

Her smile was watery but it was enough to soothe the ache building inside me.

"I'm fine, we're fine," she said, gripping my arms.

"Jess," I breathed, resting my forehead on hers and closing my eyes. "Thank God. I was genuinely scared when I saw you sitting there."

She ran her hands up and down my arms. "I know. Until I saw you through the door, I wasn't sure if any of us would be leaving this house." Her voice cracked and her tears were back.

I pulled her as close to me as I could and held her, running my hands over her hair, up and down her back. I wasn't sure if I'd ever be able to let her go again.

But, I had to let her go in order for her and Deborah to give their statements to another officer I'd only briefly filled in when he arrived. While I was grateful he had given us a moment first, I only begrudgingly let him do his job, though I didn't leave Jess's side for the entirety of his questioning.

According to Deborah and Jess's account, Marí and Cal had taken Sadie and Hayley to the park so Jess convinced Deborah she, too, needed a change of scenery. It hadn't been longer than twenty minutes that there was a knock on the front door. Without even thinking, Deborah opened the door, and Milton barged in wielding his knife. He hadn't been in the house ten minutes before I arrived. As they shared their story, all I could think was how grateful I was for the intuition and protection God had poured out over all of us.

When the women were done recounting the timeline of events, I knew I needed to head to the station and deal with the aftermath of everything that had happened. I was reluctant to leave Jess, and she definitely could not come with me. When John agreed he would take Deborah and Jess to the farmhouse and wait for Marí and Cal to arrive, I was more amenable to leaving.

Once I knew they were settled I hugged Jess likely far longer than necessary but it almost felt like it would never be long enough again. It seemed John had similar ideas about Deborah as he hadn't left her side since barging into their house.

"Hey," Jess whispered. "This isn't new to us, right? We're safe. We'll be here when you get back."

I was still battling those images in my mind of the 'what if' scenarios. "I know," was all I could get out.

Double checking the door was locked behind me when I finally left, I headed for the station. In the truck, I sat and rested my forehead on the steering wheel trying to reel in my thoughts.

God, I do not deserve the mercy you showed us today. Thank you. Give me everything I need to put this guy away for a long time.

The drive was long enough for my frame of mind to shift from worry to anger. I was going to go toe-to-toe with a man who not only murdered a woman in cold blood, but held my wife and her best friend captive and threatened them. It was time for him to meet the Mark Collins I thought I'd left in D.C.

Chapter 43

Mark

Standing across the table from Jake Milton, I glared at him with a cold fury that I struggled to contain. He tapped his fingers impatiently on the table to which his wrists were cuffed then released a sigh laced with indifference and boredom.

My pregnant wife and her best friend had been held hostage by this man, threatened with a knife, and he had the audacity to act as though he was being inconvenienced. I was seething and desperate to put a fist into the guy's face.

But my job was to get to the truth, and I intended to do just that. And if I wanted charges to stick as well as be able to pin him with Eileen's murder, I knew I had to keep my cool.

"Tell me about the night of the murder," I demanded, leaning forward, resting my hands on the table, a tan folder resting between them.

"What murder?" Jake jutted his chin out as though daring me to accuse him of something.

"Eileen Brewer."

It was times like this I could have used even an ounce of Jess's abilities. This guy was stone cold and emotionless as far as I could tell. There was not even a flicker of a reaction at the mention of her name.

With a nod of his head and a shrug of a shoulder Jake said, "What about her?"

Flipping open the folder I slid two autopsy photos onto the table. Eileen's gray face had multiple bruised areas on it and two stab wounds were visible near her shoulders. As soon as Jake's eyes landed on the photos, he jerked his head away from their line of sight.

"Any idea how she ended up like this?" I asked, trying to keep my gaze fixed on Jake.

His breathing grew heavy, and his nostrils flared once, twice, then he spat, "She was always hung up on him even when he wasn't worth the air he was breathing - which was always. He treated her like dirt most of the time and I could have given her everything. But she wouldn't leave him. Even when he's behind bars, she wouldn't let him go. He didn't deserve her."

My pulse rate ticked up. I knew we were getting somewhere but I didn't want to say anything that made him stop talking. I stood and crossed my arms over my chest and surveyed him for a moment.

"Did you deserve her?" I asked, trying to sound genuinely curious and not accusing.

His eyes snapped to mine. "More than he ever did."

"Then why did you kill her?"

With a futile attempt at pounding his fists on the table Jake growled, "Because she should have been mine."

Everything in the room seemed to freeze in place for a moment as we stared at one another. There was a dangerous rage in Jake's eyes.

Slowly, I slid my hands into my pockets as I continued watching the confessed murderer in front of me.

"And why did you hold my wife and her friend hostage?" I asked, my voice masked in a calm I was not actually feeling.

Some of the anger burned away though his tone was still hostile. "I just wanted to know where the boys were. I wanted to question them to see if they knew anything so I could wrap up some loose ends."

There were many things running through my head in that moment. What I decided to say shocked even myself.

"I wonder how Jimmy Brewer is going to feel when he finds out his friend Jake killed his wife and went after his kids."

In that instance, Jake's face went ashen, and his shoulders fell. I leaned forward and collected the photos and tucked them back into the folder before exiting the room.

When the door shut behind me, I took the deepest breath I could and held it for several seconds before slowly letting it out. Rolling my shoulders a few times, I spun on my heel and walked toward my office. There were a few more things I had to wrap up, but I had gotten what I wanted from Jake Milton. And if I were a betting man, I'd say his future was looking fairly bleak.

Chapter 44

Jess

"Please don't make me stay home tonight. It's Christmas Eve," I pleaded with Mark while Deborah sat at the kitchen island with Hayley who was coloring a picture of a llama in a Christmas sweater.

Mark was sitting on the edge of the couch cushion on which I had been sitting for far longer than I really appreciated. He held my hand in both of his. "Jess, the doctor was pretty clear about how important it was that you stayed calm and still for at least a week. And you were practically held at knifepoint yesterday. I'd say that is the exact opposite of calm."

With my free hand resting on my giant belly, I let out a frustrated sigh. I had been on the couch most of the day while Deborah hovered nearby. She had been quiet ever since the encounter with Jacob Milton and unable to be alone for long stretches of time. And now I was going to miss the Christmas Eve service. The disappointment mingled with the remaining anxiety from the last few days threatened to result in tears. It wasn't that I wanted to argue but things were starting to feel outside of my control, and this didn't feel like a big ask.

"We can sit in the back, I'll find a way to prop my feet up, and I'll be as still as shadow. I just really want us all together in church tonight. I think it would be good for us, for me."

Mark took a deep breath and studied me for several beats. I watched his reaction to every outcome to every choice in the matter play out over his face. He was uncertain about all of them including the one he finally landed on, but he knew how much this meant to me.

Letting out a heavy sigh he said, "Okay. We'll make it work, but Jess, if anything feels wrong or you find yourself ready to go, you have to tell me." He was resigned but his words held a firmness that told me he was also processing the events that had transpired the previous day.

Smiling, I pulled him toward me with the hand he was holding and planted a kiss on his lips. "Thank you. And I promise, if anything feels off or I need to go, you'll be the first to know."

"Good," he said before giving me another quick kiss. "Now, I think I need to see about this holiday llama that's being colored in the kitchen and then see about getting our own Christmas llama ready for church," Mark announced, resulting in Hayley singing her own rendition of a Christmas carol.

"Fa-la-la-la-la La-la-llamaaaaa!" Hayley giggled, as she sang.

Deborah laughed for the first time in what felt like forever as she stood and made her way to the couch. She leaned down and hugged me before asking, "Do you need anything before I go? I know you're tired of hearing that question, but I really hate not being able to do something for you."

I grabbed her shaking hand and squeezed. "I promise, I'm good. Thank you for being here and for being the best Mimi to Hayley. That is more than I could ever ask you to do, and you're amazing at it. And Deborah? We're OK. You're OK."

Tears welled in her eyes causing mine to fill, too, and she nodded. I knew she was thinking about Jacob Milton and thinking about the boys and trying to ignore the void their absence had created. My heart hurt for hers.

Deborah squeezed my hand back and said, "Okay, I will see you at church then."

With a nod and a smile, I let her go and watched her place a kiss on Hayley's head before leaving. When the door closed behind her, Mark and I exchanged a look that felt as heavy as I knew our hearts were. This was even more confirmation that we needed to be together, and we needed to be in church with our family, even if it meant all I could do was sit there and listen. There was a message waiting for us and we all needed it to remind us that our hope had come once before and, though we did not know when He would return, we could know without a doubt that He would be with us all of our days until He did.

Chapter 45

Mark

Jacob Milton was behind bars and for the first time in weeks it felt like I could take a full breath.

Jess was situated on the back row of the church with the chair in front of her turned around for a place to prop her feet if she wanted it. I knew she thought I was making too much of a fuss, but if there was anything I could do to keep her and the baby healthy and safe, I was going to do it – even if it meant making her a little crazy in the process. There had been too many close calls already.

We'd arrived an hour before the service was supposed to start so we could address any last minute needs, and Carlos could run through the music while Bob Avery tested the new sound equipment. There was a current of excitement running through me as I stood next to John and Cal and listened to Carlos strum and sing Joy to the World. I had missed this, going to church and being a part of the work.

The week Jess had returned to D.C. for her deposition after Bryan's murderer had been captured was a week that changed my life forever. She and I had spent the four months leading up to it getting to know each other over the phone. That's all it took for me to know that I was completely taken by the woman I'd worked with for years prior but had never truly gotten to know. But what's more, I met the Savior I hadn't known I needed.

In that process, John and Deborah had invited me to church where I connected with a few colleagues I didn't know were believers. We formed a small group with a few other law enforcement officers, and that's where my faith really grew. Watching men who faced the same evils I faced on a daily basis trust that God had a plan even for the lost and wandering souls like mine, reinforced my beliefs.

My attention snapped to the doors when I heard familiar happy voices outside. A smile grew on my face and I knew what came next was nothing short of a Christmas blessing.

When the door opened I was greeted by a smiling Colton. He was in my arms squeezing me almost as hard as I hugged him.

"Hey, buddy," I said with a chuckle.

I didn't have to look to know why his embrace loosened. Then he was gone from my hold. James bolted past me as I ruffled his dark hair. Both had spotted and found their way into the arms of the Parkers who ushered them inside.

"Good to see you, Kathleen," I said, holding the door open for her to enter.

"You too, Sheriff," she said smiling. "I don't think Colton stopped talking the entire drive over."

Laughing, I said, "That sounds about right."

We watched the reunion for a moment before I turned to her and asked, "How are they? I know it wasn't a long stay, but are they OK?"

Her smile faltered slightly. "They'll be OK. If they can have that," she motioned toward the Parkers, "they'll be just fine."

We continued to watch until James and Colton were seated. Of course they were at the front with the Parkers who were seated next to Carlos's family. Hayley had taken a seat next to Colton and the two were chatting as though they hadn't missed a beat. I watched Deborah really smile for what felt like the first time in a week. John had only released James's shoulder for the moment it took to change hands when he was approached for a handshake. The scene looked completely natural.

People were starting to file in, filling the seats on both sides of the room. There was quiet instrumental Christmas music playing under the hushed voices of neighbors greeting one another. The occasional laugh could be heard over the din. Scanning the room I saw the faces of my community; faces of people I swore to protect but had also grown to love. This was a good reminder that I needed to be present right now and allow myself to experience this time that was meant to be joyful and special. Everything else could wait, including the conversation with the woman sitting to my left.

"Care to sit with us?" I asked Kathleen.

She beamed when she saw Jess. "I'd love to," she said as she walked around the row then shuffled down to the seat on Jess's other side.

I took my seat next to my wife and took her hand letting the moment overtake me. Carlos's voice led the congregation in several songs and the sound of all the voices blending together filled my heart with such an overwhelming sense of calm that everything else was pushed out for the time being. That feeling was multiplied when John took the stage.

This had been a long time in the making even though on our calendars it had only been a short time. It was clear to me how perfectly God had orchestrated every circumstance that led my family, my friends, my community to this very moment. A single tear escaped down my cheek. Two years ago, that never would have happened. I was not prone to emotional displays but instead was closed off and convinced I was fine on my own. Now, I can't help but feel things and I am not ashamed to show it. There was a freedom to be had in being every part the person God created me to be.

After welcoming everyone and giving a brief history of how Redeemer Church came to be, John prayed. He prayed for the people, the town, and the future of the church. And when he thanked God for the blessings he had showered on us, the protection He'd provided, and the families he'd given us - even those not of blood, I echoed his sentiment ten-fold. This room alone contained some of my most treasured blessings, starting with the woman holding my hand.

The room was still and silent when he reached "Amen," sending a chill down my spine. It was a holy stillness that penetrated every molecule in the air. Even when John spoke again, the stillness lingered, and his words echoed through the room.

"As we consider the Christmas season, we are reminded of how Mary and Joseph were forced to leave the comfort of their own home in Nazareth to embark on a journey on foot to a town forty miles away called Bethlehem. Caesar Augustus had decreed it necessary, therefore, the couple had no choice but to make the venture. If the journey alone would be tedious and long, how much more it had to be for Mary, a young girl who was not yet married and very pregnant with a baby she had not asked to bear. That does not mean Mary and her betrothed weren't stressed or scared. It was an undertaking that neither of them could have foreseen. Yet, they made the trip because it had been ordained by the same God who had chosen Mary to bear his Son.

"Most of us know the story from there. They arrive in Bethlehem to discover there is not a real room to be had in the city, forcing Mary and Joseph to take shelter in the space where the animals were kept. As if all of that was not enough, Mary was then faced with the experience and challenge of giving birth far away from home, without the support system she'd likely had in place, potentially surrounded by animals.

"It's a shame we are not given more insight into how Mary and Joseph were feeling or what they were thinking in these moments, but we can make a fair assumption that they probably felt a little lost and overwhelmed. I would even speculate that there was fear and desperation amid their uncertainty.

"There are moments in our lives like the ones Mary and Joseph faced. You know those moments – when you check your bank account to find just how much faith you need to make it to the next paycheck; when the doctor walks in and tells you there's nothing else he can do; when everything seems lost and there's only hopelessness remaining. Here's what we often forget – that is not where Mary and Joseph's story ended.

"Just when Mary thought everything was hopeless, when Joseph felt nothing but helpless, hope found them. Help arrived. Their weary and wandering souls were found and made alive by the arrival of the Messiah who entered the world that night. I want every person in this room tonight to know that even when you feel completely lost and alone, there is a Savior who is seeking to know you and claim you as his own.

"The same Jesus we celebrate each Christmas was born so the lost could be found, the weak could be made strong, and the hopeless could have hope. All he asks is that you trust him to follow through. Will you trust him?"

Movement to my left caught my attention as the rest of the room rustled with the bowing of heads. Kathleen was digging through her purse and retrieved a crumpled tissue that she used to dab at her eyes. My heart lurched in my chest. In all of my fear and frustration that had been surrounding me and my family, I looked right over an important fact. This woman had been through her own fair share of hurt and loss. And who was there to support her? Who had her back?

Without any hesitation, Jess wrapped her arms around Kathleen whose tears had begun to fall even faster. The picture was beautiful and endearing, and how it was possible I didn't know, but it made me fall even more in love with my wife. It was a true to life representation of the unconditional compassion God had for me even when I was far from deserving of it. That thought alone humbled me.

One more song was sung, and as the crowd was dismissed, a rush of excitement rippled through the room. Families were excited to be together, discussing the plans for the evening and Christmas Day. The Parkers and the Nuñez family were corralling children including my own daughter. With a glance at Jess and Kathleen, I noticed they were still huddled together, Jess speaking in a hushed tone. I moved to retrieve Hayley from the horde but was intercepted by Helen Davis.

"Sheriff, Merry Christmas," she said with her signature smile.

"Merry Christmas to you, Helen."

Her eyes darted to the back row then back to me. "Is that Kathleen Thompkins with Jess?"

I turned to look where she had and nodded before turning to face her. "It is. The boys are up front with the Parkers," I gestured forward, and Helen turned to watch them, smiling ear to ear.

Before either of us could speak, Jess was standing with Kathleen, one arm still gently draped around her shoulders. Our attention moved in their direction. The older woman had clearly been crying.

Jess released Kathleen who had straightened her stance and dabbed her eyes one last time by the time Helen and I reached them. Her expression was a mixture of sadness and peace.

"Kathleen, it's good to see you here. Did you enjoy the service?" Helen asked.

Kathleen answered, "I did. I think I needed to be here. It was a good reminder that God always puts us where we're meant to be when He wants us to be there."

Helen's expression was kind and her voice reassuring when she said, "I think we all heard something tonight that we needed to hear. That's the great thing about God. He always tells us exactly what we need to hear when we need to hear it. We just don't always listen." Helen chuckled and I smiled and nodded in agreement.

There were days I knew exactly what God was telling me and other days I either ignored him completely or argued with him wanting him to agree with me. When God took hold of my heart and showed me how much he loved me, there was not much about me he should have considered lovable. Then he changed me and surrounded me with people to love and who loved me in return. I could already see our family expanding once more.

Clearing her throat, Jess spoke up, "I invited Kathleen to the farmhouse for dinner and she accepted. Now, I'm going to go retrieve our daughter and let Marí know we will be having another guest." She squeezed Kathleen's arm and nodded to Helen before shimmying her way out of the row and made her way to the front.

Her gaze drifted to the boys who were smiling and laughing with our family, James still standing immediately next to John who had a hand on one of the boy's shoulders. Quietly she said without looking away from the scene, "I'm so glad they have a place to belong."

The three of us stood and watched for several seconds.

Tears welling in her eyes she sniffed and went digging through her purse again successfully finding her tissues.

Helen and I made eye contact briefly, and I gave a nod before she turned and walked to where the Parkers were standing and talking to several members of the community and our family members.

"Kathleen, I don't know what kind of community you have surrounding you back home, but I hope you know that you have family here that you can call on day or night. We're all here for you and would love to get to know you. I think James and Colton would benefit from having you in their lives, too."

We were both watching the group at the front of the church. James had his arms wrapped around John who wrapped one arm around James and one arm around Deborah who had Colton squished between her and John in the sweetest family hug. Jess was crying as was Marí. Cal was smiling and holding Hayley.

"Thank you," was all she said.

I turned my attention to her. "Kathleen, take it from someone who went from not having a family to having a family that keeps expanding beyond blood-relation. You can never have enough family."

Chapter 46

Mark

It had always amazed me how many people could fit inside the farmhouse at any given time without the place feeling overrun or crowded. Tonight, we had a one-to-one ratio of adults to kids which meant the volume and energy levels in the room were extremely high. Combined with the fact that Christmas was only one sleep away, it would be safe to say the levels were off the chart. Motion was constant as some of the adults milled about the kitchen and dining areas and the kids wandered in and out of the space looking for snacks.

I had been listening to Cal tell a story about a Christmas Eve Communion service from over a decade ago about a kid who had crept into the church before the service started and drank all of the small cups of grape juice and made a huge dent in the bread that had been pieced and stored under the tablecloth on the altar table in the sanctuary. When it came time to serve Communion, the cups were empty.

My mind wandered as Cal spoke. I scanned the room, watching the smiling faces and listening to the chatter and laughter from the kids bouncing off the walls and their footsteps banging around upstairs. My gaze landed on Jess sitting on the couch with Kathleen who was holding Ana's youngest and smiling. Next year there would be another little one in the group and once again the adults would be outnumbered. At least, that was where my thoughts initially went until I remembered that there was a chance James and Colton still might not become permanent fixtures here.

I was pulled from that train of thought by the echo of laughter coming from the group in front of me. I'd have to get Cal to tell me how his story ended later as I'd zoned out halfway through. Marí clapped her hands over the noises of our family moving about the house. Cal used two fingers inside his lips to send up a whistle to call down the kids who had ventured up there to play. Footsteps banged down the steps from hungry children in a hurry to find access to the food we'd all been smelling since walking into the house. As it was his home, Cal took the moment to welcome everyone once the room had settled.

"I know I have said this before but some of y'all weren't here then," he looked around the room stopping on James, then Colton, then Kathleen. "This house holds many memories, all of which I am grateful for. And just like the memories of the past, I am thankful for the new memories being made each day, including this one right here. We talk about family a lot around here because even though a lot of us aren't actually kin by blood, we have everything it takes to make a family. We take care of each other, we put each other first, we trust one another and are loyal. But more than that, what we have is love. We love big and sometimes loud and always unconditionally. So, if you're here and you're wonderin' if you belong here, the answer is yes. Everyone who walks through that door and sits at this table is family." His gaze landed squarely back on Kathleen who looked as though she might cry at any moment.

"And with that being said, I'm gonna ask John here to bless the food and our time together, and then we're gonna eat." He slapped John on the shoulder and squeezed.

John sent up a prayer of thanks and praise and as soon as he said

Amen the noise level grew again as adults situated kids at their table and dishes were moved around the kitchen and the tables.

Kathleen had stood back away from the crowd of people milling about trying to wrangle kids and plates of food. I leaned over and whispered to Jess to save my seat and made my way to where Kathleen was standing. When I got close enough I could see her eyes were glistening with unshed tears as she wrung her hands. She looked overwhelmed.

"You know, every person in this room has a story about how they became part of this family. None of us were born into it, really." I pointed at Carlos. "Carlos and his wife Ana met Cal one afternoon when their truck had broken down in town. Carlos had just lost his job and Ana was pregnant with their second child," I motioned toward Lucia who was nine going on sixteen most days. "Cal asked if he knew anything about farming, Carlos told him he didn't, and Cal said he could teach him. That was ten years ago."

Kathleen watched Lucia as the girl rolled her eyes at something her dad said then smiled. I pointed at Jess, next. "Then there was Jess. Her first husband was practically raised by Cal." This earned me a look of shock and confusion from Kathleen. I let out an amused huff. "Yeah. His name was Bryan. This is where he was raised. A few years ago, Bryan was killed and the same guy came after Jess. Marí and Sadie had been living with Jess and helping her with Hayley when it all happened. I brought the four of them here one day for their own protection and then I went back to D.C.."

I continued, "The Parkers were Bryan's friends and virtually his second parents in D.C. and they became the same for Jess, and eventually me. I met them after Bryan but before they moved here. They took me under their wing and taught me what it was to love and be loved by God. You'll not meet two people with bigger hearts full of more love to give than they have people to give it to, but they try."

She took in the room as though for the first time before turning to look at me. "I came for Jess and Hayley. And if that's all I ever had I'd be a man wealthier than any other. But I got so much more. My family imploded when I was a teenager, so I had no idea what it was to be part of one. Now I do. The day I brought Jess and Marí and the girls to this place, I knew it was special. It's so much more than that, but I think you can tell that for yourself."

The tears she'd been holding back began to fall. I reached over and placed a hand on her shoulder. She reached up and grasped my hand as though it was the only thing anchoring her to the space where she was standing.

Her voice was barely a whisper when she said, "I haven't had a family in so long."

"I'm sorry. If you'll let us, we want to make you part of ours."

She nodded and I walked with her to the kitchen where we fixed out plates before taking our seats at the table on either side of Jess. Jess reached behind Kathleen and wrapped an arm around her shoulders and squeezed. Looking grateful and also relieved, Kathleen gave a small smile.

Jess turned her attention to me and grabbed my hand, giving it a small squeeze before pulling me toward her. I placed a quick kiss on her lips that said everything we were both thinking. There was nowhere else we would rather be and everything we needed was right here in this room.

Chapter 47

Jess

After dinner, the children dispersed to the newly empty attic that had resulted in creating the perfect playroom and hangout space. The adults had all grabbed mugs of different hot drinks Marí had made for us which I appreciated for a number of reasons. Her Dominican Hot Chocolate was heavenly – dark chocolate, cloves, cinnamon, and ginger with a little sugar in warm milk – it was easily my favorite Christmas treat.

We'd all gotten comfortable and though my eyes were heavy with an exhaustion I thought might sweep me away into dreamland for a week, I snuggled in next to Mark on the couch, careful not to hit his ponche de cafê - Marí's take on a Dominican coffee eggnog.

Before any of us knew what was happening, Deborah had set her mug on the table and was kneeling in front of Kathleen who was sitting in the arm chair. Wrapping her in a hug, Deborah only held on for a moment but remained kneeling, wrapping her hands around Kathleen's which were still wrapped around her mug.

"Kathleen, I owe you a huge debt of gratitude. You kept our boys safe. Because of you, they're here now. Thank you." Both women wiped at their eyes as Deborah continued. "John and I have talked about it so many times already and we want you to know that you are a part of our family. We want you to come for family dinners when it's convenient for you and for birthdays, and holidays. And, if I may be so bold to say so, I think you might benefit from being part of this big mixed up family, as well," she motioned to the room.

Mark retrieved a box of tissues from the end table nearest him and passed them to Deborah who held them out for Kathleen then took one for herself. Setting her mug on the coffee table, Kathleen faced Deborah looking as though she had something to say but instead wrapped her arms around her. John stood from where he was sitting and moved to join the group. He helped Deborah stand and Kathleen followed suit. The three embraced, John wrapping both women in a gentle hug, all of them sniffling through the joy and heartache and love.

I tapped Mark on the knee, and he stood then helped me from my seat. We moved into the kitchen to give the three of them some privacy. I started wrapping up the leftovers and putting them away when I froze in place finding myself out of breath as a jolt of pain hit me. Mark spun and saw me trying to catch my breath as I held a hand against my abdomen.

"Jess," his tone was laced with the panic I saw on his face. His hands reached out and grasped both of my arms.

I slowly let out a breath as the pain faded and I waited to see if there would be another. Mark watched me intently until I could relax and assure him I was fine.

"I think I overdid it today," I said, feeling mildly guilty since he had tried to convince me to stay home.

His hands moved to my back and pulled me closer. He kissed the top of my head. "I'm going to go get Hayley and take the two of you home."

I nodded and followed him out into the living room then he went up the stairs. Deborah, John and Kathleen were still standing where we'd left them but they were apart and talking. Deborah noticed me and something she saw caused a rush of concern to take over her features.

"Jess? Are you OK, sweetie?" she came toward me and placed a hand on my cheek and then my forehead as though to check for a fever. Her maternal instincts were precious.

With a weak smile I nodded. "I just overdid it today, that's all. Mark has gone to get Hayley. I assume the rest of the crew will follow."

She nodded and gave me a hug. "If you need us, you'll call." It wasn't a question and I smiled.

"You'll be the first."

Before either of us could say anything else, what sounded like a herd of elephants came rushing down the steps. James and Colton bolted toward John who intercepted them, and Deborah joined them along with Kathleen. The small group stepped into a less crowded space where they could have a quiet conversation.

Carlos and Ana were giving directions to their children to help clean up and put their jackets on because it was also time for them to depart. Cal walked with Mark to the alcove where Hayley's jacket and backpack were stowed, while Marí made a beeline for me.

"Jess, you look like you could have a baby any minute," she beamed.

I chuckled though it sounded less amused than it normally would. "Let's hope not. I at least want to make it through tomorrow. I think Hayley needs this one last Christmas before this baby gets here."

Marí smiled and patted my cheek. "Then we will pray this little guy stays put until after tomorrow."

My head tilted to the side at her words and my brows furrowed in confusion. "Little guy, huh?" We had opted not to find out the gender because we thought the surprise would be fun.

"It's just a feeling I have. Either way, we will pray you have a peaceful Christmas Day and that all will be as it should be."

I wrapped my arms around my sweet friend. "I love you, Marí. Merry Christmas."

"Merry Christmas, chica. Now go home and get some rest. Santa will not come to see you if you are not sleeping."

We said our goodbyes and wished everyone a Merry Christmas before loading up in the truck and making the short drive to our house. Hayley talked nonstop, even after Mark had her tucked into bed. Her excitement was palpable and it warmed my heart. I could hear her giggling from another room, and I couldn't stop thinking about how next Christmas we'd have two children to settle and tuck in before setting out gifts and stockings. I rubbed my belly affectionately and smiled.

Chapter 48

Mark

It took approximately three hours after Hayley finally fell asleep for us to put together the three story dollhouse Jess and I had painstakingly picked out and customized at the toy store a week ago. In my foolish wisdom I assumed it would come assembled and in a box that Jess would meticulously and perfectly wrap and I would shimmy it into place next to the tree and we would bask in the adoration and gratitude of our daughter when she opened it. Instead, I glued piece after piece of thin wooden planks together after Jess covered them in decorative contact papers that were supposed to be wallpaper or look like flooring. When the last pieces were in place all we could do was pray that the glue would dry before Hayley woke and realized what day it was.

The glue was given right at six hours to dry, which to its credit was enough for it to have remained standing through the early morning hours. Because of its unknown stability we opted not to attempt to wrap it, but we did attempt to hide it so the temptation of being played with would not be strong when our girl came downstairs. The plan worked as was evident by the soft voice I heard from the opposite side of the bed.

"Mommy, it's Christmas. We have to open presents." It was more of a whispered yell than a whisper.

I raised my head over Jess's shoulder to see Hayley practically nose to nose with Jess who had a hand resting on Hayley's cheek.

"Okay, Bug. Let mommy and daddy get up and we'll open presents. Why don't you climb up here and snuggle up in the blankets while you wait," Jess said, resulting in an excited pounce into the middle of the bed by a wide awake little girl.

I wrapped Hayley and Jess in my arms as best I could and growled, "Family hug!" causing Hayley to squeal and giggle and Jess to chuckle and groan.

"Now I really have got to get up, my loves," Jess said in a tired amusement.

She looked more uncomfortable than she had the night before, which caused me to watch her with concern. The look on my face obviously mirrored how I felt because she said, "It has been a long week and it's just starting."

While this was supposed to make me feel better, there was something different about the way she spoke and moved this morning. If I had any say, and I would definitely say something, she would be on a much stricter bedrest than she had been. My instincts were telling me that something was not right, and I was not about to take a risk or allow Jess to take a risk by overdoing the day, as she had Christmas Eve.

As Jess moved through the bathroom and closet, I kissed Hayley on the forehead and rolled out of the bed to go start the coffee and put a pan of cinnamon rolls in the oven. I could hear their voices through the walls but I couldn't understand their words. I didn't need to because I could feel the excitement throughout the house.

This was only my second Christmas with my family and I couldn't imagine it being any more perfect than the first. But, it was already better. This year I had a wife, a daughter, and a baby on the way. And Hayley's enthusiasm was greater, which seemed to be true for everything these days. I suspected it came with her age.

By the time they emerged from the bedroom holding hands, Jess was practically being dragged. I stepped in and scooped Hayley up and tickled her while Jess could get comfortable on the couch. There were more giggles and smiles and the sparkle in Hayley's green eyes was remarkable.

"Who is ready to open some presents?" I asked, feeling almost as excited as Hayley looked. She was almost bouncing with anticipation.

Throwing a hand into the air she squealed, "Me! Me!"

We let her open the gifts from our extended family which were all received with equal rapture and excitement. There was a set of beginner reading books about her favorite cartoon puppy from Marí and Cal. Deborah had picked out a few new Christmas ornaments for the tree plus some new cowgirl boots. You would have thought the girl had discovered the world's most prized treasure. My face had already started hurting from smiling and she hadn't even opened her big gift. I probably could have told her those were the only gifts she was going to receive and she would have taken them upstairs and behaved as though she had everything she could ever want from life.

Fortunately, that was not the case and we were going to have the privilege of watching her five-year-old mind explode with total shock and surprise. When I gently shifted the large sheet-covered fabrication and positioned it in front of Hayley, her eyes grew larger than the shiny globes hanging on the tree. She dragged her eyes from the gift to me, her little mouth slightly agape.

"We'll have to uncover this one together because it's fragile. Are you ready?"

She nodded as she looked back down and grabbed the edge of the sheet and lifted it upward as high as she could, gasping then screaming in delight when the dollhouse came into view. She abandoned the task of uncovering it relatively quickly, opting instead to jump up and down, hands clasped over her heart.

My gaze found Jess smiling at Hayley's reaction but doing so through a grimace. When she realized I was watching her, she faced me and scrunched her nose as she rubbed her belly. I quirked an eyebrow her way and received a shoulder shrug in return. Put together it meant she was uncomfortable but wasn't ready to call attention to it. I watched her for several beats before returning my attention to Hayley who was inspecting the small empty rooms in awe.

"One last gift. Think you're ready?" I asked.

She beamed up at me as I handed her a large felted bag. She loosened the drawstring and discovered every piece of furniture for every room in her dollhouse plus a doll-sized family to occupy the spaces. This sent her over the edge with elation.

Laying every piece out on the living room floor in front of her she began to group them by the room in which they would go.

"Would you like some help arranging the furniture in the rooms?" I asked, already knowing the answer.

"No, thank you. I want to make sure it's perfect."

I had never met Bryan Carsen, but I had read through his work. The only reason we were able to open and close the case of his murder so quickly was because of the box of meticulously organized and arranged evidence that he had sent to Jess two weeks after he died. This need for perfection and eye for detail Hayley had was all from him. I made a note in the back of mind to remember this moment for the day in the future when she asked about Bryan.

The oven timer beeped, interrupting my thoughts. The smell of cinnamon and bread filled the room and it seemed all at once the three of us realized we were hungry. Refusing to let Jess leave the sofa, I had Hayley help me set up a small table for Jess and then we spread a blanket on the floor next to the table where she and I sat to eat our breakfast. We turned on a classic Christmas cartoon and let it play in the background while we ate and talked about where the dollhouse would go after she had made her design plans.

I kept casting glances at Jess who had barely finished one cinnamon roll by the time Hayley and I had finished two each. She would occasionally catch me watching her and give me a wink or reach out and place her hand on me. My nerves were starting to fray and unease crept in, attempting to settle in my gut. I was torn between feeling happy and anxious as I cleaned up the breakfast dishes and watched Hayley cover Jess with the blanket we'd just been using. Jess's eyes had drifted closed at some point and for the moment she looked more relaxed than she had when she was awake.

The original plan was for all of us to end up at the farmhouse, but there was no chance I'd be going that far from Jess for any amount of time today. Instead, Hayley and I made a plan to get dressed and invite the rest of our family to join us in our backyard whenever they were done with their family celebrations. By mid-morning, Marí, Cal, and Sadie had come over and the girls had taken off to the wooden swing set where they chatted nonstop about their presents. By lunchtime, the Parkers along with James, Colton, and Kathleen had arrived. Kathleen had stayed at the farmhouse but Deborah had picked her up and taken her to their home before the boys opened their presents.

Marí had remastered the plan for lunch and Christmas dinner and had packed everything up and brought it to our house. Once Jess had awakened, the adults moved inside to make the preparations with the exception of Jess who was confined to her spot on the couch. We all made an effort to include her in the conversations though she seemed content to listen for the most part. She dozed off a couple of times and the combination of noise from outside and the commotion in the kitchen didn't disturb her once.

Deborah and Marí had both commented with their concern and I assured them the best I could that Jess had insisted she was fine. Marí had a look in her eye and a smirk on her face that said she knew better than any of us. I wouldn't put it past her. She probably did.

Lunch had been a simple spread of sandwich meat, cheese, and bread and some sliced fruits and vegetables. Dinner, however, had been a different story. It was a combination of traditional American foods like ham and green beans as well as Dominican fare such as pastelitos and pastelón de plátano maduro.

Space in our home was not as available, at least not in the same proportions as the farmhouse, which is why we always gathered there. However, we made it work. We created a buffet on the counters, the kids sat around the kitchen island, the women sat in the living room with Jess with their food on tv tray tables, while the men sat around the small table in the eat-in kitchen.

It was cozy, the food was good, and the company was family so it could not have been any better. As plates began to empty, people began to move again, taking dishes to the sink and talking about the different desserts in the lineup. John was in the kitchen and had just finished telling a story that resulted in a room full of laughter. When I looked over to share the laugh with Jess, I noticed her focus had gone laser sharp on the floor in front of her. Her nostrils were flaring as she breathed in and out slowly through her nose. I was kneeling in front of her within seconds.

Rather than encouraging her to talk and lose her concentration, I waited for her to indicate what she needed from me. Granted, my patience was only going to allow her a few more seconds because I was teetering between scared and terrified.

Her shoulders relaxed and she sighed out a deep breath before rolling her head from side to side.

I finally took in the breath I had been foregoing and released it before asking, "What is it?"

She smiled, still looking exhausted even though she'd slept several hours throughout the day. "Just a really strong contraction. I'm fine. It's probably going to keep happening until the baby gets here."

My hands were resting on her knees so I rubbed her thighs several times as I worked through the nerves that had built up in those seconds. "You'll tell me if it gets to be more than that." It wasn't a question.

"I promise," she leaned forward and kissed my forehead.

When I stood, I realized the adults in the room were watching us, with looks of apprehension and hopefulness. I think they were all as ready as I was for this baby to be here and we weren't the ones experiencing the throes of contractions.

Everyone had settled in the living room to visit after we had reset the kitchen. With full bellies after a full day, we were all content to sit and enjoy each other's company and if anyone decided to speak, we all listened. Sadie and Hayley were parked in front of the dollhouse. James and Colton had brought portable gaming systems they had received for Christmas. Cal shared stories from his childhood Christmases in Kentucky including one where his family woke up to one of their goats in their living room eating their live Christmas tree. These were the moments I lived for with these people. We shared our lives with one another, the past and the present, the beautiful and the ugly, the funny and the hurt.

I had wedged myself behind Jess between her back and the armrest and wrapped an arm over her shoulders. My fingers were mindlessly twirling a piece of her hair when I felt her go rigid. Another contraction was coming on and it hit me that I should have been keeping better tabs on the frequency of them. I ran the evening through my mind and could pinpoint only the one contraction. Calculating the time, it had happened close to two hours prior. I made a mental note of the time then shifted so I could whisper to Jess.

"Do you think standing or walking around would help?" I remembered Marí offering the suggestion a few weeks ago.

Jess shook her head. When the pain had subsided she leaned her head back onto my shoulder and turned to whisper back, "I do think I would like to call it a night."

Deborah had either heard her or picked up on the situation and wordlessly patted John's knee next to her. He understood immediately and stood. The rest of our guests followed suit and the process of what I've learned is known as the "Southern goodbye" began. Everyone got multiple hugs, conversations began again, and it took thirty minutes for the house to empty. By then, my heart was full.

As soon as the front door was closed, I helped Jess from the couch and pulled her into my arms. We stood there silently processing the day as well as what we both knew was coming in the near future. She had reminded me that this could go on for days but something deep down told me this was not going to be the case for us.

"I think I'm going to go get a shower and head to bed," she said as she leaned back.

"Good idea. I'll get Hayley ready for bed and tuck her in. You good?" I didn't try to hide my concern.

"I'm good," she said, lifting onto her toes to kiss me. "If I'm asleep before you come in, I love you."

"I love you. And if you need me for any reason, you'll wake me?"

"I promise."

It was too early and the day had been too full for me to be able to settle so I sat on the couch and clicked open the Bible app on my phone. The "verse of the day" was staring back at me and I knew it had been meant for me. It was Isaiah 26:3 *You keep him in perfect peace whose mind is stayed on you, because he trusts in you.*

My mind had been pulled in so many directions in the last few weeks that I realized my peace had turned into worry, anxiety, and uncertainty. I had allowed myself to become distracted from the one thing, the one Person who would have erased all of it and replaced it with a calm had I only trusted more in Him than my own abilities and competence.

Closing my eyes I sent up prayers of gratitude for having been brought to this point of reflection and reminder and repentance for having put my trust in myself. The silence was interrupted by what sounded like someone getting the wind knocked out of them coming from our bedroom. Immediately I was off the couch and headed in that direction.

In our bed, Jess was trying to sit up while controlling her breathing. I rushed to help her and caught a glimpse of the bedside clock. It had been almost two hours since the last contraction. This felt like the beginning of something big. My heart was hammering as I held her hand and she tightened her grip for several seconds before she relaxed again. Pulling her into my chest, I smoothed her hair with my free hand and kissed the top of her head.

"Can I get anything or do anything for you?" I asked quietly.

With her head pressed against me she murmured, "Come to bed and hold me?"

There was nothing I'd rather do in that moment. We settled in and spent the next several hours hovering between sleeping and working through contractions together. By 6:00 A.M., it was clear any plans we had for the day were changing.

Chapter 49

Mark

It was 6:30 A.M. and Jess was coming down from her second contraction of the hour.

Standing in front of her, I suggested, "Jess, sweetheart, I think we should at least consider driving into town where the hospital is. Just think, it will get you off the couch and out of the house for a little while." I tried not to sound as though I was talking to a child but my nerves had me overcompensating.

She growled in frustration and exhaustion. Sitting on the edge of the couch, Jess closed her eyes and breathed in, then out slowly.

"Fine," she finally sighed and she reached for my hand and I pulled her up from her seat.

She shuffled to our room to get dressed while I texted Deborah to see if she was up and able to come stay at the house until Hayley was awake. By the time Deborah had made it over, I had coffee made for all of us, Jess and I were dressed, and we were ready to take a drive.

One thing I had learned in my short time in Kentucky was that a drive anywhere was going to be monotonous and in the winter, barren. Fields that would be green in the coming months were shades of tan and brown. Trees were still empty of leaves. The barns visible from the road were filled with the remaining bales of hay needed to make it through the end of the winter. Even in the winter it was beautiful, practically untouched by anything more than nature and the occasional house, barn, and tractor. But that was the view for mile upon mile.

The drive had been quiet as I held Jess's hand over the console between us. Her grip tightened as she bolted forward, causing my attention to swing in her direction. Her chin pressing into her chest and eyes squeezed shut, she was blowing out a breath that puffed her cheeks.

My eyes went back to the road, but I started counting the seconds. I made it to fifty before I felt the tension slowly leave her body. I squeezed her hand to get her attention. I didn't want to ask the obvious question aloud so I shot her a look that I knew she'd understand.

"They're definitely lasting longer," she said, still trying to catch her breath.

"When do you think we should call Dr. Reynolds?" I asked, when it felt as though her breathing had returned to normal.

Everything I had read explained to me as best as I could understand that this was a process that went in a specific order on no specific timeline. The books and blogs I had stumbled on in the last few months also encouraged me to be present, supportive, and helpful without getting in the way. That, also, was unspecific, so this was my attempt at being helpful while also gleaning any information that could put my mind at ease. At this point, nothing felt concrete and I thrived on the objective.

Before she could answer, Jess was once again experiencing a contraction.

"Woah! Jess, are we trying to rush things here?" I asked, trying to bring levity to the situation. It had barely been five minutes since her last and we were still ten minutes from the hospital.

Jess made a sound that was a combination of a whimper and a growl and it went straight to my heart. If just hearing her felt like this,

I needed to brace myself to watch it happen. My foot laid a little heavier on the gas pedal and sent up a prayer that God got us to the hospital quickly and safely.

Panting, Jess finally said, "I think you should call the hospital and tell them we're almost there and that they might want to give Dr. Reynolds a heads up that we're coming in hot."

While I was not completely sure what she meant by that, I understood it well enough to know things had progressed very quickly and it had taken us both off guard. Letting go of her hand, I fished my phone from its holster and handed it to Jess. She pressed *Call* and I took it from there. Seven minutes later, just like last time, they were waiting for us.

By the time the truck was parked and I had run inside, Ruby, the nurse at the intake desk was waiting to give me directions. Weaving through the halls, I found the small room they had taken Jess to and they were getting her situated in the bed. The room was similar to the one we had been in days ago but I didn't recognize any of the nurses milling about.

Jess looked tired though she was attempting a smile in response to the nurse's cheery attitude as the woman was connecting wires to the monitor screen next to the bed. When she moved out of the spot she was occupying, I replaced the nurse next to Jess. Reaching out, I clasped Jess's hand and leaned down to press a kiss to her forehead. Our eyes met and through her sleepy haze, I could see the joy and excitement hiding there.

"We're doing this. You're doing this, today," I said in a half-whisper, because my voice seemed to be stuck somewhere in my throat.

Her smile was brighter for me. "We're doing this," she repeated.

Sliding my free hand onto her cheek and into her hair, she pressed her face into my palm.

"I love you so much. Thank you for giving me more than I could ever imagine wanting," I managed to say as tears filled my eyes and the back of my throat burned with emotion.

Before she could say anything else, a contraction hit. I watched a small green line rise on the monitor screen before it plateaued and hung in the air for what seemed like a full minute before descending. This was a frequent occurrence over the next two hours, growing more frequent the more time that passed. Jess's discomfort also grew more and more pronounced with every episode.

A nurse walked in soon after we passed the two hour mark. She did a quick check and announced that she was certain things were going to kick into high gear soon, to use her words. We decided to call Hayley since it was well into the morning, and Deborah had let us know they were hanging out with the rest of the family waiting for updates. Hayley was distracted which turned out to be a good thing because Jess had a very painful contraction that was immediately followed by her water breaking. We rushed off the phone and called the nurse who came in to check Jess and the baby's vitals.

"Alright, Mrs. Collins, you are doing so great right now," the bubbly nurse said. "I'm going to see if Dr. Reynolds has arrived and let him come in and check on things. I'll be right back."

Jess's eyebrows furrowed.

"What is it?" I asked.

"She was hiding something."

If there was one thing I never questioned, it was Jess's ability to know something wasn't right with one quick look.

"Something must be wrong," Jess said, a slight panic in her voice. "She said I was doing great but not the baby."

Tears had pooled in her eyes. I slid as far into the bed with her as I could and wrapped my arms around her.

"Shh," I brushed her hair back. "Let's let Dr. Reynolds tell us what is happening and we'll go from there."

Jess leaned into me as closely as she could get and wrapped her arm around mine, her grip tight, reminding me that even though I was as lost as she was in this arena, we were in it together. I held her and gently rocked her as I felt her tears drip onto my arm. This is how I knew she was physically and emotionally drained. It was a rare sight to see Jess cry.

I held her tighter and whispered, "I've got you."

Dr. Reynolds entered the room several minutes and two hard contractions later. Normally, I would stand and greet him, but my place was on the bed holding my wife.

He spoke to Jess, his tone soft and soothing. "Mrs. Collins, Nurse Adams, who was just here, updated me on some of the readouts from the monitor. Everything seemed to be moving along smoothly until your water broke. For whatever reason, it would seem something is causing Baby's heart rate to slow with each new contraction."

Jess immediately tensed against me at the information. I squeezed her shoulder hoping to remind her to relax.

The doctor continued, "It has been my experience that if we continue to wait and see what happens, there is a higher risk to the baby than if we go ahead and plan to perform a c-section."

My insides felt like ice. This was not part of any plan we had ever made and the feelings of helplessness I had before were insignificant to the ones currently working their way into my mind. I turned my attention to Jess who looked up at me, worry and uncertainty written all over her face. I didn't need a special set of skills to see it. With a squeeze of her hand, I let her know that I was with her every step of the way down whichever path she chose.

On a shaky breath, Jess nodded and said, "Okay."

Before he left the room, Dr. Reynolds joined us on my side of the bed.

"I'd like to pray with you before we take the next steps, if that's alright."

"Of course," I answered, my voice cracking.

"Our Father and Savior, I ask that you fix the minds of these two young souls on you so they might trust you and know your perfect peace. Guide our every decision and movement and we ask your will be done as it is good and perfect. Amen."

The peace that instantly flooded my soul washed every doubt and fear from my heart and displayed them in the form of tears soaking my face. There was no way Dr. Reynolds could have known how I had been meditating on the very verse he was praying over us just a matter of hours ago. Without thinking, I untangled myself from Jess and stood and wrapped the doctor in a hug. He chuckled as he gently hugged me back and I slapped his back.

"Thank you, doctor. You genuinely have no idea how much those words mean to me and to us," I said after taking a step back and retaking Jess's hand in mine.

"Sometimes God makes it plain as day," he said. "Now, the nurses are going to come in and get things rolling from here and I will see the three of you in a few minutes."

I was forced to vacate my place as they disconnected the monitors and prepped Jess for surgery. The movements in the room were quick and efficient but not hurried, which helped keep my anxious thoughts at bay. Had they been more rushed, everything would have felt more like an emergency. I was thankful for their calm expedition.

As the bed carrying Jess began to roll toward the door, a nurse approached me and suggested I follow her to scrub in and change clothes. I held up one finger to stop her and jogged forward down the hall before Jess disappeared through a set of double doors.

Grabbing her hand, I kissed her forehead. "I love you. I will see you in there."

She squeezed my hand. "I love you, too."

I pressed one more kiss to her lips before she was wheeled away and I stood there watching the greatest part of my world leave my line of sight.

The nurse who had been waiting for me cleared her throat. "Mr. Collins," she said to get my attention.

Reluctantly, I stopped watching the doors and hurried to meet her down the hall.

What felt like an hour later but had only been a few minutes, I was finally reunited with Jess in a bright room full of medical equipment and instruments. The view before me was like nothing I had ever seen before so to say it was overwhelming was an understatement. As soon as my eyes found Jess's, however, everything else faded well into the background.

All I could see was her head while the rest of her was shielded by a large curtain. Whatever was happening on the other side seemed so well orchestrated that my attention was exactly where it needed to be.

"Hi," I breathed out, feeling my heart lighten and a smile forming on my face.

"Hi," she smiled back at me.

"I know this isn't what we planned, but I'm starting to get excited again," I confessed.

"I am, too. I have thanked God over and over for you today but I haven't said it to you. Thank you for keeping me strong through all of this."

Without having any frame of reference for what was happening around us, we were both startled by the sound of a baby's cry. Jess's eyes were huge with surprise which felt like a mirror of my own expression. Tears fell from both of us and the moment we were sharing was broken when a nurse asked, "Dad, you want to tell mom what we had?"

It took me a moment to realize what she was asking. Slowly tearing my eyes from Jess, I peeked over the curtain. My breath caught in my throat and I could hardly see through my tears.

"It's a boy," I croaked.

Jess shook with sobs and laughter as her tears multiplied.

Voices swirled around us calling out numbers and words I didn't have any frame of reference for then within a few short minutes, I was being handed a tiny ball of a blanket by a nurse who appeared as overjoyed for us as we were.

"They're taking care of mom and making sure everything is as it should be so dad, why don't you sit here," she pulled up a chair that seemed to appear from thin air, "and the three of you can get to know each other."

With the tiny bundle in my arms, I positioned myself so Jess could see our son's face. We had a son and he was perfect. My heart was beating rapidly enough I was certain had I been standing, my legs would have given out on me. There was a fullness inside my chest as I watched Jess stare at the miracle in my arms. Securing him to my chest, I leaned forward and kissed Jess, then freed one of my hands to dry her face.

"You are amazing. He is amazing. I can't wait to put him in your arms," I told her as I leaned back so she could have the full view once again.

"He's beautiful," she sighed.

We stared at our beautifully perfect son in silence until the same nurse that had handed him to me showed up with a rolling crib.

"Alright, y'all, it's time for Baby's first ride. We'll wheel him down to your room and then we'll talk recovery, and all the new baby stuff. Dad, go ahead and lay him down," she instructed.

I did as told then walked alongside Jess's bed, holding her hand as we followed behind the nurse pushing the crib. Everything felt surreal as though we were walking through a mist that would soon evaporate. I knew from experience it was the result of adrenaline and that the feeling would fade soon, but it was a high I wasn't done riding. We had a son. My wife was in good health. God had done everything he had promised to do and given us perfect peace even when we didn't know what the outcome of the day would be.

Several hours after Jess had rested and the doctor was pleased with the beginning of her recovery and treatment, we called our family. The last update we had given was a quick text I had sent before Jess had been taken back to the O.R.

We had just disconnected a video call and as I was placing the phone back in its holder, Jess flailed her right arm in my direction. Her hand attempted to make a grab, but fell loosely to her side. I realized something was wrong as I watched her eyes flutter closed and the baby begin to roll sideways as her arm went slack. I reached for the baby who had been sleeping peacefully cradled in Jess's left arm before he could fall. I went into emergency response mode with our son in my arms.

"Jess!" I said loudly as I reached for the call button on her bed. "Jess!" I repeated.

Within what could only be described as the longest seconds of my life, a nurse was in the room watching monitors while checking Jess for a pulse before raising and lowering parts of the bed. All I could do was stand there and explain what I had seen happen as I held tightly to the now crying bundle in my arms.

My heart was constricting inside of my chest and breathing had become difficult. *God, please, no. Please do not let anything happen to her. Please.* These words played on a loop inside my head as I watched medical professionals work around me. I hadn't even noticed they'd multiplied until a nurse directed me to a chair in the corner of the space.

I had no concept of how much time had passed though it felt like eternity had come and gone. The sound of Jess's groan hailed my attention. I attempted to stand but my legs felt too unsteady and I was still holding the baby.

The baby!

My thoughts immediately turned to the infant I had been holding. I didn't remember the crying stopping which sent my nerves into overdrive. I began searching his tiny features for signs of distress and placing my face near his to check his breathing. The tension inside lessened slightly as everything checked out and he was sleeping.

The breath I let out was less than solid which was exactly how I was feeling. I forced myself to take several deep breaths before attempting to stand again. By this time, Jess was asking for me which helped force me into action. Gently, I placed the baby in the crib then immediately forced my way between a nurse and Jess. My hands automatically went to her face as I checked her for injuries or other conditions as though I could mitigate them in any way. Her hand wrapped around my wrist, holding tightly.

"Hi," she whispered.

A sob escaped me as I tried to process everything that had just happened. No words would form in my mind with which I could respond. I knew I needed an explanation, but I was entirely lost in needing this moment. It was likely I would not have remembered or understood an explanation had it been offered. Once I was satisfied with my evaluation, I asked the nurse to enlighten us on what had just occurred.

My focus had zeroed in on Jess intensely enough that I had not recognized Dr. Reynolds's presence in the room. He stood on the other side of the bed and was patiently observing and allowing me time to recenter and actually hear him and comprehend his words.

As he spoke, the doctor pressed buttons that raised Jess's head and lowered the foot of the bed. "Welcome back, Mrs. Collins. It would seem your blood pressure decided it did not agree with the pain medication and plummeted causing you to pass out on us. We've made some adjustments to the medication, increased your fluids to raise your blood pressure a little, and we expect everything from here on out to be smooth sailing. We'll keep an eye on things, of course, and if you feel lightheaded at all or need anything, someone is just a button press away."

The relief that washed over me felt like a tsunami wave and it was quickly followed by a swell of gratitude. My heart was over-flowing in silent thanks to God as I reached across the bed extending a hand to Dr. Reynolds. He accepted it graciously.

"Thank you, doctor," I said, with an air of reprieve.

"I'm just doing my job. You have a beautiful family and I hope you don't need me but if you do, I'll do everything I can to be here for you."

With a nod he turned and left the room.

When I looked back down, I found Jess searching the room. The crib was behind me and in it slept our son. The thought was going to take some getting used to but I was ready. I turned and wheeled the crib closer to the bed.

"Are you feeling strong enough to hold him?" I asked.

She nodded so I retrieved the snugly wrapped package and delivered it to her arms. Watching her hold him flooded my entire being with a sensation unlike anything I had ever felt before. There was love, of course, but it was mixed with reverence and awe mingled with an overwhelming sense of joy. He was so small and vulnerable and I had never been responsible for another human this small. When Hayley came into my life, she was well beyond the years of total helplessness.

Then there was Jess, who was so strong and beautiful. She had clearly done an extraordinary job with Hayley even in the face of the darkness they'd faced. And here she was, giving herself over completely once again to care for this child, our child. I could never deserve this amazing and capable woman but I was going to do everything in my power to love and protect her and our children.

"He needs a name," Jess said, without tearing her gaze from the perfectly round face she'd been staring at silently.

"Got any ideas?" I asked.

We had casually thrown out names for both boys and girls since we hadn't found out the gender beforehand. But, we both thought we had another few weeks to make a final decision.

"What do you think about naming him Michael Calvin?" she asked, then her eyes met mine.

A lump formed in my throat. Michael had been my older brother's name. It hadn't even been on the list as far as I could remember. Not because it wasn't a good name. It was a great name and it had been the name of one of my favorite people for my entire life up until I turned fifteen when one day that person had been ripped from my life. And until this moment, I had not considered it would be a name I found comfort in hearing. Now, it sounded exactly like that.

"It's perfect." I leaned down and pressed a kiss to her forehead and gently stroked Michael's face with my index finger. We sat there admiring him for another minute.

"How do you think Cal will react?" I asked.

Jess smiled. "I don't know but I can't wait to find out."

It was close to dinner time when there was a knock on the door. I had spent most of the day wedged into the bed with Jess, unwilling to leave her side. Most of that time, we traded Michael back and forth, both of us wanting to acquire as much snuggle time as possible while not wanting the other to miss out on any. When a nurse would come in, I'd vacate my spot just to return to it once she had completed her tasks. I didn't attempt to move when we heard the knock until a familiar voice followed it.

"Daddy!"

I sat up as quickly as I could without jostling Jess, a jolt of happiness surging through me. I stood to swing Hayley up into my arms and kissed the side of her head.

"Hayley-bug!"

Behind her, our entire crew shuffled into the room that seemed large enough until this moment. Immediately, I was overcome with emotion at the sight of our family. Their voices were all hushed and excited as they moved into the room. Deborah quickly embraced me then practically shoved me out of the way to get to Jess, causing me to chuckle. Marí was next and followed Deborah's lead. John and Cal both offered handshakes and shoulder claps. James and Colton hung back behind John, but Colton was clearly interested in discovering the object to which the attention was being given.

I walked with Hayley to the other side of the bed so she could lean down and kiss Jess and see her baby brother. Wordlessly, I inquired if Jess wanted Hayley to join them on the bed.

When she nodded, I asked, "Do you want to sit with mommy and your brother?"

Hayley was all too excited to make herself comfortable under Jess's free arm.

"Want to hold him?" she asked.

Hayley's eyes lit up and she nodded excitedly.

Together, we got him positioned on Hayley's lap and the entire room seemed to melt at the picture. Deborah was using her phone to snap photo after photo, for which I was grateful. Hayley giggled as Michael squirmed and yawned. It was taking every ounce of willpower I had to hold back the tears threatening to make themselves known.

The precious moment was fleeting as Hayley grew less enthusiastic about the baby brother who wasn't very interactive at the moment. I left Hayley on the bed with Jess and picked up our son since I was certain everyone in the room was being polite by not asking to get their hands on him.

Because it was unexpected, I walked him over to Cal with every eye in the room on me.

"I'd like you to meet Michael Calvin Collins," I said, holding the baby out to Cal.

Cal blinked several times before holding his arms out to receive him. When he looked down at the baby sleeping in his arms, it was as though he had disconnected from the rest of the world entirely. A few tears dripped onto the blanket swaddling Michael. That was when the entire room filled with the sound of sniffles and the wisp of tissues repeatedly being pulled from a box.

After a few silent minutes, Cal cleared his throat and with a nod to Jess then to me, he handed the baby to John before taking a step back and pulling out a handkerchief to dry his face. Michael was passed from person to person, including Colton who sat in the plastic cushioned chair and took the instructions to be gentle to the extreme. We all hid our amused smiles as he sat stark still, barely breathing, arms curled up around the blanket. The relief that washed over

Colton when Deborah took Michael from him was felt for him by all of us.

When Jess's dinner tray arrived, the exit process began. Hugs were given and plans were made for Hayley. It took seven minutes for the room to clear out so the poor woman delivering the food could get the tray inside the room.

It was obvious Jess was exhausted and I was amazed she had lasted as long as she had. When she was done eating, I suggested she get some rest and I would call a nurse to take Michael to the nursery. She was reluctant to let him leave the room, but I insisted she at least get a little uninterrupted sleep. It had been the right call as her eyes closed and her breathing deepened moments after the door closed behind the nurse.

Needing to release some of the pent-up energy that had compounded during the day, I took a few laps through the hospital courtyard. The sun was on its way down and the air was getting colder. The breeze was sharp but refreshing, cleansing. I inhaled deeply, letting the fresh air fill my lungs. The day, as stressful as it had been, had ended perfectly. I had a wife, a daughter, and now a son. It was a life I could have never earned, but I would be eternally grateful to the God who allowed me to have it.

Chapter 50

Jess

Four Months Later

When I poked my head around the corner of the doorway, my heart took flight at the sight of Mark sitting in the plush glider in the corner of the room with Michael tucked into one side, Hayley on the other, and his arms wrapped around them both holding a book in front of them. One might think I'd grown accustomed to the picture in the last few months because it's one I saw every day. Instead, I found myself continually reminded how blessed I am to not only be here but to watch and experience it. And as much as I wanted to stand and remain an observer, we had a schedule to keep. When Mark uttered the words, "The End," that was my cue to move into action.

"It's time," I said, smiling and walking toward the chair to help Mark maneuver both children.

"Mommy! Do you like my bow?" Hayley asked, trying to make a quick escape from her laid back position.

I chuckled as Mark removed his arm at the same time I reached down and hooked my hands under Hayley's arms and lifted her upward. It was a move we'd almost perfected in the last couple of months once I'd been physically cleared to pick anything up that weighed more than Michael.

" I love your hairbow. Mimi Deb did a great job picking it out for you. I bet she can't wait to see it," I told her as I straightened her dark yellow dress.

Michael had fallen asleep during storytime, so Mark stood and carried him straight to the car seat and fastened the harness.

"You look sharp," I told Mark as he straightened, car seat in one hand and Hayley's hand in his other. His smile rivaled the spring sunshine that was surrounded by white fluffy clouds in the cerulean sky.

I picked up the diaper bag from the counter then stepped forward and smoothed his tie. It had been a while since any of us had been this dressed up, but it was a special day. Not that I minded seeing Mark in a nice pair of Wranglers or his tactical work pants, but there was just something about him in a tie that gave me heart eyes, like the ones in the old cartoons I grew up watching. Maybe it was also a little reminiscent of our early days when he wore a shirt and tie everyday. Even with a healthy appreciation for the nostalgia, however, nothing compared to the sight of him holding both of our babies.

Although Hayley would turn six in a few months and start Kindergarten in the fall and would argue valiantly that she was not a baby, when I saw her, I still saw her as small and dependent as her brother. Mark had missed those days of her life because we'd had Bryan. And while it's never been a subject we've dwelt on because the past is merely a point of reference and not where our hearts continue to exist, I was always aware that Mark was affected by not having the same connection to Hayley. Granted, Hayley had been his and he had been hers from the day they met, even if she was the only one who had known it to the extent an eighteen-month-old could know anything. Their bond had been instant and strong.

Digging my phone from the side pocket of the backpack, I

snapped a quick picture of my whole world before asking, "Shall we?"

The four of us got situated in the car and made the short drive into town. Hayley was extra chatty which meant she was nervous on top of being excited. She wasn't the only one. I wasn't nervous but I'd definitely felt the excitement building throughout the morning.

The parking area was full, so we had to walk a little ways to get to the entrance which allowed some of our nervous energy to wear off. As soon as we walked through the double doors of the courthouse, Hayley slowed down and clung to my hand and arm. We held on to each other as we'd done so many times before but this time, it was in anticipation of something wonderful.

Mark navigated the halls quickly, our footsteps echoing in the hall. When we reached the small room, we were greeted by a group of familiar faces huddled together. Marí, Cal, and Sadie were chatting with the Parkers, Kathleen, James, and Colton. As soon as we walked in, the already humming room erupted with excitement. The adults exchanged hugs with one another while the kids all went for the high fives.

Hayley eagerly claimed the spot between Mark and Colton, who couldn't contain his excitement as he animatedly shared their plans to hunt for artifacts that afternoon. Deborah sat on Colton's other side, fussing with his hair while he remained oblivious to her actions. James was wedged as close to John as he could get between the Parkers.

Theirs was a bond I'd enjoyed watching develop. James had been the caretaker and protector for Colton for so long, it was sweet to watch him learn and lean into his role as a child and a son. It had been a new experience for both he and John but it was one they both took to with open hearts and open arms. And John was made to be a dad. That much had been evident soon after I'd met him.

As we settled into our seats, the buzz of chatter around us slowly quieted down when Judge Casey made his entrance and took his seat on the stand. The next thirty minutes passed by in a whirlwind of emotions, as we laughed, cried, and smiled our way through some of the most memorable moments of our lives.

As the judge turned to Hayley and asked if she understood what was happening, she beamed with excitement and replied, "We're all getting the same last name." The judge chuckled at her response and proceeded to make the announcement that would change her life forever. "Then it is my great honor to officially give you the name Hayley Grace Collins," he declared. Hayley threw her fist in the air and shouted, "Yes!"

The judge congratulated us on our beautiful family and proceeded to call the Parkers, James, and Colton forward. Each member was asked questions about their lives and their wishes. When the judge turned to Colton and asked if he understood what was happening, his response moved the entire room to tears. "I thought I had lost my family forever. But my family found me. And now we'll always be together."

The judge paused for a moment, straightening papers on his desk and rearranging objects in front of him. He cleared his throat and gazed at Colton with a warm smile. "Son, I hope you will always remember that all lost things deserve to be found. And finding a family is like finding a hidden treasure. Once you have found it, it's yours." He then turned to John, Deborah, and James. "And it is my great honor to declare James and Colton Parker sons of John and Deborah Parker, their forever family."

The room erupted into cheers, sniffles, and happy sobs. I reached over and took Kathleen's hand, and she gave me a watery smile in return. Watching her thrive as James and Colton's aunt had been a joy. There was a newfound freedom in it that she would not have had if she had attempted to remain their guardian.

And of course John and Deborah had already fallen into step as parents as naturally as we're born knowing how to breathe. They'd mastered the art of a preteen's birthday party, copious amounts of boy laundry, and instilling gentlemanly manners. Each day had been an adventure and I was beyond grateful for the front row seat. I even told Deborah I was counting on her learning and experience when it came to raising a boy. We'd both laughed and agreed to muddle through together.

The sun was bright and overhead as we pulled up to the farmhouse, our voices mingling with the excited chatter of kids already running around outside. The new outdoor dining area, built by Cal and Carlos, was impressive - long picnic tables and a pole barn for shade and lighting. We were here to celebrate, and as we stepped out of the car, the rest of the crew had already arrived and the excitement surrounding us was unmistakable.

The older kids rushed off to play, the parents yelling after them to change their clothes. Mark picked up an empty car seat since Cal had already claimed Michael as soon as we had arrived. I slung the backpack over my shoulder and met Mark at the front of the car, taking his outstretched hand. He leaned down for a kiss, and his simple "Thank you" said it all - gratitude for all the love and effort that went into making this moment possible. I smiled, feeling the warmth of his hand in mine, and replied with a heartfelt "Thank you" of my own.

As we walked hand in hand towards our family, I looked around at the familiar faces and knew that this was home. The bond we shared was unbreakable, and as long as we had each other, we were home.

Epilogue

Jess - Two Years Later

As we exited the restaurant, Mark and I were laughing at the fortunes we'd each gotten in our fortune cookies. His fortune suggested he would be well suited for a career that utilized his artistic flair. Mine encouraged me to pursue my dreams within reason. We'd started laughing before getting up from our table and were still giddy and smiling as we held hands walking through the parking lot. Whether it was the delirium of being out alone for the first time in months or just the happy bubble we typically found ourselves in when we were together, I didn't care. I felt on the verge of skipping the rest of the way to the car. My heart was full and I was happy.

The purse slung over my shoulder started vibrating, drawing my attention. I swung the bag to my front and pulled out my phone with my free hand. A feeling of surprise followed by curiosity niggled in my brain. I turned the screen to show Mark.

"Were you expecting a call from him?" His tone was as surprised as I felt.

I shook my head. "If Dr. Thorne is calling me, he has a reason. Want to take the call with me?"

Mark nodded toward the car. We slipped into the front seats of the vehicle before, I slid my finger across the screen to answer then hit the speaker button.

"Dr. Thorne, what can we do for you?" I asked.

"Jess," there was a strained panic to his voice I didn't recognize followed by a sound of papers rustling.

"Dr. Thorne, is something wrong?"

"I need your help."

That was all we heard before the line went silent. Several seconds later, the call failed on his end. Mark and I looked at each other before I immediately attempted to call back but it was to no avail multiple times.

Mark had already pulled out his phone and was making a call of his own.

"Washburn," he said. "Yeah, hey. How's retirement treating ya?"

After several seconds Mark answered, "That's great. I really wish this was a catch up call because there is a lot to catch up on. But I need a favor."

Another pause.

"Great. Listen, you know Dr. Thorne over at the university? Any chance you have time to head over to his office and do a well check. I know it's not something you'd normally do, but Jess just got a phone call that ended rather abruptly after a cryptic message. It isn't sitting well for either of us."

Mark listened and nodded. "Thanks, man. Yeah, I owe you one. Give me a call when you get there, if you don't mind. Yeah, same number. Thanks, again."

Seeing Mark shift into his serious mode confirmed for me what I was already feeling. Dr. Thorne was in trouble.

A hundred thoughts swirled in my brain. If Dr. Thorne was in trouble and he needed my help, did that mean I was going to have to travel back to D.C.? Was he in danger or just in need of my skills? I had children. Even if there wasn't a potentially dangerous threat looming, I wouldn't leave them to go that far away for an extended period of time. My life was different now. I was a consultant who worked from a screen or as an instructor. My investigative days in person ended the day I left D.C.

My thoughts were spiraling and Mark must have sensed it. He grabbed my hand and ran his thumb over my knuckles. "Hey, let's wait and see what Washburn finds. It may be nothing."

I nodded, knowing full well that he also understood it could be something. I appreciated his attempt at soothing my nerves.

Raising my hand to his lips, Mark pressed a gentle kiss to the back of it before giving it a squeeze.

"I want ice cream," he announced with a half smile, knowing I wouldn't argue.

His distraction game was sweet. I smiled back and said, "That sounds like an excellent idea. Think this counts as pursuing my dreams within reason?"

His eyebrows raised and his blue eyes sparkled with amusement. "Do you dream of ice cream?" he asked.

"All the time," I answered with an exaggerated sigh.

"Then it absolutely counts. I'm looking forward to making your dreams come true," he said with a wink.

As always, it sent a jolt of electricity through me.

"Now, what kind of artistic flair do you think I could bring to the Sheriff's Department?"

<hr>

Want to take a look into the future?

Check out the Bonus Epilogue

Afterword

As of this publication, there are over 400,000 children in America's foster care system by no fault of their own. These children are just like any other children. They have hopes and dreams, and they deserve to be treated with dignity and respect. Unfortunately, due to circumstances beyond their control, they have been thrust into a system that can be overwhelming and confusing. As a result, many of these children struggle with feelings of abandonment and low self-esteem. By supporting the foster care system, you're not only providing the basic necessities of life to these children, but you're also showing them that they are valued and loved.

The foster care system is not without its challenges. There is a shortage of foster homes, and many children end up bouncing from one placement to another, which can cause further trauma and instability. In addition, foster parents often face financial burdens in providing for the needs of the children in their care. That's why it's important to support the foster care system, even if it's only through monetary means. Your donation can help provide resources and support to foster parents, and ensure that children in the system have access to the care and services they need.

If you're interested in making a donation, becoming an advocate, or just learning more about foster care and adoption, here are some links to help you learn more about how you can support foster care in your community.

Foster Love - (www.fosterlove.com)
AdoptUSKids - (www.adoptuskids.org)

Maple Bacon Pecan Cinnamon Rolls

INGREDIENTS

CINNAMON ROLL DOUGH
- 1 cup warm milk (about 115 degrees F)
- 2 1/2 teaspoons instant dry yeast
- 2 large eggs at room temperature
- 1/3 cup salted butter** (Melted, but make sure it isn't over 110° Fahrenheit. Just softened is fine.)
- 1/2 cup granulated sugar
- 1 teaspoon salt
- 4 1/2 cups all-purpose flour (divided)
- ½ cup heavy whipping cream

MAPLE BACON PECAN FILLING
- 1/4 cup (55g) unsalted butter, room temp
- 1/2 cup (100g) light brown sugar, packed
- 1 tbsp cinnamon
- 2 tbsp pure maple syrup
- 1 tsp maple extract
- 1 cup finely chopped pecans

• 6 strips of thick bacon cooked until crispy (crushed and divided)

MAPLE ICING
• 1 cup (120g) powdered sugar
• 2 tbsp heavy cream or milk
• 2 tbsp pure maple syrup
• 2 tsp maple extract
• 1 tbsp water to thin (optional)

INSTRUCTIONS
CINNAMON ROLL DOUGH

1. To start the rolls, dissolve the yeast in the warm milk in a large bowl.

2. In a separate bowl, add sugar, butter, salt, eggs, and flour, mix well.

3. Pour the milk/yeast mixture in the bowl and if using a stand mixer, you will want to use the dough hook. Mix well until well incorporated.

4. Place dough into an oiled bowl, cover and let rise in a warm place about 1 hour or until the dough has doubled in size.

5. Roll the dough out on a lightly floured surface, until it is approx. 16 inches long by 12 inches wide. It should be approx. ¼ inch thick.

6. While the dough rests for 10 minutes, make the filling by mixing the butter, brown sugar, cinnamon, maple syrup, maple extract, and half the bacon together with a fork. It should form a soft paste consistency that's perfect for spreading.

7. When the 10 minutes is up, spread the filling into a thin and even layer, leaving about 1/2 inch border all around the outside of the dough.

8. Sprinkle with an even layer of the chopped pecans.

9. Roll the dough up into a log. Place your hands at each end of the log and give it a gentle squeeze in to compact the log of dough. It

may have stretched out a bit during the rolling process, so this brings it back together.

10. For best results, use unflavored dental floss to cut the rolls. If you don't have floss, you could also use really thin sewing thread. If using a sharp knife, gently saw back and forth and try not to press straight down into the rolls. This will squish them into an odd shape.

If using the floss, slide it under the roll and toss both ends of the floss over top. Pull them through to create a cut. Cut off the two ends of the log and then cut the remainder into additional pieces.

11. Place the rolls in a buttered or greased 9×13" dish (you could also use two 9" round pans). It's OK if all of the rolls are touching. ***See notes for overnight instructions**

12. Place in a warm spot and cover with a towel to rise for 1 hour. If you live in a colder climate, preheat the oven to the lowest temperature. Once it's ready, turn the oven off and place the rolls inside. This creates a warm environment for the rolls to proof.

13. Preheat the oven to 350F (remove the rolls if you proofed them inside). The rolls should have doubled in size.

14. Bake for 25-30 minutes or until the tops are a light golden brown. While they cool, make the icing.

MAPLE ICING

1. In a small bowl, whisk together all the ingredients (minus the water). If you like a thinner icing, add the water.

2. Drizzle onto the warm rolls then sprinkle with remaining bacon.

NOTES

OVERNIGHT CINNAMON ROLLS – After step 11, cover the rolls in plastic wrap and place in the refrigerator overnight. Before baking the next day, allow the rolls to rest at room temperature (covered) for about 45 minutes. Preheat oven to 350 (F) and bake 25-30 minutes or until tops are light golden brown.

Acknowledgments

Thank you, Jesus, for the creativity and time you gave me.

Thank you, Rob, for being my constant, my cheerleader, my alpha-beta reader, my everything!

Thank you, Ashley, for taking on this project and making it the best version of itself. Stanley 🐻 and I are forever grateful and look forward to many more projects alongside you!

To my beta readers - THIS IS FOR YOU. You inspired me and here we are. THANK YOU.

About the Author

A wife, mom, author, marriage and family counselor, a former AP Psychology teacher, and a podcaster, Jennifer draws from her life experiences and imagination to connect with her readers and listeners through the written and spoken word.

When she's not wearing one of her many hats, you'll find her tucked away with a book and what's likely her third coffee of the day.

Find her on social media under @jcarrwrites

Also by Jennifer Carr

A STORY OF LOVE, LOSS, AND RESTORATION

Get to know Mark and Jess before they moved to Owenston.

No Matter What